Oliver Optic

The Sailor Boy

Or, Jack Somers in the Navy

Oliver Optic

The Sailor Boy
Or, Jack Somers in the Navy

ISBN/EAN: 9783337209896

Printed in Europe, USA, Canada, Australia, Japan

Cover: Foto ©Andreas Hilbeck / pixelio.de

More available books at **www.hansebooks.com**

Jack Somers's Promotion   Page 123

THE
SAILOR BOY.
OLIVER OPTIC
LEE & SHEPARD.
BOSTON.

THE SAILOR BOY;

OR,

JACK SOMERS IN THE NAVY.

A Story of the Great Rebellion.

BY

OLIVER OPTIC,

AUTHOR OF "RICH AND HUMBLE," "IN SCHOOL AND OUT," "THE BOAT CLUB,"
"ALL ABOARD," "NOW OR NEVER," "TRY AGAIN," "POOR AND PROUD,"
"LITTLE BY LITTLE," "THE RIVERDALE STORY BOOKS," ETC.

BOSTON
LEE AND SHEPARD PUBLISHERS
10 MILK STREET NEXT "THE OLD SOUTH MEETING HOUSE"

TO

CHARLES A. B. SHEPARD, ESQ.,

This Book

IS RESPECTFULLY DEDICATED

BY HIS FRIEND

WILLIAM T. ADAMS.

PREFACE

"The Sailor Boy," the second volume of "The Army and Navy Series," was written before the War of the Rebellion had ended in the surrender of the Army of Virginia under General Lee, April 12, 1865. Like its predecessor in the series, it was written, in a certain sense, in the midst of the scenes which it describes, for they were transpiring while the writer was engaged in preparing it.

The atmosphere of peaceful New England, though not actually pervaded by the sulphurous fumes of the battle-field, was warlike, and was filled with reports and rumors of war from the scenes of operations on the land and on the sea. Even if the worker with the pen in his library had not been an intense loyalist, wholly devoted to the preservation of the Union, he could hardly have escaped the influence of the times; for though far removed from the "fire-eaters" of the day, the patriotic sentiment of the people blazed up at its brightest.

The volume was written in the glow of this prevailing sentiment; and though the writer is not in the least tempted to recede from the opinions he held during the war, he would soften some of the minor details if he were to do the work anew, at the present time, with the light of over a quarter of a century shining upon the events of that period. He believes with all his heart that "the war is over"; he has become acquainted with prominent civilians who sustained the Southern cause, and with military and naval officers who "fought on the other side," and has found they were not the demons the popular fancy had depicted them. Some of them were the mildest, gentlest, sweetest-tempered gentlemen he ever met. There were butchers and cold-blooded monsters on both sides; but neither the North nor the South is to be judged by the wretches of this type who drifted into the war.

About the time the third volume of this series was published, the preface of which is dated April 30, 1865, one of the author's most valued friends strongly advised him to hasten the completion and issue of the remaining books of the series, because he said the war was over, and the demand for such works must soon cease altogether. The writer was disposed to accept his view, and did accept it, so far as the demand for the series was concerned. He had his " Young America Abroad " in contemplation at the time, and went to Europe that year to gather his material; but as soon as possible he finished his work on the books, dreading the catastrophe predicted by his friend. More to his own than to the prophet's astonishment, the demand for the volumes has not ceased up to the present day.

Instead of abruptly terminating, as the author thought it would, the demand exists the present year, and has not ceased at any time. On the contrary, a few years ago his publishers invited him to furnish another series of the same kind; and the fifth volume of it, " Fighting for the Right," he has just completed.

In looking over the first pages of " The Sailor Boy," the writer finds the title-page graced with the names of those who have been his publishers during the lifetime of a generation. But a glance at the dedication gives a feeling of sadness. Charles A. B. Shepard, the junior of the firm which has stood as sponsor for nearly all his works, passed away from the scenes of earth some four years ago. The author's associations with him in business and social relations were of the most intimate character. He was a true and faithful friend, fair and upright in his dealings with all men, and his death was felt as a loss to the community in which he lived.

The author has often had occasion to return his grateful acknowledgments to the boys and girls for the favor they bestowed upon the series of which this book is one; and he takes this opportunity to thank the men and women of to-day again for their generous appreciation of his work, not only when they *were* boys and girls, but for what they have shown in their mature years.

WILLIAM T. ADAMS

DORCHESTER April 1893

CONTENTS.

CHAPTER		PAGE

THE SAILOR BOY.

THE SAILOR BOY;

OR,

JACK SOMERS IN THE NAVY.

———

CHAPTER I.

THE VICTORY AT PORT ROYAL.

"HURRAH for the navy!" shouted John Somers, as he rushed into the house, threw his cap upon the floor in the entry, and bolted into the room where the family were just sitting down to supper. "Hurrah for the navy!"

"What is the matter now, John?" demanded Mrs. Somers, placing the teapot on the table, and suspending all further proceedings till the excited young man had told the news.

"'The army and navy forever! Three cheers for the red, white, and blue!'" added John, swinging his

handkerchief, and singing lustily the words of the patriotic song.

"Why don't you tell us what the news is, John? You
act just like a madman when any thing has happened."

"Fort Walker and Fort Beauregard captured! The
navy gave 'em fits down there," replied John, pulling
the "Boston Journal" from his pocket, and tossing it
upon the table, to the imminent peril of the milk
pitcher, which, however, maintained its gravity, in spite
of the rude assault.

"Massy sake! I thought the whole Southern consarn
had broke down," added Gran'ther Green.

"It will break down and cave in now. Our folks have
got a footing in South Carolina now, and they'll soon
bring the rebels to terms," said John, who was fully
imbued with the enthusiasm, as well as the spirit of
prophecy, which pervaded the earlier period of the great
American Rebellion. "Let me tell you, gran'ther, the
navy has done a big thing down there. Commodore Dupont will bring 'em to their senses in double-quick time.
Charleston will have to take it next."

"Eat your supper, John, and talk about it afterwards,"
interposed Mrs. Somers.

"Supper!" exclaimed John: "who can eat with such
news as this? Let me read it to you."

Mrs. Somers and the rest of the family were quite
willing to hear what the navy had done at Port Royal;

and John was permitted to read the stirring account of the action, which he interpolated with comments of his own, expressive of his admiration of the flag-officer and the blue-jackets generally, who had achieved the glorious victory.

" I wish I had been there !" exclaimed John, when he had completed the reading of the narrative. "How I wish I had been there !"

"You had better eat your supper now," quietly remarked Mrs. Somers, who did not seem to relish the turn which the conversation had taken.

" Here I am rotting on the stocks, lying round like a lubber, when the ship's in a gale of wind," said John, as he stuffed half a hot biscuit into his mouth, apparently to mollify the dissatisfaction with which he regarded his position.

" Have some apple-sauce, John ?" added Mrs. Somers.

The young aspirant for distinction took some apple-sauce, and continued to eat, for a few moments, with a desperation dangerous to the well-being of the digestive organs, and which might reasonably have awakened a fear in the mind of his anxious mother that he would choke himself to death, instead of being killed by a splinter or a shell on board a man-of-war. John was silent for a time ; but he kept up a vigorous thinking, and it is doubtful if he could have told whether he was eating hot biscuit or " salt horse." It would not have required a conjurer, either, to tell what he was thinking about; and the poor mother, with her husband far away in the rebel country (if, indeed, he was still living), and one son exposed to the perils of battle and march, walked mechanically from the table to the closet, as she proceeded to clear off the table, looking as sad as a vision of sorrow; and it needed no conjurer to tell what she was thinking about.

She was a patriotic woman; but no doubt she wished the glowing news from Port Royal had never reached the ears of her son. She had endured all the agonizing suspense which only the wife of an absent husband and the mother of an absent soldier-boy can comprehend; and she would fain keep this remaining son by her side to sustain and soothe her by his presence. She hoped he was not needed; she tried to persuade herself that John belonged to her, now that his twin-brother had joined the army: yet the New-England blood in her veins would not let her be selfish, if the country needed his services.

She knew what John was thinking about, and she knew that the oft-repeated question was about to be proposed with more emphasis than ever before: Would she consent to his entering the navy? He had asked her permission twenty times during the summer and autumn, and she had as often silenced him by pointing to the work required to be done upon the little farm. But now the corn and cabbages, the potatoes and the apples, had all been harvested, and she could no longer detain him upon the plea that his services were needed at home; for there was hardly work enough about the place to give Gran'ther Greene, who was now in better health than usual, the exercise which was needed to keep him alive.

"Mother, aren't you ashamed of me?" said John, suddenly dropping his knife and biscuit, and looking steadily at Mrs. Somers, who was gathering up the dishes on the other side of the table.

"Ashamed of you, my son? What ails the boy?" exclaimed she, pausing in her occupation, and gazing at him with all a mother's pride visible in her expression.

"Aren't you ashamed to have a son loafing about home when the navy is short of sailors? I can hand, reef, and steer, and I know the mainmast from the jolly-boat. I've been one voyage with father in a square-rigged vessel, and two in a 'fore-and-after.' I can make a long splice, a short splice, an eye-splice, a Turk's head, or a Jacob's ladder. I know where to find the halyards and braces, the clewlines, buntlines, and bowlines. I know all about it, mother. Now, aren't you ashamed to have me lubbering round here like a dandy in a hay-field?"

"No: I'm sure I am not," replied Mrs. Somers with emphasis. "You have been a good boy, and worked hard all summer."

"But I haven't had any thing to do for a week but stow my grub and pick my teeth."

"It won't hurt you to lie still for a week or two."

"Well, mother, I want to go into the navy; and I think I shall be just as safe there as I shall at home, and be earning something all the time, too."

"I should think you'd rather be at home than off to sea this winter. Don't you hear the wind howl out-doors?"

John did hear the wind howl, and he had heard it before, and it did not disturb his bright vision of life on the wave: on the contrary, he rather liked its music. He suggested, in reply, that the coast of South Carolina or the mouth of the Mississippi would be a warmer and pleasanter place to spend the winter than the cold hills of New England. While they were debating the question, a loud knock at the front door interrupted the discussion; and John bolted the balance of his supper, while his mother went to answer the summons.

"Does Captain Somers live here?" inquired a gentleman at the door.

"Yes, sir, he does; but he is away from home now," replied Mrs. Somers. "Won't you walk in, sir?"

"Thank you: I wish to see his son, John Somers," added the stranger, as he followed Mrs. Somers into the little front parlor.

"Yes, sir: I'll call him," said she, as she glanced nervously at the shoulder-straps which the gentleman wore; for the "foul anchor" on them indicated that he was an officer in the navy.

Leaving her lamp in the parlor, she returned to the kitchen, where John had just swallowed his second cup of tea, and was at that moment thinking, that, on board a man-of-war, he should drink his "slops" out of a tin cup, and not indulge in the luxury of plates, knives, and forks.

"There's a gentleman wants to see you, John," said his mother; and her heart was full of misgivings, and that foul anchor still haunted her imagination; and she could not persuade herself that the officer had not come to carry off her boy, and ship him in the navy.

"Wants to see me?" exclaimed John, who was not in the habit of receiving many visitors through the front door.

"Yes, and he is an officer in the navy."

"What can he want of me?"

"Don't you know who he is, John?" asked the anxious mother, who had more than half suspected that there was a plot to rob her of her remaining son.

"I don't; I haven't the least idea, mother.'

"Well, don't keep him waiting, John, whatever he wants; but I hope you won't do any thing without consulting me."

"Of course not, mother," replied John, as he left the room.

Mrs. Somers sat down in a chair near the parlor door, and tried to hear what the stranger said; for she was very nervous and uneasy. She could not make out what the gentleman wanted : so she concluded that the small lamp she had left in the parlor would not afford sufficient light on the subject of the meeting ; and she lighted a large kerosene lamp, and carried it into the apartment herself. The conversation did not seem to be interrupted by her appearance ; and she therefore concluded that the officer and her son were not engaged in any plot or conspiracy against the peace and comfort of the present head of the Somers Family.

" Madam, perhaps I ought to speak to you as well as to your son about the object of my visit," said the officer, as Mrs. Somers deposited the lamp on the mantel-piece.

" Well, I don't know, sir," replied she, fully expecting to hear a proposition for John to go into the navy that very night.

" Captain Barney sent me after your son," he continued.

" That was not very kind of Captain Barney," thought the poor mother, now fully convinced that John was doomed to the navy ; but she did not say any thing.

" I reside in the next town to this, and am at home for a short time on a furlough. My father was suddenly taken very ill this forenoon ; and, about an hour ago, the doctor declared he could not live till to-morrow morning."

" I'm very sorry," said Mrs. Somers, beginning to be deeply interrested in the sad story of the stranger ; " and, if I can do any thing to help you, I'll go right over."

" Thank you : we do not need any assistance at home. My brother is a captain in the garrison down at Fort Warren, and my father has expressed a very strong desire to see him. I hastened over to Pinchbrook to take the cars for Boston ; but I was too late. All I could do then was to take a boat, and go down to the fort. Captain Barney, who is a friend of mine, offered to let me have his boat ; but I don't know any thing about Pinchbrook Harbor, and must have a skipper. I am informed that your son is one of the best boatmen in the place, and knows every rock and shoal in the bay."

" I think I do, sir," replied John quietly.

" But it is an awful night to go upon the water," added Mrs. Somers, as she glanced at the windows, the loose sashes of which were beating a tattoo against the frame.

" I know it is a bad night, Mrs. Somers ; but I have been afloat in many a worse one. It is not a pleasure excursion ; and I would not ask such a favor with a less reasonable excuse than that which I have offered."

" John knows best about such things ; and, if he is willing to go, I shall not object," added Mrs. Somers.

" Of course I am willing to go, mother. But you are not going yourself, are you, sir?"

" I feel that I must."

" I thought you would want to go back to your father."

"I do; but I am afraid you would not be able to gain admission to the fort without me."

"I guess they would let me in."

"I am afraid not; and if my brother should fail to reach home in time to see my father, through any neglect of mine, I should never cease to reproach myself. I will go with you."

"Dress yourself warm, John, before you go: it is an awful night on the sea," added his mother.

Leaving Mrs. Somers with the stranger, John hastened to put on his "sea rig," and in a few moments returned to the parlor, with an oil-cloth coat on his arm, and a fisherman's hat in his hand.

"All ready, sir," said he.

"Ay, ay, my lad," replied Lieutenant Bankhead, as he rose, and bade adieu to Mrs. Somers.

"Now be careful, John," added Mrs. Somers, as she followed them to the door.

"I'm always careful, mother. Don't be a bit scared about me," replied the young salt confidently.

"I wish that man didn't belong to the navy," said Mrs. Somers to herself as she closed the door: "he will be certain to fill the boy's head full of notions afore he gits back, and he'll be more'n ever for going. Well, well, it can't be helped. I hope the poor soldier will see his father afore it's too late;" and she resumed her household duties in the kitchen.

CHAPTER II.

THE DASHAWAY IN A NOVEMBER GALE.

JOHN SOMERS had been as uneasy as a fish out of water ever since his brother went into the army; an event which had occurred the preceding spring. He was quite as patriotic as Thomas, and was just as desirous of doing something to help his struggling country in the hour of her peril. His tastes were for the sea; though he would rather have joined the army than not had a part in the glorious work of putting down the Rebellion. But his mother had steadily resisted his importunity, and the month of November found him still at home, an unwilling resident beneath the parental roof, discontented and unhappy even in the midst of those hallowed associations which make home the dearest spot on earth.

If the summoning voice of his country was powerful, the gentle tones of his mother were more potent. Though he did not reason and philosophize on the subject, he felt that his mother was nearer to him than his country; yet he hoped that she would yet give her consent to his going into the navy.

Pinchbrook was situated a few miles from Boston ; and its port, which was dignified by the title of Pinchbrook Harbor, was located upon one of the arms of the sea connected with Boston Bay. It was a thriving little place ; and, during the summer, John, besides taking care of his father's little farm, had contrived to earn a few dollars by doing odd jobs in the village, and especially by acting as skipper, cook, or foremast-hand, on board the sail-boats and yachts of the place. He was a skilful boatman, and was thoroughly proficient in the science of nautical cooking. His chowders, fries, and battered-clams were entirely unexceptionable ; and, at a pinch, he could bake a bluefish or make a batch of biscuit.

But John was not satisfied with his achievements at Pinchbrook Harbor and in the bay, nor with the proceeds of his labors. His wages in the navy, not to mention sundry huge expectations which he entertained of pocketing some enormously large dividends of prize-money, would yield a far better return for his labor. He was satisfied that he could do more for the support of the family away from home than he could by " loafing about Pinchbrook," as he modestly designated his humble operations ; and, when he left the cottage with Lieutenant Bankhead, he fully believed that the something had turned up for which he had so impatiently waited for months.

To make the acquaintance of a lieutenant in the navy was a piece of good fortune which he had not anticipated, and he was convinced that he should make a favorable impression upon the mind of his passenger before they returned from the fort. It was, as his mother had remarked, an awful night to go upon the sea; but he had weathered some heavy gales in a fore-and-aft schooner, and he was satisfied that he could keep Captain Barney's little yacht right side up in any thing short of a West-India hurricane.

As they walked down to the harbor, Lieutenant Bankhead questioned his young skipper in regard to the boat in which they were to venture upon the stormy bay, and the dangers they would encounter on the passage. These inquiries, however, were only intended to "bring out" the young salt, and develop his knowledge of the business he had undertaken. His replies were so satisfactory, that the officer soon became as confident as his skipper; and, moreover, he began to entertain a very high respect for the character and ability of his new companion.

"You'll do, Jack," said Mr. Bankhead, after he had fully tested the knowledge of the boy, and the peculiar seamanship necessary for the safe management of a sail-boat; "you'll do. I can handle a ship: but I never attempted to work a boat under sail; that is, I never

made a business of it.   If you put me through all right,
I'll give you a ten-dollar bill, and be much obliged to you
besides."

"I'll do the best I can ; but it blows pretty heavy, and
there's an ugly sea running."

"I know it, my boy ; and so much the more credit to
you if you take me through handsomely."

"I don't think there'll be any trouble about it, sir.
Captain Barney's boat's as stiff as oak and iron can
make her, and she works like a lady in a sea.   Here is
the wharf.   I don't know your name, sir."

"Lieutenant Bankhead, of the navy.   Yours is Jack
Somers ; at least, everybody calls you so."

"Yes, sir ; and it's a good name enough for me.   I
wish it was written on the shipping-papers in the navy."

"Perhaps it may be yet.   We want all the likely lads
of your build and spirit that we can get."

"I should like to go in," added Jack, as he cast off
the painter of a small dory, in which they were to pull
out to the moorings of the sail-boat.

"Why don't you, then ?"

"My mother don't want me to leave home.   If you
will step into this dory, sir, I will pull you off to the
Dashaway."

"Dashaway ! is that the name of the captain's boat ?"

"Yes, sir : he christened her himself."

"Well, it's a smashing name.   By the by, I will speak

to your mother about your going into the navy, if you wish," added Mr. Bankhead, as he stepped into the dory, and seated himself at the stern.

"Thank you, sir; but I don't think she will let me go."

"Perhaps she will. I am ordered to the Harrisburg, and very likely I can induce your mother to let you ship in her. Well, this comes heavy," added Mr. Bankhead, as a wave dashed its spray all over him.

But the passage from the wharf to the Dashaway occupied but a few moments: and John soon placed his passenger upon the half-deck; and, after making fast the dory to the moorings, he joined him. The skipper opened the cuddy, which was large enough to contain two berths and other conveniences, and invited him to enter, and thus protect himself from the cold wind and the dashing spray: but Mr. Bankhead was too much of a sailor to shun his own peculiar element; and, enveloping himself in a heavy pea-jacket he found in the cuddy, he offered his services to assist in getting the boat under way.

"You are the skipper, Jack, and I will obey your orders," said he. "What shall I do?"

"You may knot these reef-points in the foresail, if you please, sir, and I will put a couple of reefs in the mainsail. It will help us get off the quicker."

"But you don't intend to carry a reefed foresail and a reefed mainsail, do you?" asked the officer.

"No, sir: we will try it under jib, and mainsail with two reefs. I think she will carry it; but, if she won't, we shall be all ready to put her under a reefed foresail."

"Just so; I understand you; and your calculation is a very good one."

In a few moments these preparations were completed, and the mainsail was hoisted. The wind blew even fresher than John had supposed; but he still believed that the Dashaway would carry her jib and double-reefed mainsail.

"Now, sir, if you will stand by the helm, I will let go the moorings, and hoist the jib," said the skipper, when every thing was in readiness for a start.

"Ay, ay, my lad. The jib-sheet leads aft, don't it?"

"Yes, sir."

John then cast off the moorings, and, seizing the halyard, ran up the jib in the twinkling of an eye. Mr. Bankhead then made fast the sheets, and the Dashaway, catching a heavy flaw, heeled over till her washboard was nearly submerged,—an antic which caused the lieutenant at the helm to cast loose the mainsheet, under the impression that she was going over.

"She can stand it, sir," shouted John, as he hauled in the sheet again, and took his place at the helm.

"She makes cantering work of it, anyhow," added Mr. Bankhead, whose nerves were somewhat shaken by the heeling-over of the boat.

"She's good for a bigger blow than this. Now, if you will take a seat on the weather-side, or lie down in the cuddy, we shall soon get our bearings. There, sir, she jumps over the waves like a feather."

Captain Barney was too much of a sailor himself to own any other than a stiff, weatherly boat; and such was eminently the character of the Dashaway. She breasted the big waves like a mass of solid oak; and though the spray dashed furiously over her, as she leaped over the angry billows, John Somers felt as safe in her as he would in the kitchen of his mother's cottage. The wind was east, and the sky overcast, which made the night exceedingly gloomy and dark. The intrepid young skipper could only discern the sombre outlines of the islands and the headlands of the main shore; but these were sufficient to enable him to lay his course.

Lieutenant Bankhead, though an older and perhaps a better sailor, did not feel so much confidence in the weatherly qualities of the Dashaway. He was accustomed to large vessels, and he could not help realizing that his life was in the keeping of the bold youth at the helm. He was silent and thoughtful. His father was dying at home; and, without this solemn fact, a man with a soul could not but be impressed and awed by the wild war of the elements, within the circle of whose contending forces the little bark that bore him on his mission of parental affection was struggling on her course.

He was silent and anxious; and John, fully alive to the responsibility which rested upon him, was too busy and too earnest to talk. The roaring of the wind, the surging of the waves, and the thumping of the boat against the sturdy sea, were the only sounds to be heard; and they were enough to occupy the whole mind of a thinking being, and idle words seemed to be an insult to the majesty of the storm.

On flew the Dashaway, till the dark form of Fort Warren appeared like a gloomy shadow upon the eastern sky. They were soon sheltered from the fierceness of the blast by the high walls of the fortification, and the boat came into comparatively still water. The spell seemed to be broken; and the lieutenant, who had hardly spoken a word since the boat got under way, uttered some hearty commendations of the skill of the boatman.

By the exercise of the same good judgment which had enabled him to bring his little craft in safety through the darkness and the storm to her destination, John, with the assistance of his passenger, laid her alongside the wharf which forms the only landing-place at the island. Here, as Mr. Bankhead had anticipated, a serious difficulty presented itself. The fort was at that time, as it is at present, used as a place of confinement for political prisoners. Messrs. Mason and Slidell had just been placed within its strong walls, to meditate upon the folly and crime of rebellion against the best government on earth ; and the military regulations, which excluded the curious and the lawless, were necessarily very stringent.

"Keep off, keep off!" shouted the sentinel on the wharf, as the boat rounded up by the pier, — "keep off, or I'll fire into you!"

"I am Lieutenant Bankhead, of the United-States Navy ; and I come on business of pressing importance."

"Show your pass," replied the guard hoarsely.

"I have no pass."

"Keep off, then, or I will fire! My orders are very strict."

"Will you pass the word for the officer of the guard?"

"I can't do it. Keep off, or I must fire!"

"One word, and I will go. Who is officer of the day?" demanded the lieutenant.

"Captain Bankhead."

"He is my brother. His father is dying. You can put the boatman and myself under guard."

This statement seemed to produce an effect upon the sentinel, and he ordered both John and his passenger to come upon the wharf. The corporal of the guard was sent for, and soon appeared with a lantern in his hand, which enabled him to see the shoulder-straps of Mr. Bankhead. He directed them to get into the boat again, while he despatched a man for Captain Bankhead. It was some time before the latter appeared ; and then half an hour was consumed in seeing the commandant of the fort and obtaining the necessary furlough.

It was after ten o'clock when the two brothers were embarked on the Dashaway for the return trip. If there was any change in the weather, it was for the worse. The rain had begun to fall, and the gale had not decreased in violence.

"Now, my lad, you have two lives besides your own, instead of one, in your keeping, and you must have a sharp eye to windward," said Lieutenant Bankhead.

"I shall do the best I know how. We will run up under the reefed foresail; but a small boat going before the wind makes worse weather than on any other tack. She will shake you up a good deal; but she will land you at Pinchbrook Harbor in two hours from now, if nothing happens," added John, as he cast off the painter, and pushed off from the wharf.

"This is an awful night," said Captain Bankhead, who, being no sailor, began to be filled with doubts and fears as the Dashaway leaped forward upon her course.

But, notwithstanding the doubts of the sailor and the fears of the soldier, the brave little bark bore them safely over the stormy waves, till in mid-channel, just below Fort Independence, a dark object on the water, dead ahead, attracted the attention of the watchful skipper.

"Sail ahead!" said Lieutenant Bankhead.

"I see it, sir."

"I will go forward, and see how she heads."

The naval officer went out to the heel of the bowsprit to determine the course of the approaching vessel.

"Steady," said he.

"Steady," replied John.

CHAPTER III.

THE SAILOR AND THE SOLDIER.

THE approaching vessel, which appeared to be a pilot-boat, was close-hauled, and was beating down the harbor. Her course, at the time she was discovered on board the Dashaway, was at a sharp angle across that of the little schooner. She was going off on the port side of the Dashaway; and all danger of a collision seemed to be over, though Lieutenant Bankhead still retained his position on the forecastle.

"Hard a-port the helm!" shouted the naval officer suddenly: "she is going in stays!"

"Hard a-port it is!" replied John promptly, as he put the tiller in the direction indicated.

"Keep her away, keep her away! Up with your helm!" screamed Mr. Bankhead, as the stranger came about, with her sharp bows close aboard of the Dashaway.

John had obeyed the order of the lieutenant: but, at the instant he did so, he realized that it was a mistake, which, if executed, would be likely to swamp the boat;

and, the moment the foresail began to shake, he jammed the helm hard down, at the same time hauling on the fore-sheet, thus bringing her up to the wind. The Dashaway began to draw again, and swept round in a graceful curve: but the stranger was upon them; and, to the eye of the officer at the heel of the bowsprit, a collision was inevitable.

"Jump for your lives!" shouted he, as he sprang from the forecastle of the Dashaway, intending to grasp the bob-stay of the pilot-boat; but he missed his mark, and went into the water.

Captain Bankhead was about to follow the example of his brother, and save himself from the impending wreck of the Dashaway.

"Stay where you are!" exclaimed John, seizing him by the arm, as the Dashaway swept round, barely grazing the bows of the stranger. "We are safe!"

"But my brother is lost!" replied he in an agony of suspense.

"He leaped aboard the vessel."

"No: he fell into the water," gasped the captain.

The pilot-boat had swept by on her course; but, on discovering the accident, she came up with the wind.

"Boat ahoy!" cried a voice from the rolling waves.

John put the Dashaway about, and came up again before the wind, heading for the spot, as nearly as he could judge, whence the sound proceeded.

"Go forward, and haul him in, if you see him!" said John, sharply, to the soldier.

"Boat ahoy!" again cried the lieutenant.

"I hear him!" replied the captain, as he sprang forward. "I see him!"

A huge wave bore the struggling sailor upon its crest, and his brother attempted to grasp his extended hand; but the boat swayed off, placing him out of reach of the willing soldier. But, fortunately, John saw the poor fellow, as the wave lifted him up; and, putting the helm down, he rushed to the side, and succeeded in grasping the lieutenant by the arm. With the aid of the brother, he was hauled on board, nearly exhausted by his struggles with the angry billows.

John sprang to the helm again; for the boat had nearly swamped by getting into the trough of the sea. Without loss of time, he put her upon her course again. The Dashaway had shipped a great deal of water; and the young skipper, without regarding the dignity of his passengers, ordered the captain to take the bucket, and bale out the standing-room.

"Do it, Fred," said the lieutenant. "I can take care of myself now."

"We are all right now. How do you feel?" asked John of the sailor.

"I am almost used up; but I shall be better in a few moments," he answered feebly.

In a short time he had recovered his breath, and was able to assist the soldier in the labor of clearing the standing-room of the water. When this work was completed, the boat rode easier over the seas, and confidence was in a measure restored in the minds of the passengers, who had seated themselves by the side of the skipper.

"I have been overboard twice before; but I was never so near being drowned as I have been to-night. My lad, you have saved my life, and I shall never forget it as long as I live," said Lieutenant Bankhead.

"I did the best I could for you, and I am sorry you had such hard luck."

"If it had been I, that would have been the end of me," added Captain Bankhead: "I should have gone to the bottom like a stone."

"So should I, if Jack hadn't hauled me in just as he did. My wind was about gone, and I should have given up in half a minute more. Fred, do you know that minutes seem like years when a man is overboard in a heavy sea?"

"I never tried it."

"When you missed your grasp, I gave up for lost; for I knew I couldn't hold out till the boat went round and came up again. Jack, you are the pluckiest little fellow I ever saw in my life."

"I tried to do what I could," replied John modestly.

"No one could have done more or better; but, my

lad, why didn't you put the helm hard a-port, as I told you?"

"It would have gybed the boat, and she would have filled and gone down if I had."

"Perhaps you are right. You know your boat better than I do."

"Besides, I was satisfied she would go clear if I brought her up to the wind," added John. "If you had stuck by the Dashaway, you would have been all right."

"But I was sure the schooner would come aboard of us."

"It was a close shave: we only escaped by the skin of our teeth. I wouldn't try it again for a hundred dollars."

"I wouldn't for a thousand."

"We may well thank God that we are still alive," said the captain.

"With all my heart I do thank him," replied the sailor reverently. "I shudder when I think of our poor mother: what a blow it would have been to her in the midst of her woe if only one of us had returned to close the eyes of our dying father!"

The brothers were silent during the rest of the passage; for thoughts too solemn and holy for utterance were stirring their souls. Without further incident or accident, the Dashaway reached her moorings. Lieutenant Bankhead assisted John in making all snug on board of her, after which they pulled ashore in the dory.

"I never was so glad to set my foot on land before," said Captain Bankhead, as he stepped upon the wharf. "I am half frozen, as well as frightened out of my wits."

"I don't feel very comfortable; but we have no time to spare."

"I suppose not: it must be two o'clock in the morning," added the captain, whose teeth were chattering with the cold.

As they walked up from the wharf, they discovered a person approaching them. It was Captain Barney, at whose stable Lieutenant Bankhead had left his horse. He had been anxiously awaiting the return of the boat; for the howling wind and the cutting rain had raised some doubts in his mind concerning the prudence of his action in permitting Mr. Bankhead and John to venture upon the bay on such a night. He had not expected to see them yet, and was merely walking down to the wharf to take an old sailor's glance at the sea and the weather.

"Is that you, Jack Somers?" said he, as he approached the party; for it was too dark to make them out with his eye.

"Yes, sir: we have come back safe and sound," replied the young skipper, proud and happy that he had succeeded in executing the duty imposed upon him.

"I am glad to see you, Bankhead; for I've been worrying about you. It has blowed heavy ever since you went away, and I began to be afraid that I had made a mistake in letting you go. Well, I see there are three of you : so I suppose you found your brother."

" Yes, sir, — Captain Barney, my brother," added the lieutenant, introducing the parties, who were strangers to each other.

" Happy to know you," replied the old gentleman. " You are not a sailor, and I suppose you don't take this kind of a night as kindly as your brother."

" It's a terrible night to go to sea, and I'm thankful to be once more on the solid earth."

" So am I," added Lieutenant Bankhead. "But, captain, we have no time to lose."

" Come into the house and warm you, while I get your horse ready," said Captain Barney, as they reached the hospitable mansion of the old shipmaster.

John volunteered to get the horse ; and the two officers went into the house, where their kind host insisted upon providing them with dry clothing. By the time the horse was ready, they had not only put on dry garments, but they had related the history of their perilous cruise, and given John Somers the highest commendation for the skill, coolness, and energy with which he had discharged his duty.

" He saved my life, and I shall never forget him," said Lieutenant Bankhead in conclusion.

" He's a smart fellow," added Captain Barney.

" He wants to go into the navy : and, if I can have any

influence with his mother, he shall go; for we want as many such fellows as we can get."

The two brothers shook hands with Captain Barney and John, and the lieutenant promised to visit Pinchbrook again as soon as he could. Though it was only half-past twelve o'clock, instead of two, the sad mission which had induced him to venture upon the water in such a night urged him to the utmost haste, and he drove off at a rapid pace.

"Jack, you are a smart boy!" said the captain bluntly, as the vehicle disappeared in the gloom. "You have done a big thing to-night, and it may be the making of you. Come into the house and warm yourself now. I've got some hot coffee and a lunch on the table."

"Thank you, sir; but mother will be worrying about me, and I think I had better go home as soon as I can."

"That's right, Jack: you are a good boy. Always look out for your mother. But you must have a cup of coffee and a bite before you go."

The old gentleman insisted; and John concluded that the coffee and eatables would enable him to walk enough faster to make up for lost time: so he followed Captain Barney into the house, and consumed a marvellously large quantity of bread and ham in a marvellously short space of time, very much to his own satisfaction, and not less to that of his bountiful host.

"Jack!" said Captain Barney, who sat in his armchair, watching the busy jaws of his young friend.

"Sir," replied he, not in a very clear tone; for his mouth was too full for a favorable exhibition of the human voice.

"You have made a good friend to-night."

"Yes, sir; but I only did my duty."

"Did your duty, you dog!" roared the captain, laughing heartily. "That's just what I've been saying. It's every man's duty to do the best he can, blow high or blow low; but blow me, Jack, if there's one man in a thousand that does it. Why, Jack, if every man did his duty, we should all be angels, and every rogue would be fit to make a parson of."

"I couldn't do any less than I did; but I thought the lieutenant had piped down for the last time when I saw him go overboard," replied the happy boy, as he finished his lunch. "Now I must go home, sir. I will come down in the morning, and put the boat in order."

"Well, go home, Jack, and quiet your mother; and within a month you will be a reefer on board a man-of-war. Good-night, Jack."

"Good-night, sir."

John walked home as fast as his legs would carry him; for he knew his mother was worrying about him, and would not go to bed till he returned. I need not tell my readers how gladly she welcomed him home after the dangers through which he had passed, nor with what a motherly interest she listened to the story of the cruise, nor record the exclamations of wonder and alarm with which she interlarded the exciting narrative. But, before two o'clock, John was sound asleep, dreaming of batteries and broadsides, bobstays and bowlines, great guns, cutlasses, and boarding-pikes.

CHAPTER IV.

THE NAVAL RENDEZVOUS.

BOUT a week after the events recorded in the preceding chapters, Lieutenant Bankhead paid another visit to Pinchbrook; but the way had already been prepared for him. Mrs. Somers, finding that she should be compelled to yield to the tremendous pressure which would be brought to bear upon her, had already decided to yield gracefully and without a struggle. Captain Barney had used his eloquence to some purpose; but the strong desire of John to serve his country was the most powerful influence acting upon her mind.

On the morning after the captain's visit, John was somewhat surprised to hear her open the subject herself, without any prompting on his part.

"I have been thinking about your going into the navy, John, ever since I waked up this morning."

"Have you? Well, what do you think about it, mother?" replied John.

"I have come to the conclusion **that you had better go, if you want to.**"

"Of course, I want to go; but I don't want to go if you are not willing. I shouldn't have a moment's comfort if I thought you were worrying about me all the time."

"I don't think I should worry any more if you were gone than I have for the last two or three months."

"Well, I didn't mean to drive you into letting me go."

"You haven't. I've made up my mind that you will just be as well off in the navy as you will be at home. You always was a good boy; and I expect you will behave yourself wherever you go."

"I always mean to do that, mother. A fellow can't be a very bad boy in the navy, they are so strict."

So it was decided that John should go into the navy; and there wasn't half so much friction about the matter as he thought there would be when the final action should come. His mother seemed to be entirely satisfied to have him go; and she was more cheerful for the few days following the decision than she had been before. All doubt and anxiety on the subject were removed, and she was disposed to look on the bright side of the case

When Lieutenant Bankhead appeared, there was no occasion for the array of excellent and convincing arguments which he had provided to overcome the mother's repugnance to the proposed step.

"Is your son at home, madam?" said he, after the introductory remarks were concluded.

"Yes, sir: he is out in the garden. I have sent Jenny after him, and he will be here in a few moments."

"I suppose you know what kind of a time we had upon the water the other night," continued the visitor.

"Yes, sir: John told me all about it."

"And, of course, he told you how deeply I am indebted to him for the service he rendered me?"

"He didn't say much about that," replied Mrs. Somers, who did not know but that he might think her son had criticised the conduct of his passenger on that eventful night.

"He is a brave little fellow, and I owe him a debt I shall never be able to repay."

"Oh, well! John don't mind that."

"But I mind it; and I should have been here before to repeat my thanks, if the death of my father had not prevented."

"John thought ever so much of you; and I rather think he is much obliged to you for falling overboard, and giving him a chance to pull you into the boat. But you are not the first man that John has pulled out of the water," added the mother proudly.

"I am very glad to have obliged him, though it is not every young man whom I should be willing to oblige in that manner. But, madam, your son wishes to go into the navy."

"Yes, sir; he has been wanting to go ever since the

war broke out: but I couldn't make up my mind to let him go before; and John isn't a boy that would go without his mother's leave."

"Good boys always love and respect their mothers."

"But I've made up my mind to let him go just as soon as he has a mind to He wanted to go off and sign the papers yesterday; but I told him he had better wait till he saw you."

"Indeed! I am very glad you have consented.

"Yes, sir; I thought it would not do any good to hold out any longer: and John is a good boy, and will behave himself wherever he goes. Here he comes: he can speak for himself.'

Lieutenant Bankhead rose, and grasped the hand of John as he entered the room; and, after they had talked a while about their trip to Fort Warren, the subject nearest to the young man's heart was again brought up for consideration. His grateful friend gave him all the information necessary for his guidance in the important step he was about to take. It was decided that John should enter the navy on the following day; but, as the ship to which Mr. Bankhead had been ordered would not be ready for sea for a few weeks, it was thought best, for several reasons, that the young sailor should enlist in Boston, and spend the period of his probation on board the receiving-ship at Charlestown. The arrangements having been completed, and an appointment made for

John to meet his friend in the city at noon the next **day,** Mr. Bankhead rose to take his leave.

" Jack, I dare say you may think I am a very forgetful man," continued the lieutenant, with a smile upon his handsome face.

" Forgetful? I don't understand you, sir. I'm sure I never thought any thing of the kind," replied John, blushing up to his eyes.

" You know, I promised to give you ten dollars if you brought me back safely from the fort the other night."

" I never thought of it, sir."

" Well, I did ; though the illness of my father drove it out of my head for the time," added the officer, taking out his porte-monnaie.

" Really, sir, I don't want you to give me a cent. I don't ask any thing for what I did."

" I don't care what you want, Jack. My conscience wouldn't let me sleep at night, if I didn't keep my promise. Oh ! you needn't blush, my boy : I'm not going to pay you ; but I want to make you a small present, and my brother insisted upon adding something to my little gift. Here is mine, and here is my brother's ; " and Mr. Bankhead handed him first a hundred-dollar bill, and then a fifty-dollar bill.

" Why, sir, I " —

" Take them, Jack, just to oblige me," added the lieutenant.

"No, sir: I can't take all this money. It will burn my fingers if I keep it."

" If you feel afraid of it, just hand it to your mother, who, I dare say, will find a good use for it."

John protested, and Mrs. Somers protested; they protested singly and together: but the officer was resolute, and positively refused to take back the bills.

" If I thought I could pay you, Jack, in money, I should have given you a thousand dollars. There is an elderly lady, who lives only seven miles from here, who is just as grateful to you as I am; and, when she feels able to leave home, she is coming over to see your mother; and I know they will be the best friends in the world."

" Who, sir?" .

" My mother, Jack. She already thinks a great deal of you, my boy; and, when she sees you, she will not think the less of you."

Lieutenant Bankhead took his leave; and John and his mother were so bewildered when he had gone, that they hardly knew what had happened during his visit. But there were the two bank-bills to attest the reality of what had occurred; and the rest of the day was spent in making preparations for the sailor-boy's departure. The question of what should be done with the hundred and fifty dollars caused considerable discussion; for Mrs. Somers thought it should be placed to John's credit in the Savings Bank, and he declared she must use it to make herself comfortable until he could get some money to send home. John was the stronger party in the argument; and the money was carefully deposited in the bureau-drawer, to be expended as the necessities of the family might require.

The next morning, John rose very early, and did his "chores" about the house as usual. These were his last hours at home; and, though he was not a very sentimental lad, he couldn't help visiting all the familiar spots in the vicinity, and recalling all the pleasant little incidents of the past. He might never see them again; and, when he left the little chamber which Thomas and himself had occupied since they were old enough to leave the trundle-bed, he was weak enough to shed a few tears He compared his comfortable bed with a hammock or the berth-deck of a sloop-of-war; but, when he thought that he was going forth to fight for the glorious stripes and stars, he was reconciled to any privations which he might be called upon to endure.

The hour for his departure came; and after his mother had given him a few words of counsel, and a blessing warm from her heart, he kissed his sisters, shook hands with Gran'ther Greene, and rushed out of the house before any one had an opportunity to shed many tears. At the railroad station he found many of his young friends who had come to see him off: but the train was approaching; and after Captain Barney had wrung his hand, and his friends had given him a hearty God-speed, he stepped into a car, and, as it seemed to him, actually entered upon his career as a sailor-boy.

If our space would permit, we could, no doubt, tell what Jack Somers was thinking about as the train hurled him along into the arms of his future destiny. He was a good boy, and I suppose he thought of every thing that would be likely to occur to the mind of a good boy leaving home to take a part in the most momentous war in which a nation ever engaged. But, of whatever else he thought, I am sure that his mother was uppermost in his mind. For her sake he was resolved to be true to his God, his country, and himself.

At the appointed time, he met Lieutenant Bankhead at the hotel where he was boarding while in the city; and after dinner they repaired to the naval rendezvous, where John was duly presented for examination under the auspices of his influential friend.

"Your name, my lad?" demanded the recruiting agent.

"John Somers," replied our hero with a promptness which was part of his nature.

"How old are you?"

"Seventeen, sir."

"Have you been to sea?"

"Yes, sir."

"How long?"

"One voyage to the West Indies, and two to Charleston. I have been about boats ever since I was a baby."

"I can vouch for him that he is every inch a sailor," added Lieutenant Bankhead; "and the smartest lad in a small craft I ever came across in my life."

"Looks like it," said the agent. "What can you do, my lad?"

"Hand, reef, and steer. I know something about rigging; but I don't want to ship as an able seaman."

"Good: ordinary seaman, then; though you are rather young."

"Better than half of them in the service," said Jack's friend.

"All right, Mr. Bankhead. We will take your word for it."

"I ought to know: I have sailed with him when I wouldn't trust myself in the hands of many a skipper that I have known."

John was then taken into another room, where he was ordered to "strip," and was thoroughly examined with regard to his physical condition. A minute description of his person was then written out, including his height, complexion, color of his eyes, and other distinguishing marks, which would enable his officers to identify him if occasion should require. He was pronounced sound in every respect, and fit to serve the United-States Government in the capacity of an ordinary seaman.

The men on board a ship-of-war are shipped in three classes: landsmen, who know nothing about a ship; ordinary seamen, who can " hand, reef, and steer," and who are sent aloft to perform the ordinary work of a sailor; and seamen, sometimes called " able seamen," who are competent to do every thing required in fitting out and working the ship; who know all about rigging, splicing ropes, making and mending sails; who can rig and unrig any spar; and who understand the lead.

Landsmen, at the time of which we write, received twelve dollars a month. They remain on deck, haul the halyards, braces, and other ropes which are worked on deck, clean up, and do general work. The pay of an ordinary seaman was fourteen dollars a month; and of a seaman, eighteen. There are also three classes of boys, called first, second, and third class boys, — according to their knowledge and physical ability, — who received, respectively, nine, eight, and seven dollars a month.

When a sailor ships for the navy, he is supplied with clothing, and other articles of comfort and luxury, upon credit; that is, the value of the goods is charged to him, to be deducted from his future wages. As my readers may be curious to know the contents of Jack Somers's bag, I shall add a list of the articles with which he was supplied, and the prices of them : —

1 Pea Jacket, ...$12 00
1 Blue Cloth Jacket, ...10 00
1 pair Blue Cloth Pants,....................... 4 00
1 "   "   Satinet do. 3 00
1 Blue Cap,..................................... 1 00
2 "   Flannel Shirts, ... 4 00
2 White Frocks,................................ 3 00
2 "   Inside Shirts, ... 3 00
2 pairs Drawers,.............................. 3 00
2 "   Duck Pants,............................ 3 00
2 "   Stockings, ... 1 00
1 pair Shoes,................................. 2 00
1 Neck Handkerchief, ... 1 50
1 Tin Pot and Pan,...........................   75
1 Jack-knife and Spoon, ...   50
1 Bar Soap and Scrubbing-Brush, ... 1 00
1 Shoe-brush and Blacking, ...   50
1 Razor, Shaving-box, and Soap,..............2 15
                                             ______
                                             $55 40

Jack blushed when the last-named articles were handed
to him; but, as he had already made some efforts to
coax a little feathery down upon his upper lip to vegetate
more rapidly than Nature was disposed, he determined to
persevere, in the hope that he might surprise his friends,
at the expiration of his term, by presenting himself before them with a full-grown beard.

Men may draw two pounds of tobacco; but it is not
allowed if the sailor is under twenty.

Our hero was appalled at the extent of his wardrobe: but Mr. Bankhead assured him he would find a use for every thing he had, unless it was the shaving implements; which made Jack blush again, as though it were wicked to shave.

CHAPTER V.

ON BOARD THE OHIO.

ON board the receiving-ship Ohio, to which all naval recruits in the vicinity of Boston are sent, Jack reported to the officer of the deck; and after his name had been registered, and sundry particulars in regard to him entered upon the ship's books, he was sent forward. A number for his hammock, and another for his clothes-bag, were given him; and he was assigned to a mess. Mr. Bankhead, having done all he could for his *protégé*, and stated his intentions in regard to him, took his leave; and Jack found himself alone, though there were hundreds of men on board the ship.

Though Jack was alone so far as acquaintances were concerned, there was no opportunity to be lonesome; for the gun-deck was thronged with men. There were old sailors who had been fifty years in the navy, and " green hands" who had just come from the country, and had never seen a ship till within a few days. There were rough, hard-visaged men, and those with no small pretensions to gentility. There were men of all colors and of every nation.

It was a lively scene, whichever way he turned; and Jack sat down upon a mess-chest to observe the strange sights, and listen to the strange sounds. Some of the men were walking up and down the deck for exercise; some were playing cards, dominoes, and similar games; some were reading, and some were mending their clothes. It was an interesting prospect to a young man full of life; but he could not help thinking of the happy home in Pinchbrook, and the devoted mother who was the central figure in the picture. On the whole, he did not like his surroundings very well. The place did not seem much like a ship, and he hoped he should not have to be confined a great while on board the old hulk.

While he was thinking of home and friends, and trying to bring his imagination to bear upon the future, a ringing blow on the top of his head confused his ideas, and completely upset the air-castle which he had erected in his vivid fancy.

"Heave up, my hearty!" exclaimed the author of this wanton mischief, as he brought the large tin pan he carried in his hand down upon Jack's head a second time.

"What are you about?" demanded the contemplative young man, springing to his feet.

"Get off the mess-chest, then, so I can get at the grub," replied the man in a surly tone.

"Why didn't you say so, then?"

"I did say so."

"Well, you had better not hit me in just that style again," added Jack angrily.

"Shut up, you young monkey! Do you think I'm going to bow and scrape to every lubber that chooses to moor his carcass on the mess-chest? Now sheer off, and keep out of the way."

Jack did not move, and, withal, wore so dignified and independent an air, that the man, who had charge of the mess to which the recruit was ordered, struck him once more, on the side of the head, with the tin pan. This was rather more than Jack's warm blood could endure, and more than his philosophy was proof against. Regardless of the rigid discipline of a man-of-war, he instantly squared off, and planted a smart blow of his fist upon the face of the surly fellow. With a volley of heavy oaths, the cook of the mess sprang at him with the ferocity of a tiger. Jack, who was cooler, defended himself on scientific principles, and repeated his "practice" upon the physiognomy of his antagonist with such effect, that either because his blows were tremendous, or because there was a spot of grease on the deck, his assailant went down.

"Avast there, Spriggs!" shouted an old and dignified salt, who was mending his pants near the scene, — "avast there, and let the youngster alone!

For a moment, the blue-jackets on the gun-deck revelled

iu the anticipation of a fight.   A crowd began to gather, but the sport was quickly nipped iu the bud by the appearance of a couple of marines with cutlasses in their hands, each of whom seized one of the belligerents.

"What's all this about?" asked one of the marines.

"What's it about?" replied Spriggs. "Why, that young lubber hit me side of the head; and I don't let any man this side of Gibraltar do that."

"He struck me three times on the head with the tin pan," added Jack; "and no man this side of Gibraltar, or the other side either, can do that."

"I shall report you to the officer of the deck," said the marine, as a couple of ship's corporals appeared, and were left to enforce a strict neutrality between the parties.

In a few moments the master-at-arms presented himself, and Jack and Spriggs were ordered to the spar-deck for examination. The parties were conducted into the awful presence of the officer of the deck, before whom all of them, including the master-at-arms, and Tom Longstone, the old seaman who had witnessed the affray, reverently touched their hats; which is the usual token of respect to an officer on board a ship-of-war.

"Well, my lad, you have made a bad beginning," began the officer of the deck, who was no doubt pained to see the *protégé* of Lieutenant Bankhead thus early implicated iu a disturbance.

"It was not my fault, sir," replied Jack.

"I beg your honor's pardon: but the youngster hit me side of the head; and what I did, yer honor, was in self-defence," said Spriggs.

"How's that, my lad?" demanded the officer.

"It is not true, sir. I was sitting on the chest, when he came up behind me, and struck me over the head with a tin pan."

"Yes, your honor: he was sodgering on the mess-chest, and wouldn't get out of the way, so I could get the hard-tack out for supper."

"Then you struck him first?" asked the officer sternly.

"He wouldn't move till I did," added Spriggs sourly.

"He didn't ask me to move, and I did not know he was near me till he struck me."

"That's a fact, yer honor," interposed Tom Longstone. "The youngster was peaceable enough till Spriggs hit him, and he did not strike back till he was hit three times."

The two marines fully confirmed this testimony, though they had not witnessed the scene which preceded the affray. Spriggs was immediately ordered to the place of confinement on the orlop-deck, there to subsist for twenty-four hours on bread and water, with irons on his ankles.

"Now, my lad, you are a green hand on board of a man-of-war," said the officer of the deck, when the guilty party had been conducted below. "You must learn that fighting is never tolerated under any circumstances. This is your first offence, and I shall let you off."

"I beg pardon, sir," stammered Jack, his face as red as the crimson bunting in the ensign at the peak, — "I beg pardon, sir; but I could not help it."

"Yes, you could help it. We don't tolerate fighting. If you have any complaints to make, you will have a chance to be heard. Now go to your mess, and remember what I have said."

Jack touched his hat as he saw the others do, and went below. He was perfectly willing to remember what the officer had told him: but it did not exactly accord with his ideas; and he was very much afraid, that, under the same temptation, he should be likely to repeat the offence.

"There, youngster, you've larned a lesson," said Tom Longstone, as he settled himself upon the mess-bench, and resumed his labors at the dilapidated trousers he was attempting to restore to their former state of usefulness.

"I'm much obliged to you for what you said for me," replied Jack, as he took a seat by the side of the old salt.

"You're welcome, my hearty. I hope you won't need a word from me again to keep you out of the 'brig,' which is the prison on board a man-of-war."

"I hope not; but I can't stand it to be thumped round, as Spriggs began with me."

"You are smart and spunky, my lad; and I like you for't: but, when one of them ere flunkies strikes you foul, you must sarve 'im out some other way."

"I don't know any better way to serve out a bully than to give him as good as he sends, on the spot."

"Nor I neither, my lad; but 'twon't do board a man-o'-war. That's beatin' to wind'ard for the sake o' runnin' on the rocks Sheer off, and sarve 'im out some other way."

"A fellow will be bullied and trodden upon by every petty tyrant in the ship, if he submits to it."

"No, he won't, youngster. A man finds his level board a man-o'-war just as he does everywhere else. If a man behaves himself, everybody — officers and all — will treat him with respect. I've been in the navy thirty years, and I know it's a fact."

"What could I do, when that man struck me? If I had submitted, he and others around would have repeated the insult."

"Sarve him out some other way," replied old Tom mysteriously.

"I don't understand what you mean."

"You'll larn, my fightin'-cock," added Tom with a cunning smile.

"What would you have done if Spriggs had struck you on the head with a tin pan?"

"He wouldn't have done that to Tom Longstone, nor any other man board this 'guardo.'"

" Perhaps not; but suppose he had ?"

" I should have knocked him over, just as you did, my spunky one."

" But then you would have gone into a fight."

" Not I, my lad. I should have sheered off as soon as I had a done it; and left the ship's corporals to take care of him, if he wasn't satisfied. I might have cut down his hammock arter he turned in, or dropped a belayin'-pin on his toes, or something of that sort; but I shouldn't get up a fight with him. The fact is, my crank little one, an ill-tempered fellow is sarved out so many ways, board a man-o'-war, that he soon larns to mind his own business."

" Well, I dare say I shall soon learn the ways of my new shipmates; but I don't half like the fashion of hitting a fellow in the dark."

" You can't fight it out board the ship, and you won't stand it to be bullied by a flunky. As to hitting 'im in the dark, my little breezer, that's all in your eye. Your flunky knows who does it, and so does every man in the ship. That's our way of sarvin' 'im out."

" Very likely I shall get used to it in a short time : at any rate, I mean to do my duty faithfully, obey orders, and keep up to the discipline of the ship."

" That's right, my jolly bantam : that's the way to get along in the navy."

Tom Longstone was a veteran in the navy, and knew

every rope in the ship, as well as every quirk in its discipline, and was thoroughly posted in all the superstitions and traditions of the service. For some reason or other, — perhaps because he had displayed the spirit of a man, — the old salt was strongly prejudiced in Jack's favor at the first interview, and proceeded, in due form, to take him under his protection. Tom pumped him dry in regard to his parents, his native place, his antecedents upon the sea and the land. He examined him in seamanship, inquired carefully into his moral and religious principles, — as carefully as though Jack had been a candidate for the situation of chaplain instead of ordinary seaman, — and was particularly nice in his inquiries into the incipient hero's patriotism.

"You see, my jolly little clipper, I believe in two things: one on 'em is the Bible, and t'other the 'Meriken flag. I never throwed a vote in my life, and never had nothin' to do with politics; but the man that says any thing agin the 'Meriken flag, why, smash my cutwater, but he's my enemy! Them's my sentiments, Jack. I haven't got no other creed, in politics or religion. Stand by the Bible and the 'Meriken flag, my hearty, and it'll be all right with you in this world and t'other one too. Steady! there's the boatswain's whistle piping to supper. Here, my jolly biscuit-nibbler, stow your little carcass in here, and I'll see that the sharks don't gnaw your walking-timbers off."

Tom Longstone seated himself at the mess-table, upon which the grub had been placed, during the conversation, by a steward *pro tem.*, who had been deputed to serve in the place of Spriggs. They did not have hot biscuits and baked apples for supper; but the fare was good, wholesome, and abundant in quantity. Jack was introduced to his mess-mates, in man-of-war style, by Tom; and very soon the conversation turned upon the events which had occurred before supper, and our hero was duly commended and admired for his manliness.

"He'll larn better how to sarve out a flunky one of these days," said Tom, who was proud of his *protégé*. "That's just the way you'll sarve out the rebels, my lad: lay 'em aboard, and carry 'em all standing."

"I hope I shall behave myself on such an occasion," replied Jack modestly. "I came into the navy to fight for my country, and I intend to do my duty."

"That's the idea, my merry little piper. Stand by the stars and stripes as long as there's a plank left."

"I reckon some of us will be drafted before long," added Ben Blinks, a weatherly old tar, who had just returned from a foreign cruise, and shipped again for three years.

"The sooner the better," said Jack with enthusiasm.

"I've been aboard the guardo about as long as I want to be," continued Bob Rushington, a man-of-war dandy, who wore ear-rings, and had shining black curls.

"I say, Jack, who's the officer that convoyed you aboard?" demanded Tom Longstone.

"Lieutenant Bankhead."

"Bankhead? He is a gentleman and a scholar. I've heard good things of him."

"He promised to have me drafted into his ship," added Jack.

"Good, my little honey-bee; and, if he takes you, he must take me," said Tom, bringing his fist down upon the mess-table.

"I think he would be very glad to have you."

"Suppose you put in a word for me."

"I will, with pleasure."

"And for me," added Blinks.

"Likewise for me," suggested Rushington.

Half a dozen others made a like request; and Jack did not know but he should have the pleasure of drafting the whole crew for Mr. Bankhead's ship. But, after consultation with Tom, he decided to use his influence only for Blinks and Rushington: first, because he liked them; and, second, because Tom said they were first-rate seamen.

CHAPTER VI.

JACK TAKES A LESSON IN DISCIPLINE.

ON the following day, Spriggs was released from confinement; having served out his twenty-four hours upon bread and water. He was ordered to resume his duties as cook of the mess. He looked at Jack with an evil eye: but, as our hero was under the powerful protection of three old men-of-war's men, he behaved tolerably well; and Jack, willing to forgive him, treated him as handsomely as though nothing had happened to disturb their friendly relations.

"Just keep an eye to windward, my lad," said Blink after supper. "Spriggs looks as though he meant mischief."

"Thank you, I will," replied Jack; "though I am willing to let by-gones go for nothing."

"Spriggs isn't: so just keep your weather-eye wide open."

"Do you think he will attempt to whip me?"

"Not he; he has got enough of that: but he'll upset a pot of hot tea in your lap, or do some dirty trick of that sort."

"I'll look out for him."

"Just keep right up stiff into the wind, and we'll see you through if he attempts to fool you."

Jack paid no apparent attention to Spriggs, though he kept a close watch upon all his movements. When the hammocks were piped down at night, he observed that his enemy kept a sharp eye upon him, and he had no doubt he intended mischief. He mentioned his suspicions to Blinks, whose hammock was slung next to his own."

"All right: he's got your bearings, and he means to cut you down."

"I don't see that I can help myself, unless I keep awake all night."

"Yes, you can: we'll rig a dummy for you."

Blinks explained his plan; and, with the assistance of his other friends, they deposited four twenty-four-pound shot in Jack's hammock. Another shot was slung over the hook, in such a manner that the ropeyarn which held it in position would be severed when the revengeful villain cut the lanyard of the hammock. Bob Rushington then stowed himself away under the lee of the mainmast, and Jack occupied his hammock. All these preparations had been very carefully conducted, so as to avoid the keen scrutiny of the master-at-arms and the ship's corporals, who form the active police of a man-of-war; but it is more than probable that one of the latter officers knew all about the proceedings, and was quite willing that Spriggs should be " sarved out " in his own coin.

The conspirators kept themselves wide awake, though they were careful to avoid an open breach of discipline. The lights were all put out, so that nothing could be seen ; and silence reigned upon the decks of the Ohio, on which were berthed not less than a thousand men. Jack was nervous and expectant. Four bells — ten o'clock — struck ; and he began to be very sleepy, and impatient for the trap to be sprung. At five bells, he began to think that he had mistaken the purpose of his malignant enemy ; and he was just going to sleep, when down thundered the cannon-balls upon the deck, rolling off into the scuppers with a noise like the mutterings of a distant tempest. At the same time, a heavy groan saluted the ears of the aroused sleepers, as well as of the ingenious conspirators who had plotted and executed the mischief.

" What's the row ? " demanded Blinks, as innocently as though he had just been awakened from the slumber of innocence itself. " Who's hurt ? "

" Oh, my foot ! " groaned the sufferer, who appeared to be unable to retreat from his position.

" What's the matter with your foot ? " asked Rush-ington, who had come forward from the mainmast to ascertain the issue of the plot.

" It's smashed to a jelly ! " groaned Spriggs, whose tones were readily recognized by the occupants of the hammocks in the vicinity.

" How did you do it?   Did you roll out of your hammock?   I heard an awful fall of something out here just
now," added Rushington, whose voice seemed to melt
with sympathy for the afflicted cook of the mess

Spriggs made no reply to these direct questions; for
we doubt not his conscience was as sore as his foot. One
of the ship's corporals on duty upon the berth-deck presently appeared, and demanded the cause of the disturbance.

" Spriggs has tumbled out of his hammock," replied
Rushington. " The ship gave a lee-lurch, and pitched
him out."

" Oh, my foot!" groaned Spriggs.

" I don't exactly see how you could smash your foot
tumbling out of a hammock," added the ship's corporal.
" There aren't a very heavy sea runnin' just here alongside the wharf, nuther."

" I didn't fall out of the hammock," said Spriggs in
savage tones.

" Didn't you? Then maybe you can tell how it happened?'

" I don't know what it was: somebody dropped a shot
on my foot."

" What were you doing her?" demanded the officer
of police.

Spriggs declined to answer this question; and the un-
pitying official, for some reason or other, did not press

the question, but ordered the sufferer to come with him to the hospital, and have the injured member examined.

"I can't walk," sighed Spriggs, as he attempted to rise. "My foot is smashed to a jelly, I tell you!"

"If that's so, Spriggs, I reckon you'd better stick to your hammock another time, and not go skylarking about decks at this hour of the night," added Rushington, whose advice was certainly good and well meant. "If you can't walk, we will carry you to the sick-bay."

The ship's corporal and the seamen picked up the discomfited conspirator, and bore him to the hospital. As soon as they had disappeared, Blinks carefully concealed the ropeyarn by which the cannon-ball had been suspended; and, having repaired as well as he could the damage to Jack's hammock, they all turned in, and slept without further disturbance.

Spriggs was confined to the sick-bay for a week; and it was a month before he could walk without limping. On his return to the mess, he seemed to be satisfied, and treated his companions with proper respect and consideration. When he came back, Jack was taking his turn as cook of the mess; a position in which each man in succession serves for one week. He felt that his predecessor in office had been amply "sarved out;" and, though he did not like the man, he wished to be at peace with him. He treated him respectfully and kindly, and used every means in his power to conciliate him. His efforts were not in vain ; for, before our hero left the receiving-ship, Spriggs had forgiven, and perhaps forgotten, the past : at any rate, they were on as good terms as two persons not mutually respecting each other could be.

Jack had not seen Mr. Bankhead since they had parted on the deck of the Ohio ; for the latter had gone to Philadelphia, where his ship was fitting out : but our sailor-boy had written to him in regard to his future prospects, and, in his letter, had taken occasion to mention his three friends who had desired him to intercede for them. He had received a favorable reply, and for several weeks had been impatiently waiting to be summoned to a more active field of labor.

At the time of which we write, there was a deficiency of seamen at the navy-yards of Philadelphia and Washington, and drafts were occasionally made on those at Charlestown and Portsmouth. After Jack and his friends had waited till their patience was nearly exhausted, they were delighted to hear that Lieutenant Bankhead, first-lieutenant and executive officer of the United-States steam sloop-of-war Harrisburg, was upon the spar-deck, and would immediately draft a number of seamen for his ship.

"Now, my breezy little reefer, your time has come," said Tom Longstone, as the word was passed along among the men : " Mr. Bankhead is on deck."

"I will run up and see him," replied Jack hastily, as he started to execute his purpose.

"Avast, there, avast! Belay every thing!" exclaimed Tom, as he grasped his *protégé* by the arm, and detained him.

"What's the matter, Tom?" demanded Jack, rather surprised at the conduct of his friend.

"Don't be in a hurry: just moor your hulk alongside of Old Tom on this mess-chest, my sentimental little skipper, and let us overhaul this matter a little."

"But Mr. Bankhead is on deck, Tom; and I want to see him."

"All right, Jack: so he is. If he wasn't, I wouldn't say a word. Mr. Bankhead is first-lieutenant and executive officer of the sloop-of-war Harrisburg. Now, my lively little pap-consumer, what are you?"

"What am I? What am I? Why, I'm an ordinary seaman in the navy, and hope soon to be drafted into the Harrisburg."

"Precisely so; but you don't know no more nor a marine. Are you goin' for to go for to throw yourself into the arms of Mr. Bankhead, just as though he was your fust cousin, and you'd been off on a long v'y'ge?"

"He will be very glad to take me by the hand," said Jack, rather mystified at this representation of his own insignificance.

"Jack, don't you stick your flipper out to Mr. Bankhead any more'n you'd put your leg into the maw of a ground shark," continued Tom earnestly.

"Why not?" demanded Jack, who thought Tom's suspicious were an insult to his friend, and a reflection upon his sincerity.

"Why, you young monkey, you are as green as a horse-mackerel! You don't know no more nor a landlubber!"

"Mr. Bankhead has seen the time when he was glad to obey my orders," replied Jack smartly.

"Ha, ha, ha!" laughed Tom, taking off his cap, and pitching it down upon the mess-table; while Blinks and Rushington roared till their sides ached at the self-sufficiency of the young sailor.

"Well, you may laugh as much as you please; but says he, 'Jack, you are skipper, and I will obey your orders. What shall I do?' says he. 'Knot these reef-points in the foresail,' says I; and he did it."

"All that may be, my noisy little boatman; but things is changed since you and Mr. Bankhead went on your last cruise. I s'pose you think he'll take you into the cabin, rig you out in long togs, and mess you with the ward-room officers."

"I don't expect any thing of the sort, Tom: I don't want him to do any thing of that kind. I am willing to do my duty like any other fellow on board."

"So much the better, my darling; for Mr. Bankhead is too sensible a man for to make a baby of you. He aren't a-going to feed you with warm milk. If he's your friend, he's going to make a man of you."

"I expect to fare just like my mess-mates,—no better, no worse; but I expect he will treat me like a Christian."

"He'll do that, my jolly little beef-eater; but if you go sticking your flipper out to him, just like as if you was a wardroom officer, I'll bet a month's wages he won't know you. Don't you do it, Jack. You hain't been thirty years in the navy, my precious little infant; you never saw Cape Horn; you never went up the Mediterranean; you never walked round a capstan board a man-o'-war. You don't know no more about discipline nor a heathen do about Watts's Hymns."

"What shall I do?" asked Jack, not a little puzzled by this exemplification of man-of-war discipline; and perhaps he was disposed to inquire if there was any use in having a friend in the wardroom, if he was not to be permitted to know him.

"What shall you do? There, now, my sweet little bone-cracker, them's the most sensible words you've spoken for half an hour. What shall you do? That's jest what the publiken wanted to know when he smote his breast. He smote his breast bekase he wanted to know. He didn't spile his shirt-bosom for nothin', Jack. What shall you do, my blating little lamb?

"Yes, Tom; what shall I do?" asked Jack, highly amused as well as deeply edified by the profound remarks of the old blue-jacket. "And, if you don't answer me pretty soon, I shall begin to think you are nothing but an old blower."

"Vast heavin', Jack : respect my bald head, and never let that little tongue of yourn unkile any thing that sounds like a nick-name. It's a bad practice, and nothin' but lubbers and marines ever does such things," replied Tom sagely.

Jack had his doubts upon this point, though he did not venture to express them, but again pressed his question.

"What shall you do, my little snivelling milk-sop?—what shall you do?'

"Yes; what shall I do, Tom? That's what I want to know ; and, if you don't answer pretty soon, the boat-swain's whistle will cut short your yarn, as it did yesterday."

"I'll tell you, Jack. Just throw your ear-ports wide open, and belay that frisky little tongue of yourn, and I'll tell you in less time than it would take a monkey to run up the main-to'-gallant-mast backstay."

"Blaze away, Tom !" replied Jack impatiently.

"Ay, ay, my lad : here goes. When you're mustered, and Mr. Bankhead goes round lookin' at every man from keel to truck, and gazin' down into his peepers as though he'd lost his jack-knife down them,—I say, my oily little butter-chops, don't you do so much as wink at him. I say, Jack, you mustn't know Mr. Bankhead from Adam's great-grandfather. If he wants to know you, he'll tell you on't. If he wants to shake hands with you, he will send the ship's cook to let you know it three weeks aforehand, so't you can be all ready for the honor that's in store for you. Mind that, Jack; and you've larnt a lesson that'll make a seaman of you."

And just then the " people " were mustered, and Jack and his friends tumbled up on the spar-deck to undergo the scrutiny of the executive officer of the Harrisburg.

CHAPTER VII.

THE HARRISBURG.

IT was fortunate for Jack Somers, that, when the crew were mustered to enable the officer to make his selection, he was prepared by the lesson of Tom Longstone for his interview with Mr. Bankhead. As the old man-of-war's man had suspected, our sailor had fully anticipated a very cordial greeting from his friend, the first-lieutenant of the Harrisburg; and, without the explanation he had received upon the gundeck, he would have been very much hurt by the cold and stiff manners of that gentleman. As it was, he expected nothing in the nature of a courteous acknowledgment of their former acquaintance. But in this he was happily disappointed; for though Mr. Bankhead did not indulge in any thing like familiarity with him, and did not even shake hands with him, he was greeted with a pleasant smile, which was sufficiently significant to him.

"I am glad to see you again, Jack," said he, in addition to the condescending smile which made our sailor-boy the envy of a score of blue-jackets who noticed it. "Of course you will go with me."

"Thank you, sir," promptly replied Jack, as he touched his cap to the lieutenant with a degree of respect which exhibited the remarkable progress he had made in discipline.

"Where are your friends, Jack?" added Mr. Bankhead.

"This is Tom Longstone, your honor," answered Jack, giving an extra flourish of discipline to his reply.

Tom was accepted, and so were Blinks and Rushington, very much to the satisfaction of all these worthies; for the Harrisburg was a crack ship, and to be drafted into her was a stroke of good fortune worthy the highest appreciation of the gallant tars. That evening, those who were selected by Mr. Bankhead were sent to Philadelphia in charge of an officer, where they arrived on the following day. Jack wrote a letter to his mother before his departure; but he had no opportunity to see her. His friends, including Captain Barney, had been to see him once on the regular visiting-day; and he had hoped that they would come again before his departure. He was disappointed in not being permitted to look once more upon the face of his mother, though he rejoiced in the prospect of soon engaging in active duty. The affectionate letter which Jack wrote to her no doubt assured her that he was still the same loving son; that the new life upon which he was entering had not blotted from his remembrance the hallowed associations of home.

Jack had but little chance to see either New York or Philadelphia on his journey : but he was more desirous of fighting for his country than he was of seeing its great cities ; more inclined to think of the active career before him, than of the vanities and pleasures of a large town The draft of seamen was duly transferred to the receiv ing-ship at the navy-yard, and our hero again found himself subjected to the discipline of the " guardo."

Fortunately for his peace of mind, he was not long condemned to this idle and distasteful life. The Harrisburg lay at anchor near the receiving-ship,— a beautiful vessel, exhibiting every element of strength and endurance ; and, as Jack occasionally glanced through the open port at his future home, he admired her fair lines, and longed for the time when he should be transferred to her. The welcome order came in due time, and the crew of the gallant ship were sent on board.

Jack and his friends were disposed to give three cheers when they reached the deck of the Harrisburg ; but, as this would have been a breach of discipline, it was not attempted. Our hero soon had enough to think of ; for the executive officer immediately mustered the men, to give them their stations, and assign them to their messes.

On board a man-of-war, every thing is arranged with the nicest precision. A thorough system pervades the ship, and every thing is done by rule. The Harrisburg had a hundred and twenty men crowded upon her spar-deck at this muster: but in a short time, under the efficient and methodical arrangement of Mr Bankhead, order came out of chaos; and, when he had finished his work, every man knew where he belonged during each hour of the day and night; where he was to go when the ship went into action; when she was to tack or wear; when the sails were to be set, furled, or reefed; where he was to take position if the ship caught fire, or was boarded by an enemy. Every one knew where he was to eat and sleep, where he was to stow his hammock and clothes-bag, and every thing else which was to enable him to discharge his duty as one of the wheels in the complicated machine of which he was an essential part.

If our readers are not familiar with ships, we shall find it very difficult to make them comprehend Jack Somers's position and duties on board the Harrisburg; but we shall endeavor to give them some ideas upon the subject. A ship, and especially a man-of-war, is a complicated structure; and our young friends must not expect any more than a partial view in these pages, for the whole volume would be no more than sufficient to do justice to the subject.*

The Harrisburg was a screw-steamer of about two

---

* We refer those who are curious to know more about ships-of-war to Master Brady's "Kedge Anchor;" to Herman Melville's "White Jacket, or the World in a Man-of-War," and, for ships in general, to Mr. Dana's "Seaman's Friend."

thousand tons burden, and usually denominated a sloop-of-war. She was a full-rigged ship; that is, she had square sails on her fore, main, and mizzen mast, and could be worked under sail or steam, as occasion or necessity might require. She carried twenty-eight guns, all of which were placed upon her upper or spar deck. Some large men-of-war, called ships-of-the-line, have four decks. The Ohio, in which Jack had spent several weeks, was of this class. The upper deck is then called the spar-deck; the next below it, the gun-deck; the third, the berth-deck; and the fourth, or lowest one, the orlop-deck.

The decks, which in a house would be called floors or stories, are not divided off into rooms; so that, forward of the officers' cabins, they look like long halls. The square holes, or windows, through which the muzzles of the cannon are pointed, are called port-holes, or ports. They are closed by two doors,—one swinging up, and the other down.

The Harrisburg had two decks, properly so called, — the spar-deck and the berth-deck. On the former, where the guns were placed, all the working of the ship is done, as well as the fighting. There is no house or other structure upon it, as is generally seen on board a merchant-ship. Upon the berth-deck the men eat and sleep. The after-part of this deck contains the cabins of the officers. The captain occupies a cabin by himself in the aftermost part of the ship Next forward of this is a large apartment, having small staterooms on each side of it, called the wardroom, which belongs to the commissioned officers of the ship. Next to the wardroom is an apartment called the steerage, divided into two parts, the port and starboard steerage, in which live the midshipmen and master's mates, the assistant engineers in a steamer, and the "forward officers,"—viz., the boatswain, gunner, carpenter, and sailmaker. Down in the bottom of the ship are placed the boilers and engines.

The hold, or place under the berth-deck, is divided into a great number of rooms; such as the paintroom, the storeroom, the breadroom, shot-locker, shellroom, sloproom, magazine, lightroom, coal-bunkers, chain-lockers, tier gratings, and other cells and holes. The magazine contains the powder, and is lined with copper. It is so constructed that it can be filled with water—flooding the magazine—when the ship takes fire. No man is allowed to enter it unless clothed in a dress prescribed for this duty, with no nails in his shoes, or metal buttons upon his garments. The lightroom adjoins the magazine, and is simply a small room to hold the powerful reflecting-lamp, which throws its light into the magazine through a large pane of heavy glass. This arrangement is intended to prevent the necessity of taking a lantern into the magazine, where the slightest spark might doom the noble ship to instant destruction, and her gallant crew to an untimely death.

The principal officer of the Harrisburg was the captain, whose rank in the navy, at the time of which we write, was that of commander. Under the old system, the highest grade in the navy was captain, who, when he commanded a squadron (two or more vessels) was called a commodore ; but this title was not authoritatively recognized in the Navy Department. A captain who had been in command of a fleet or squadron was thereafter called " commodore," as a mark of distinction, in the same manner that a member of Congress keeps his "Hon." after he has ceased to hold his office.

Whatever the nominal rank of the chief officer of a ship-of-war, he is called the captain He is supreme in his command, being subject only to his orders and the naval regulations Everybody on board must obey his orders, and without asking any questions. Being " monarch of all he surveys," he does not give his orders to the men who are to execute them, but to the first-lieutenant ; who is also called the executive officer, because it is his duty to execute all orders from the captain. For example : If the captain wants the ship put upon the other tack, he does not give the order, " Ready about," to the seamen ; " Put your helm down," to the quartermaster who cons the helm : but he simply directs the first-lieutenant to " Come in stays ;" and this functionary gives the

various orders to the officers and men who are to execute them.

The first-lieutenant is the *working* commander of the
ship. The other wardroom officers of the Harrisburg
were the second, third, and fourth lieutenants, the sailing-
master, the surgeon, the paymaster, lieutenant of marines, and chief engineer.

The ship's company are divided into two watches, each
of which serves alternately on deck for four hours during
the day and night. At all times, the deck is in charge of
an officer; and the period that he serves is called his
watch. He is then the officer of the deck. The first-
lieutenant does not keep a watch : this duty is performed
in turn by the second, third, and fourth lieutenants, and
the master. For ordinary ship's duty, each watch-officer
serves four hours on deck, and twelve below ; but, when
all hands are called, every officer must be at his station,
and the first-lieutenant take command of the deck. The
master, who has charge of the navigation of the ship, is
not necessarily a watch-officer.

The surgeon, besides the obvious duty of such an
officer, has the entire charge of the sanitary condition of
the ship. He not only prescribes for the " people " when
they are sick, and dresses their wounds in battle, but he
must inspect the ship at times, and report any thing
which may tend to injure the health of the crew.

The paymaster — formerly called the purser — not

only performs the duties which his title implies, but he has the charge of all stores and goods, clothing and provisions, belonging to the Government, on board the ship. He has a clerk to assist him; for he must keep all the accounts with the officers and men, charging them with clothing or other stores with which they may be supplied, that it may be deducted from their wages when they are paid.

The lieutenant of marines has the command of the marines, or soldiers, on board the ship, of whom there were twenty in the Harrisburg. These men are employed as sentinels in various parts of the ship. One is always stationed at the wardroom door, one at the "brig," and one at the scuttle-butt, or pump. At anchor, one is on duty at the gangway, or place where the ship is entered; and one on the forecastle. Between sailors and marines there is a mortal antipathy, which the officers do not seek to abate; for the soldiers are depended upon in case of mutiny and insubordination.

The chief engineer has the sole charge of the engines and boilers, and the subordinate engineers are under his command. On board our ship there were one first, two second, and four third assistant engineers; these officers having the actual charge of the engines, keeping watch like the other officers: but their chief does not keep a watch.

Master's mates and midshipmen, who occupy the steerage, are aids to the various officers, and have miscellaneous duties.

The forward officers are, the boatswain, who has charge of the rigging and cordage ; the gunner, who has charge of the guns and ammunition ; the carpenter, who does the joinery-work ; and the sailmaker, who makes and mends sails. The boatswain has four mates, one of whom is called chief. The gunner has one mate, and one quarter-gunner for each division of three guns on a side. The carpenter and sailmaker have each one mate, and each his gang, selected from the crew.

All ranking below the forward officers are called petty officers, of whom there is a host : such as captain of the fore, main, or mizzen top ; captain of the hold, of the forecastle, of the after-guard ; quartermaster, master-at-arms, ship's corporal, yeoman, armorer, &c.

Quartermasters have charge of the wheel, or steering-apparatus, of the signals, and of the lead. The master-at-arms is the chief of police, assisted by the ship's corporals. The yeoman has charge of the ordnance and stores. Each of the boats is in charge of a petty officer called a cockswain. The duties of the other petty officers will be understood from their names.

CHAPTER VIII.

"ALL HANDS, UP ANCHOR!"

JACK SOMERS had a very correct idea of the interior of a man-of-war, and of the various officers and their duties, when he went on board the Harrisburg; but he was not a little confused by the many numbers he had to remember, which were used to indicate his various stations at the guns and the mess, on deck, in the top, in the boat, and in his hammock.

He was placed in the starboard watch, stationed in the mizzen-top, belonged to the third division of the battery, attached to gun No. 9, was first loader, and second boarder. In furling sails, he belonged on the starboard-yard arm of the mizzen-top-gallant yard. In reefing topsails, his place was on the port-yard-arm of the mizzen-topsail yard. In tacking or wearing ship, his position was at the lee main-brace. In loosing sails, his place was the same as in furling. In getting up the anchor, his duty was at the capstan. In boat, he pulled the bow-oar of the captain's gig.

Jack Somers was a good boy, and was determined to know and do his duty. As soon, therefore, as he had a chance to sit down by himself, he began to think over and fix in his mind his various stations, and to rehearse all that had been said to him. But he found that he had already forgotten some of his numbers; yet, by the grace of the first-lieutenant, he was permitted to consult the station-bill, a document in which the position of every man in the ship is recorded. As perseverance always overcomes every obstacle, he soon made himself proficient in all his numbers.

While the ship remained at her moorings in the river, the crew were daily exercised in their various duties, and Jack soon became practically familiar with every thing required of him. After he had been on board about a week, the proper signal was hoisted, every fire and light in the ship were extinguished, and the powder was taken in, and stowed in the magazine.

"Now, my little roisterer, we shall soon be in blue water," said Tom Longstone, as they gathered around the mess-table that afternoon.

"The sooner the better," replied Jack. "I want to tand by that gun No 9 when she pours shot and shell into the rebels"

"You will have a chance one of these days, my bantam, if you are patient."

"We may be sent off on blockade duty," said Ben

Blinks, who, by some contrivance of interested parties, was in the same mess.

"Then we shall have a chance to gather up some prize-money," added Bob Rushington, who, by the same contrivance, was a member of mess No. 4.

"I should like the prize-money very well," continued Jack; "but I don't like the idea of hugging a sand-bar for the next six months."

"Well, my hearties, old Tom ain't no prophet: but I really don't think this ship is going on the blockade; and, if she don't have some rebel shot through her in less than three months, I'm content to give half my grub to the jollies."

"Where do you suppose we are bound?" asked Ben.

"Don't know; don't care: but this ship ain't a-going to burrow in the mud, no how. Now, mind what old Tom says, and write it down in your log-book."

It was quite impossible to tell whether Tom was right or wrong: but his words were accepted for all and more than they were worth; for the speaker was a kind of oracle among the seamen, on account of his long experience in the service. The next morning, the engineers and firemen were observed to be very busy; and soon the smoke was seen to issue from the smoke-stack. The fires roared for several hours in the furnaces, and the steam hissed in accord with the impatience of the crew to be off.

After Jack's patience had been sorely tried by the long delay, he welcomed with a thrill of delight the pipe of the boatswain.

" All hands, up anchor ! "

It seemed to him just as though the beginning of all things had come, and he sprang to his station at the capstan. The first-lieutenant was now in charge of the deck : he had received his orders from the captain, and was proceeding to the systematic execution of the details. The second-lieutenant was on the forecastle, with the boatswain near him. The third-lieutenant was in the waist, and the fourth on the quarter-deck, near the mizzen-mast. These were the stations which these officers took when any manœuvre which required all hands was to be executed.

" Ship the capstan-bars ! " said the first-lieutenant.

The order was repeated by his subordinates ; and all the sailors assigned to this duty seized the bars, and inserted them in the drum of the capstan.

" Bring-to, forward ! " continued the executive officer ; which order was repeated by his juniors as before.

Our non-nautical readers will not, perhaps, understand this command ; and we will try to render it into English. The cable to which the anchor is attached, and which holds the ship to the bottom, is a very large iron chain. A rope, called the " messenger," is attached to this chain by a contrivance called a " selvagee." The messenger extends from the cable to the capstan, around which it is passed several times. When the capstan is turned by the men, of course it winds up the messenger, and hauls in the chain fastened to the anchor. "Bring-to, forward," was the order requiring the men to attach the messenger to the cable, and pass it around the capstan.

"Are you ready forward?" shouted the first-lieutenant, after he had waited a sufficient time for his former order to be executed.

"All ready forward, sir!" responded the second-lieutenant.

"Walk round with the capstan!" added the first-lieutenant.

The men went round with a will; and Jack would fain have sung his "Yo-heave-oh!" as he had been accustomed to do at the windlass on board his father's vessel: but the "people" of a man-of-war are required to execute their duties in silence. The music of a fife, playing Yankee Doodle, as an accompaniment to the movement, was, however, some consolation, and assisted him very much in keeping the needed "stopper on his jaw-tackle."

"Anchor away, sir!" said the boatswain, who was on the forecastle, ready to report what progress the cumbrous anchor was making in its passage upward to the regions of daylight.

"Anchor away, sir!" repeated the second-lieutenant.

"Strike one bell!" continued the first-lieutenant, addressing the quartermaster, who was stationed at the wheel.

Old Tom Longstone, who was in charge of the wheel, struck one bell, which was the signal for the engineer on duty to "go ahead slowly."

"Anchor's up, sir!" added the boatswain, after the men had walked round the capstan a while longer.

"Anchor's up, sir!" repeated the second-lieutenant.

"Pawl the capstan!" ordered the first-lieutenant; which meant that it was to be secured, so as to keep the anchor where it was. "Unship the capstan-bars!"

This order was repeated by the under-officers, and executed in good order by the men. There was no crowding or treading upon each other's corns; but every one knew his place, and did not get in anybody's way.

"Cat the anchor!" said the first-lieutenant.

The ponderous anchor was now hanging at the hawse-hole; and the execution of the order last given would secure it upon the top of the bulwarks, ready to be dropped overboard when occasion should again require its use.

"Lay forward to the cat-falls!" said the boatswain; and those whose duty it was to do this work attached a purchase-block to the anchor, for the purpose of hoisting it up to the cat-head, which is a timber projecting out over the bow of the ship.

"All ready with the cat, sir!" reported the second-lieutenant.

"Walk away with the cat!" replied the executive officer.

On board a man-of-war, the ropes are not pulled hand over hand; but the men walk away with them: that is, they run along the deck with them as firemen do with the engine.

"Strike four bells!" continued the first-lieutenant to the quarter-master at the wheel; which meant. "Go ahead at full speed!"

The Harrisburg was now actually in motion, and gliding down the Delaware upon her mission of destruction among the rebels; if, indeed, such was her mission: for none of the crew had the remotest idea where the good ship was bound, or upon what kind of duty she was ordered. If the officers knew, they did not condescend to inform the men; for the "people" are as far removed from their superiors in social rank in the ship, as though they were not all equals before the democratic law of our land.

"Here we are!" said Jack enthusiastically, as he placed himself by the side of Bob Rushington, who was gazing through one of the open ports into the water.

"Yes, my lad, we are off," replied the dandy sailor, who looked very sad and sentimental for the moment. "Has it occurred to you that not every one who is full of life and hope to-day will return alive and well from this cruise?"

"Well, I hadn't thought any thing about it," replied Jack with a smile, as he glanced at the wry face of his friend, "and, what's more, I don't mean to think any thing about it."

"You are a thoughtless boy," sighed Bob. "Some of us will lose the number of our mess before many weeks have passed by"

"Very likely, Bob: but we are going out to fight fo; our country; and, if we are not ready to die for her, we have no business here."

"Very true, my lad; but the future is dark and un, communicative."

"Come, Bob, you splice too many syllables on your words. You are a brave fellow, and ready to do your duty."

"I trust I am; but sad thoughts come like the autumn of the year."

"Avast there, Bob!" said Ben Blinks. "Don't frighten the lad."

"He doesn't frighten me," added Jack. "I put my trust in God; and, come what may, I know it will be all right with me as long as I do my duty to my God and my country"

"Why, darken my toplights, if the lad don't talk like a parson!" said Ben.

But, while they were laughing at Jack for his pious expression of faith, the drum beat to quarters; and, in a moment more, the great guns were belching forth the customary salute. This was a new experience to our sailor-boy; for, though he had been through with all the forms of firing the guns, he had not before heard them "speak." The sound was perfectly stunning: but Jack was a lad of too much spirit to exhibit any signs of dislike; and, though he could not hear himself speak, he worked like an old man-of-war's man at his post.

The Harrisburg continued on her course down the river under steam alone. The strict discipline of sea service commenced, and every thing went along on board like clockwork. The regular watches were set; and the second-lieutenant, who was the officer of the deck, walked up and down on the weather-side, upon which no idlers, and no officers or men not on duty, were permitted to intrude.

In a ship-of-war, as in a merchant-vessel, the twenty-four hours are divided into watches of four hours each. Commencing at eight o'clock in the evening, the starboard watch is on duty till twelve. At half-past eight, one bell is struck; at nine, two bells; and so on till the end of the watch, when eight bells indicate the time for the port watch to relieve the other.

The port watch is then on duty till eight bells, or four o'clock in the morning. From four till eight is the morning watch; from eight till twelve is the forenoon watch; from twelve till four is the afternoon watch.

From four till eight are the "dog-watches;" that is, the four hours are divided into two watches of two hours each. By this arrangement, the watch which came on duty at eight o'clock the preceding night will be below during the first part of the night. If it were not for the dog-watches, the starboard watch would be on duty every night during the cruise from eight till twelve, and again from four. till eight in the morning, thus obtaining but four hours' sleep each night; while the port watch would sleep every night from eight till twelve, and from four till seven in the morning. By the change which the half-watches introduce, every man obtains four hours' sleep on watch-nights, and seven hours on other nights.

At four o'clock, when the hands were piped to supper, the Harrisburg was off Cape Henlopen, and standing out to sea.

CHAPTER IX.

"ALL HANDS, MAKE SAIL!"

SUPPER comes at four o'clock, in the dog-watches: rather an early hour, when it is remembered that Jack pipes to breakfast at eight bells, or eight o'clock in the morning. The three meals are taken within the space of eight hours; leaving sixteen hours between supper and breakfast. Jack Somers did not like the arrangement very well; but custom adapts us to every emergency, and he soon learned to lay in a stock of grub which would last him two-thirds of a day.

"All hands make sail, ahoy!" shouted the boatswain, as his shrill whistle rang through the ship after the men had concluded their evening meal.

"Lay aloft, topmen!" was the first order given by Mr. Bankhead, which was repeated by other officers at their stations. "Lower-yard men in the chains!"

The topmen ran up the shrouds, while the lower-yard men placed themselves in position to do so when the order should be given.

" Aloft, lower-yard men ! " added the executive officer at the right time. " Man the boom tricing-lines ! "

The studding-sail booms are spars which extend out beyond the yard-arms, when used ; but, when the sails are furled, they lie upon the top of them. The boom tricing-lines are attached to the inner ends of these spars, by which they may be hauled up so as to get them out of the way, and enable the men to work upon the sail

" Trice up ! " continued Mr. Bankhead ; which order, as usual, was repeated by the proper officers.

" Lay out ! " he added, when the studding-sail booms were out of the men's way ; and, in obedience to the command, they extended themselves along the whole length of the several yards, standing upon the foot-ropes, and holding on to the sail or ropes with the hands.

Jack Somers, as we have before stated, in loosing sails, belonged upon the mizzen top-gallant yard, which is the third cross-spar from the deck ; and, further, his place was at the starboard yard-arm, which is the end of the spar, on the right-hand side of the ship, looking forward. He was as much interested in the operation as though he had been in command of the ship ; for it was the first time he had performed the duty when it really meant something.

" Loose ! " said Mr. Bankhead ; and, at the word, the men " passed the gasket," which is a rope wound round the sail, to confine it to the yard when furled.

"All ready in the mizzen-top!" added the captain of the top, when the operation was performed; and the men stood holding the sails in place upon the yard.

The captains of the main-top and of the fore-top indicated, in like manner, that they were all ready for the next order, and, when the lieutenants upon deck had reported the fact to the executive officer, he proceeded with the manœuvre.

"Let fall!" and, at the word, all the sails to be set were shaken out at the same moment, and dropped down from the yards.

"Overhaul your rigging aloft!" proceeded Mr. Bankhead; and his order, translated into the shore vernacular, meant that the men on the yards were to arrange the sheets, buntlines, clewlines, and other ropes, so that they could work freely, or not impede the progress of the sail when it should be hoisted up.

"Man your sheets and halyards!" was the next command.

The sheets are the ropes on the topsails, by which they are hauled down to the yards. For example, — the mizzen-top-gallant sail was fastened to the mizzen-top-gallant yard, upon which our hero was stationed. Attached to the lower corners of this sail were two ropes, passing over a sheave, or pulley, in the mizzen-topsail yard. These two ropes were the sheets; and, when the sail is set, they are drawn tight, to keep it in place.

All the yards of the ship, except the lower one on each mast, slide up and down. When the sails were loosed, the yards were *down*. The rope attached to the yard, passing over a sheave set in the mast, by which the spar is hoisted up, is called a halyard. Any rope by which a sail is hoisted is called a halyard.

When the men appointed for the purpose had taken hold of the sheets and halyards, the various officers reported that they were ready.

"Haul well taut!" said Mr. Bankhead.

The effect of the execution of this order was to bring every thing to its bearings.

"Let go, and overhaul your rigging aloft!" continued the first-lieutenant.

"Sheet home, and hoist away!"

At this order the yards were hoisted up, and the sheets hauled down to their places. The operation was thus completed; the ropes, with a whole vocabulary of cabalistic names to designate them, were belayed and flemished down; and every thing was in apple-pie order.

At eight bells in the evening, the starboard watch went on duty; and Jack, muffled up in his pea-jacket, came on deck. The wind was blowing a stiff breeze; and the Harrisburg, under sail and steam, was driving through the great waves of the Atlantic at the rate of twelve knots an hour. On board a man-of-war, men are stationed at all times in the tops; which are the platforms on the masts, just above the lower yards. In large ships, they are capacious enough to hold quite a squad of men, who are on duty there in readiness to perform any service that may be required of them.

The topmen of the starboard and port watches are each divided into first and second parts, called " quarter watches," one of which relieves the other in the tops at the appointed time. When Jack came on deck at eight bells, — as he belonged to the first part of the starboard watch of mizzen-topmen, — his place was in this airy perch above the deck. It was a very safe and comfortable position, notwithstanding any prejudice which our shore friends might have against such an elevated roosting-place, in a dark night, and in a rolling sea, when the ship pitches so that a landsman would hardly be able to keep his feet on deck, much less in the tops, where the motion of the vessel is more sensibly experienced.

Jack Somers had his sea-legs on, and felt perfectly at home on the topgallant-yard arm, in the tops, and in his close quarters on the berth-deck. In fact, he had made up his mind to be a good seaman, and to conduct himself like a true patriot. The honor and glory of the American flag on board the Harrisburg had been intrusted to him, in common with about a hundred and fifty others; and he was fully alive to the responsibility which this trust imposed upon him. He had braced himself up to endure any discomforts and hardships which this new position might impose upon him; and he was not likely to be dismayed by a gale of wind or a sharp set-to with a rebel battery, much less by the ordinary life of a man-of-war's man.

Jack took his place in the mizzen-top: and, as he ascended the rigging, he began to think of home; for this was his first night at sea, and his thoughts naturally reverted to his mother's cottage in Pinchbrook. He often thought, in his leisure moments, of the blessed associations which cluster around the abiding-place of parents and brothers and sisters. It was a blessed influence which these reflections exerted upon his mind and heart. They preserved him pure and unsullied from the contaminations which surrounded him; for, with many true and good men in the ship, there were those of low and vile tastes, who lived only for the joys of the present moment. Thus far, our sailor-boy had set his face and his heart against the vices and sins of his more debased shipmates.

Of the friends that Jack had made on board the receiving-ship, there was only one among his topmates, — Bob Rushington. All three of them had been rated as petty officers; for they were really superior hands. Bob was a captain of the mizzen-top, Ben Blinks was a captain of the main-top, and Tom Longstone was a quartermaster.

"What are you thinking about, Jack?" said Bob,

when they had been in the top about half an hour, during which time his companions had been carrying on a conversation in a low tone.

"I was thinking of home," replied Jack.

"Wishing you were there," added Bob.

"No: not exactly."

"You ought to brought your ma with you," added Sam Becket with a low, chuckling laugh.

"I'm not homesick,—I hope, not yet," said Jack; "but it is pleasant to think of home."

"So it is—to babies," sneered Sam. "You haven't got larn't yet, my lad."

"I never shall learn to forget my home."

"Yes, you will; just clew down your ideas, and be a man-of-war's man. Milk for babies, rum for men, my lad. Have you got any coppers in your pocket, my boy?"

"I have three," answered Jack, thrusting his hand down into the depths of his trousers-pocket. "Do you want them?"

"Perhaps I do: that will depend upon circumstances. Do you see my hand, Jack," said Sam Becket; "if you can't, you can feel it: there it is."

"Well, what of it?"

"Odd or even?" continued Sam.

"Odd," replied Jack, not understanding the purpose of his companion.

"Odd it is: there are three of 'em, and they are yours;" and Sam took Jack's hand, and attempted to place the cents in it.

"What do you mean by that?" demanded our hero.

"What do I mean? Don't you know a boom from a bobstay? You said odd, and the coppers are yours. You won them."

"Won them!" exclaimed Jack: "I don't want to gamble."

"Hush up! Do you want to tell the officer of the deck what we are about!" protested Sam in an energetic whisper.

"I'm perfectly willing to tell him what I'm about."

"Well, you young monkey, I should think you were hailing a frigate in a nor'-wester. You are as green as a yaller squash-bug. Here, take the coppers: they belong to you; you won them."

"I never gamble," repeated Jack resolutely, but in a lower tone than before.

"Take 'em, Jack, or you're my enemy."

"I cannot take them. I'd rather go into the brig for a week than gamble for a single cent."

"Silence in the mizzen-top!" said Mr. Midshipman Dickey, who had been pacing the lee-side of the quarter-deck in the capacity of aide-de-camp to Mr. Granger, the officer of the deck.

"There, you young milksop!" said Sam in an angry whisper. "Do you see what you have done?"

"Avast there, Becket!" interposed the captain of the top. "Don't get up a quarrel with the lad. He means right."

"I won't have no quarrel with him; but he won the money, and he must take it, or he is my enemy."

"Friend or enemy, I won't take your money," added Jack firmly, as he settled his back against the mizzen-topmast rigging, and folded his arms as if to prevent the coppers which he had inadvertently won from being thrust upon him by force.

"Won't take 'em: won't ye, my hearty?"

"No, I will not: I did not mean to win them."

"Didn't mean to? Don't you know what odd and even means?"

"I didn't know it meant gambling."

"All I got to say is, that I take it as an insult."

"I did not mean to insult you."

"Then take the coppers."

"I can't do that."

"Take the coppers, and give me a chance to win 'em back, and then we'll call it square. After that, if you want to go about on the other tack, all right."

"I will not gamble to please you or any other man."

"Very well, my hearty: I'll sarve you out for this. There's two ways to insult a seaman: one is not to drink his grog when he axes you; and t'other is not to take his money when you've won it. You insulted me, Jack Somers; and I'll sarve you out the first time the wind comes from the right quarter. D'ye hear, ye little snivelling rat-catcher? Why didn't you bring your ma with you to keep you from falling overboard?"

"Because I can take care of myself, and because I want to keep my mother out of bad company," replied Jack sharply.

"Bad company! What do you mean by that, you little splatterbrains? Did you mean me?"

"I didn't mean anybody else in the mizzen-top," answered Jack in a low but stiff tone.

"Did ye? Then I'll smash your toplights!" said Sam, springing forward, apparently with the intention of inflicting summary vengeance upon his topmate.

"Avast there, Becket! Now, batten down your gab-port, and don't say another word. The lad has the rights of it. If he don't want to play, he needn't. It's agin all orders to play on board. Now let him alone," interposed Bob Rushington, taking the angry seaman by the arm.

"I'll be"—

"Belay all!" said the captain of the top firmly. "If you say another word about it, I'll report you to the officer of the deck."

Becket, in the face of this threat, did not dare to pursue his vindictive measures any further ; and, during the remainder of the watch in the top, Jack was permitted to consider without interruption the enormity of the vice of gambling, and the results to which it inevitably leads.

CHAPTER X.

"MAN OVERBOARD!"

"ALL the starboard watch, ahoy!" shouted the boatswain's chief mate, at eight bells, on the following morning.

Jack rubbed his eyes open as quick as he could, and slipped out of his hammock; for the first thing that came to his mind was his resolution always to be prompt and faithful in the discharge of his duties. As he tumbled up the ladder, and made his way aft to the mizzen-rigging to relieve the quarter-watch in the top, he saw that Sam Becket was the next man before him. This circumstance recalled the incident of the preceding evening, especially as he saw the man who had promised to be his enemy glancing over his shoulder at him. It was still quite dark; but Jack saw, or thought he saw, a very malignant expression in the countenance of his topmate.

He was determined not to give Becket any cause of offence, and therefore kept well away from him. He permitted his enemy to mount the rail, and go up several ratlins, before he ventured to follow him, fearful that the gambler would attempt to "sarve him out" by treading upon his hands as he went aloft, or kicking him in the head.

"Lively, Jack, lively!" said Bob Rushington, who was next behind him.

"Ay, ay, Bob; but I mean to give my enemy a wide berth."

"Heave ahead, Jack! Don't stop there!" added the captain of the top; for our sailor-boy had halted for a moment till his dangerous companion should get out of his way.

At that instant, Jack felt the whole weight of Becket come down upon him, and his hold upon the shrouds was wrenched off. The instinct of self-preservation prompted him to seize the nearest object, which happened to be the long legs of Sam Becket. The additional strain upon the hands of that worthy was more than he was competent to sustain; and Jack, realizing that he had grasped an insecure substance, released his hold, and recovering his balance, leaped down upon the quarter-deck of the ship.

Sam Becket, unable to obtain a new hold upon the rigging, was pitched over backwards into the sea. Jack saw with horror the catastrophe which had overtaken the gambler, and jumped upon the rail to ascertain his fate.

"Man overboard!" shouted several of the watch.

The officer of the deck gave the orders to the quarter-master at the wheel necessary for stopping and backing the engines, while the man stationed at the taffrail for the purpose detached the life-buoy.

Jack Somers stood on the rail, gazing down into the dark and treacherous sea where his topmate had disappeared. He was a courageous lad; and, without thinking of the consequences to himself or of his own weakness, plunged into the water just as Becket rose to the surface. The latter was but an indifferent swimmer, if he could swim at all; and, instead of taking his misfortune like a reasonable man, he commenced kicking and struggling in the most unaccountable manner, evidently having no control over himself in the agonies of fear.

The steamer went ahead some distance before she stopped; and Jack and his struggling enemy were left far astern in the rolling waves. Our hero, as heroes always are, was cool and self-possessed. He could not help wondering at the stupidity of his topmate in making such a fuss at such a momentous time, when his safety absolutely depended upon a careful husbanding of all his strength. But Sam continued to kick and struggle till his wind gave out; and then, when he could kick and struggle no more, he began to take the thing more coolly: in other words, he was on the point of going to the bottom, mystically rendered in seamen's vernacular as " Davy Jones's locker."

Jack, who had all the time behaved himself in a very orderly and circumspect manner, kept his eye on the burning fuze of the life-buoy, which had been ignited by the act of being detached from its beckets at the stern of the vessel. It was quite near him; for it had been dropped into the water the instant the cry which indicated the accident had sounded through the ship. When Sam showed signs of the exhaustion which rendered it safe for his topmate to approach him, Jack swam up to him, and seized him by one of his hands.

The convulsive clutch with which the drowning man closed his hand upon his enterprising deliverer assured the latter that the danger of being carried down with him was not yet over. Jack was compelled to " pay out" well to avoid this peril : but, after one more desperate struggle, the unfortunate man was quiet again; and Jack succeeded by the exercise of a great deal of well-expended strength in towing Becket to the life-buoy, to the supporters of which he secured him as well as he could.

Jack Somers was not made of iron, though he is the hero of our story ; and, by the time he had placed Becket in a position of comparative safety, he began to think it was about time for a boat to come to his relief. He was thoroughly worn out by his exertions ; and when he glanced over the tops of the waves, which were tumbling the life-buoy about in a very unceremonious manner, he was appalled to see the steamer apparently a mile off. To add to his consternation, the pyrotechnic apparatus on the life-buoy had been extinguished, either by the spray or by the limitation of its material.

The prospect was exceedingly dark and gloomy, and there were some strong indications that the career of Jack Somers in the navy would be completed with the close of the tenth chapter. Our sailor-boy could not help thinking of his mother, and the assurance he had given her that he was just as safe on board a man-of-war as in the cottage at Pinchbrook; and perhaps he might have been if he had had the worldly-minded prudence to remain on the deck of the Harrisburg, instead of trusting his carcass to the uncertain mercies of an Atlantic sea to save the life of a worthless fellow who had taken the trouble to publish himself as his enemy.

It is true, it was a sublime and Christian act to attempt to save the life of an enemy: but we are quite sure that Jack did not think of his religion, or reason upon the subject, before he dashed into the water; though a soul influenced by the pure gospel of love does not have to consider in an emergency which requires an act of prompt self-sacrifice. The atmosphere of love with which the Christian heart surrounds itself inspires the thoughts, words, and deeds; so that self-sacrifice, like a heavenly impulse, requires no cold and calculating reflection.

It was a rash act, unquestionably, however noble and sublime it may appear. It had been performed from impulse. Our sailor-boy had done, at this time, no more than he had on three similar occasions in his previous experience, though never under circumstances of so great peril. To save a boy from a watery grave by jumping over the stern of a yacht in Pinchbrook Harbor, and leaping from the rail of a ship far out to sea in the sombre shades of a winter morning, were two entirely different affairs, as Jack was now fully assured while clinging to the life-buoy exhausted and chilled.

We might transcribe some of the great thoughts which rushed through the mind of our hero, or give words to the simple prayer which his heart rather than his lips breathed to Him who holds the waters in the hollow of his hand; but, while every moment seemed a week, he saw the lights of the ship moving on the rolling ocean. The sight gave him hope; and he watched them with an intensity of feeling which no one, not clinging to a life-buoy in mid-ocean, can appreciate or comprehend.

But the lights moved not towards him. Those on board had lost his bearings, or he had drifted far from the spot where he had first committed himself to the waves. He was chilled by the cold, and exhausted by the violence of his exertions; and when he saw the steamer backing by him, and too distant to be hailed, he felt a sinking sensation of despair creep into his soul, which began to drive the life from his body. When all hope seemed to have departed, a sound, welcome as the music of the flowing rill to the thirsty, dying pilgrim, attracted his attention, and gave him strength for one more struggle for life. It was the measured thump of oars in the rowlocks of a boat. He looked in the direction from which the sound came, and discovered a blue light, which had just been fired, casting a lurid glare upon the rolling billows.

" Boat ahoy!" he shouted with all the strength of his lungs; but his voice sounded to him like that of a pygmy. He repeated the call several times, and his heart was gladdened by the answering hail of his friends.

" Where — away!" came in hoarse tones across the long, sweeping surges of the ocean.

" Boat ahoy!" repeated Jack with desperate earnestness; and he continued to shout, while the gleams of rapidly expanding hope seemed to shoot warmth and life through his chilled veins.

" I see him!" shouted the bow-oarsman, as the boat approached the buoy, still bravely bearing up its freight of human life and hope. " Steady, cockswain! Lay on your oars! Avast pulling! Back her! You will run 'em down!"

By this time the boathook of the bowman was made fast to the buoy, and in another moment Jack and his companion in misery were dragged into the boat

8

"God bless you, Jack, my boy!" exclaimed Ben Blinks, folding our hero in his arms as a mother does her child.

"Give way!" said the cockswain; and the boat came about, and pulled to the ship.

On the passage, Ben worked vigorously upon the benumbed limbs of Jack, while two others performed a similar service for Becket. When the boat reached the gangway, our sailor-boy was able to grasp the man-ropes, and ascend to the deck with the assistance of Ben Blinks; but Sam was hoisted up in slings just like a barrel of hard-tack. The sufferers were both handed over to the care of Dr. Sawsett; while the boats were recalled, hoisted up to the davits again, and the ship went on her course as though nothing had happened.

In a couple of hours, Jack Somers was as good as new; and Becket, when "the water was pumped out of him," as Ben Blinks expressed it, began to improve, and, after "general quarters," was able to give an account of his cruise.

It had been whispered about among the people that there was some foul play connected with the affair; and, the report having reached Mr. Bankhead through the officer of the deck, he proceeded to examine into the case at the first practicable moment.

"How came you to fall overboard, my man?" demanded the executive officer. "You are an ordinary seaman, and you ought to be able to go aloft without accident."

"Foul play, sir!" replied Becket in surly tones.

"What do you mean?"

"The topman below me pulled me off the rigging, sir."

"Who was he?"

"Somers, sir," replied Becket with the most unblushing effrontery.

"Somers!" exclaimed Mr. Bankhead, astonished at the charge against his *protégé*.

"Yes, sir: he caught hold of my legs, and pulled me off the rigging," added he, looking up from the hammock in the sick-bay, where the examination was in progress.

"Do you know who saved your life?—who jumped overboard after you?"

"No, sir. Who was it?"

"No matter who it was. Did Somers pull you off by accident?"

"No, sir: I think not. We had some trouble in the mizzen-top last night, and I think he has a grudge against me. He was sarvin' me out, sir."

"Marine, pass the word for Somers," added Mr. Bankhead.

Jack presently appeared, and had no difficulty in divining the occasion of the summons. The first-lieutenant stated the charge, which Jack promptly denied, giving a full explanation of the affair as it was.

" Pass the word for Rushington," said Mr. Bankhead ; and the captain of the mizzen-top appeared, and substantiated Jack's story. The trouble in the top was also ventilated.

" They are lying on me, sir ! " said Becket.

" You black-hearted scoundrel ! " exclaimed Mr. Bankhead warmly ; for his indignation could be no longer controlled. " Would Somers push you overboard one minute, and dive after you the next ? "

The wretch was taken all aback when he learned that his injured topmate had saved his life at the peril of his own : and, having convicted the culprit, Mr. Bankhead went on deck, followed by Jack and Rushington ; for the ship was now approaching the capes of Virginia.

CHAPTER XI.

THE COCKSWAIN OF THE CAPTAIN'S GIG.

THE Harrisburg stood in between the capes, and, in the course of the forenoon, dropped her anchor off Fortress Monroe. Jack, from his lofty perch in the mizzen-top, obtained a fine view of that celebrated fortification, of which he had heard and read so much. As he gazed upon the " sacred soil " of Virginia, now consecrated by the ashes of heroic martyrs who had fallen in defence of the glorious old flag, his thoughts reverted to his soldier-brother; for there had occurred the stirring events in which Tom Somers had been an actor.

Jack was proud of his brother, and thankful that he had done his duty bravely and faithfully in the army. He hoped he should soon have an opportunity to do something for the old flag; and, as he glanced at the ensign floating at the peak of the Harrisburg, he felt more than ever devoted to the good cause, and ready to die in defence of the cherished emblem.

There was Virginia; and Tom could not be a great way off. He longed to see him; and he could not help thinking how smart he should feel in presenting himself before his soldier-brother in the uniform of the navy. But every thing was very uncertain in time of war ; and a bullet might kill Tom, a splinter or a round shot place the gloomy " D. D."* against his own name on the ship's books. What would his poor mother do if either of them should be killed? His eye grew dim at the thought. His father too, if living, was probably some-where in Virginia ; and these reflections had a very strong tendency to give him a fit of the blues. He felt like crying a little, — just as though a few tears would do him good.

"What's the matter, Jack?" demanded Bob Rushing-ton. "You are foggy about the toplights."

"I was thinking of my father and my brother," re-plied Jack.

"Well, aren't it pleasant to think of, my lad?"

"I haven't seen my father for nearly a year. I sup-pose he is in the hands of the rebels, if he is alive."

"Don't cry about it, Jack! The old gentleman will turn up all right one of these days," added Bob in sym-pathizing tones.

Just then, the boatswain's whistle piped away the crew of the captain's gig ; and Jack, who was one of them, ran down the mizzen-rigging, and was one of the first to report on the quarter-deck. In anticipation of this duty, the oarsmen of the gig had been ordered to dress in clean clothes. They were young, fine-looking, athletic men, who had been selected, on account of their personal appearance, to pull the commander of the Harrisburg wherever his duty or his inclination should lead him.

While the men were waiting for orders, Jack saw Lieutenant Bankhead point to him; and the captain seemed to be very anxious to have him carefully designated, so that he could identify him. Now, our hero, like all brave and noble-hearted young men, was as modest and bashful as a school-girl. His cheek glowed with blushes when he became conscious that he was the subject of the officer's remarks. He wished himself at that moment on the mizzen-top-gallant yard-arm, or surrounded by the favoring darkness of the fore-hold.

The idea of being looked at and particularly noticed by so magnificent a person as Captain Mainwright, commander of the United-States steamer Harrisburg, was rather too much for Jack's susceptible nature; but I am happy to inform my sympathizing readers that he did not faint, or commit any other foolish act. It wasn't his fault that he was a handsome young man; that he was well-formed, and had an exceedingly pleasant countenance, with bright blue eyes, through which his soul, as the novelists would say, proclaimed its own nobility. I am not quite sure it was his fault that he blushed; but, considering his youth and inexperience, he may well be pardoned for this display of feminine weakness. Jack was opposed to blushing on principle, and he felt exceedingly awkward while his cheek tingled with the warm blood that did not belong there; and, in his efforts to appear indifferent, he was on the point of committing a breach of discipline, and of sinning against the immaculate stainlessness of the quarter-deck, by whistling,—an expedient to which people on shore as well as on board ship resort to make their looks belie their actions.

If it was a sin to blush, the captain and the first-lieutenant of the Harrisburg had determined not to see it, or not to punish it on the present occasion; for they continued their remarks, without the least regard to the agony they were causing our sailor-boy. They were even cruel enough to utter some very flattering commendations upon the conduct of Jack that morning, in a tone so loud, that the whole gig's crew couldn't help hearing them.

"Bully for you, Jack Somers!" said the stroke-oarsman in a whisper.

"Poh!" replied Jack contemptuously; but, at the same time, his cheeks glowed with a ruddier tint, and his heart beat a more lively tattoo against his ribs.

The first and second cutter and the captain's gig were already moored to the swinging-boom, to which the boats of a man-of-war are fastened when she lies in port. Jack wished the order would be given to pipe over the side into the gig; for he felt just as though he should sink through the deck-planks, if this scene continued much longer. But there stood the captain and Mr. Bankhead, talking about him, just as though he had been some great man. The executive officer was evidently giving his superior a history of Jack's cruise on the life-buoy; and our hero thought he was spinning out the yarn to a very unnecessary length.

At last the story came to an end. The two great men of the ship wheeled round upon their heels, and walked aft. They paused a few moments at the taffrail, and continued the conversation in a more earnest manner. Suddenly the captain wheeled round again, — just as naval officers do who have spent years of their valuable lives in pacing the weather-side of the quarter-deck, — and walked briskly towards the boat's crew, who were — all but Jack Somers — patiently waiting for a further expression of his mighty will and pleasure.

" Cockswain ! " said Captain Mainwright sharply; for he was an officer who always spoke quick and to the point.

" He's on the sick-list, your honor," replied the stroke-oarsman, touching his cap.

" Sick ! " exclaimed the captain with well-feigned astonishment; for every one of the gig's crew was perfectly well aware that the captain knew where his cockswain was at that particular moment, and also what had occasioned his sudden illness.

"He's very bad, your honor," added the stroke-oarsman, touching his hat again with a smile which indicated that he was presumptuous enough to understand and appreciate the joke that the majesty of the quarter-deck was engaged in perpetrating.

"What business has my cockswain to be sick?" added he, turning to the executive officer; for the captain of a man-of-war never jests with the denizens of the berth-deck.

"Mutiny!" replied Mr. Bankhead with a smile.

"What's his name?" asked the captain, who could not be expected to know the cognomen of so humble an individual as the cockswain of his own gig, especially as the ship had been in commission less than a fortnight.

"Becket," replied the first-lieutenant, who might possibly have consulted the station-bill within half an hour. At any rate, his information was sufficiently accurate to enable him to answer the question without any embarrassing hesitation.

"That's the man that fell overboard, and was saved by Somers!" added Captain Mainwright with apparent astonishment; but it is more than probable that he was not half so much astonished as he appeared to be.

"The same, sir."

"He had no business to fall overboard, and I shall disrate him for doing so."

Mr. Bankhead bowed with becoming reverence to the fiat of his superior.

"I want a new cockswain," continued the captain.

"Bully for you, Jack Somers!" said the stroke oarsman in an awful whisper.

"Somers!" said the captain in a tone which seemed to be fearfully majestic to our blushing, trembling sailor-boy.

Jack stepped forward, and touched his cap, as much awed as though he had stood in the sublime presence of the Autocrat of all the Russias.

"Somers, I am told you did a foolish thing this morning."

Jack touched his cap again, as deferentially as before: and the captain's view of the act, at least as he expressed it in his remark, was really a relief to him; for he was one of that sort, who, if it were not for the name of the thing, had rather be blamed than praised.

"Never jump overboard after a man again, if he is the best friend you have in the world," added the captain, in a tone so decided, that the gig's crew began to pity poor Jack, and to think that the captain was using him very harshly after he had behaved so handsomely.

It is true, Tom Longstone and Ben Blinks had told him the same thing; and their advice must certainly have been good, since it was enforced by such high authority as the captain. Jack touched his cap before the admonition of his commander, and really began to think that he had done a mean thing, instead of a noble and magnanimous deed.

"Never do it again, Somers," continued the captain. "We can't afford to lose a man like you, especially for such a fellow as Becket. Henceforth you will be rated as cockswain of my gig. Pipe away your crew, Somers!"

Jack would not have been more astonished if the Minnesota, which lay at anchor near the Harrisburg, had poured a broadside into the ship, than he was when he found himself so suddenly and unexpectedly promoted to the elegant and dignified office of cockswain of the captain's gig. He was amazed, confounded, bewildered, at the magnificent position to which he had been elevated.

"Thank your honor!" stammered Jack, pulling off his cap, and bowing as low as though he had been in the presence of the Sultan of Turkey.

Captain Mainwright turned, and walked aft; leaving Jack standing like a statue, as immovable as the mainmast of the ship.

"Away with you, Jack." said Mr. Bankhead in a low tone, as he walked by him towards the waist.

"Gig-men, away!" added Jack, giving his first order in virtue of his new position.

He was perfectly familiar with the duties of a cockswain, though he had never performed them, or even, in his wildest dreams of future distinction, aspired to such a splendid position. In a moment more, he was over the side with his crew; and the gig was brought up to the gangway, ready to receive its distinguished passenger.

While he was waiting, the new hand appointed to fill his place entered the boat.

" Bully for you, Jack !" said the stroke-oarsman, while the new cockswain was adjusting the cushions in the stern-sheets of the gig.

" Good on your head, Jack !" added another. " You desarved it ; and there is not a man in the ship that won't be glad of it."

" That's so."

" Except Becket."

" Becket's only fit for shark's meat," added the first speaker.

Jack was very glad to find there was no ill feeling towards him among his shipmates on account of what had been done, which added very much to his satisfaction. He was as happy as a boy of seventeen could be ; and he longed for the time when he could sit down on the mess-bench, and hear Tom Longstone's comments on the matter. And what a topic for a letter to his mother ! Wouldn't she feel good when she heard all about it! He intended to write that letter as soon as he returned from the shore ; but in it he intended to promise his mother never to jump overboard after a shipmate again, in accordance with the injunction of the captain and the advice of his best friends. He should have a word to say about the increased pay he would receive in his new capacity.

While he was thinking over the bright prospects which had suddenly dawned upon him, Mr. Dickey, midshipman, — the elegant and accomplished bantam of the quarter-deck, — came over the gangway, and installed himself in the stern-sheets as the officer of the boat. Jack paid him the homage due to so important a personage, and the distinguished Mr. Dickey subsided upon the cushions in languid consciousness of his own magnificence. On ordinary occasions, our hero could not look upon this notable young gentleman without a strong tendency to exercise his risibles: but at this time he actually felt a profound respect for him; probably because his own position, being a peg higher, placed himself so much nearer to the ineffable grandeur of that held by Mr. Midshipman Dickey.

The captain came over the side next, and was received with due honor by all in the boat.

"Toss!" said Jack. "Let fall! Give way!" and the gig was dashing over the waves towards the sallyport of the fortress.

Our innocent readers must not suppose, from the elevated position to which our hero had been exalted, that he was admitted to the counsels of the captain. Not even the magnificent Mr. Dickey could aspire to this honor; and both of them had to wait in the boat till Captain Mainwright had finished his business on shore.

CHAPTER XII.

SHIP ISLAND.

CAPTAIN MAINWRIGHT remained so long in the fort, that it is quite probable he forgot that Mr. Midshipman Dickey was waiting for him at the pier. Perhaps it would have made no difference with him, if he had thought of it: at any rate, he stopped a long time; and, when he came down to the boat, he did not apologize to Mr. Dickey for detaining him so long. Mr. Dickey did not seem to be offended with him for his want of consideration; for he touched his cap as politely, when the captain stepped into the boat, as though his patience had not been sorely tried.

Jack Somers touched his cap very reverently; for he was so grateful to the commander of the Harrisburg for his kindness to him, that he would willingly have waited all day and all night in the boat for him. As Captain Mainwright was engaged in the business of the nation, it is likely that he did not care whether Mr. Dickey was satisfied or not. In fact, officers in the navy are not in the habit of consulting the wishes of their inferiors : and we are inclined to think that they are perfectly right in doing so ; for, if they attempted to please all who chose to differ from them, the old flag would be the greatest sufferer by the operation.

Jack wanted very much to know how long the ship was to remain at Fortress Monroe : but he did not think it prudent to ask the question even of Mr. Bankhead, much less of the captain; for, even if these gentlemen had known themselves, they had a provoking habit of keeping things to themselves. It is not certain that any officer below the captain knew when or where the ship was going ; and it was a fact, that not a man outside of the cabin and wardroom had the remotest idea whether they were going to Gibraltar or the South. This may seem very strange to our readers ; but the destination of a ship-of-war is seldom made public in time of war. Sometimes the seamen can form a tolerably correct idea from the amount and kind of stores put on board, and other circumstances. Vessels often sail with sealed orders, which the captain is permitted to open only when the ship reaches a certain position. The information is not often communicated to the people, though they sometimes obtain it by accident.

On board the Harrisburg, everybody wondered where they were going ; but the whole subject was a sealed book to them, and Jack was obliged to content himself without knowing any thing at all about the matter. As he stood behind Captain Mainwright, with the tiller-ropes in his hands, he tried to read the expression of his face; yet, when he gave the order to " toss oars," he had made no headway whatever in the operation. The captain's face was as uncommunicative as his lips.

The side was manned when the monarch of the quarter-deck went over the gangway, and was received in due form by the officer of the deck, and others who were present. The commander of a man-of-war is always received with a great deal of ceremony when he comes on board of the ship, though he may not have been absent fifteen minutes. The " side boys" form a double line, and touch their caps as he passes through the lines. He is treated with a great deal of respect at all times. Every man, from the first-lieutenant to the third-class boys, touches his cap to him, as every officer and man must do when he approaches his superior.

Boat-keepers at the swinging-boom stand up, and salute officers arriving or departing in boats. If Captain Mainwright's gig, in going to or coming from the shore, had met a boat containing a flag-officer, — that is, the commander of a squadron, — etiquette would require that his crew should toss oars (hold them up, perpendicularly), and the captain would touch his cap to his superior. Commissioned officers, in passing him, would lie on their oars, and warrant-officers would toss oars to him. These are tokens of respect which every inferior must yield to his superior. Custom or particular regulations adjust all these matters with the most punctilious care.

When Captain Mainwright had gone up the side, and the accomplished Mr. Dickey had also disappeared over the bulwarks, Jack secured his boat, and went on deck. As he passed along the crowd of idlers, he was roughly congratulated upon his good fortune. He made his way down to the berth-deck, where he found Tom Longstone.

"Give us your flipper, Jack!" said the veteran, as he rose from the mess bench. "I give ye joy, Jack! It's a good thing to have some one in the wardroom to speak a good word for you."

"Then you think I owe my promotion to the favor of Mr. Bankhead?" replied Jack, as Tom wrung his hand.

"Sartin of it, my pretty piper."

"Then I would rather throw up my new rating," added our hero.

"Why, you lollipop! I don't say you didn't desarve it; for every man aboard knows as how you did. It is not every man that desarves promotion as gets it."

"I don't ask any favors," continued Jack.

"Yes, you do, my lively gigsman. You want your de-sarts, and you'll find that's the greatest favor you can get."

"I don't see it in that light."

"Are you going for to kick because you've got a good friend in the wardroom?" demanded Tom sternly.

"No; but I don't want any favors not bestowed upon the rest of the men."

"It's all right: no mistake about that. The whole crew would like to give you three cheers for what you did; and every mother's son on 'em would vote to make you boatswain this minute, if they could."

"Doubted!"

"Yes, they would: we'll except that piratical Becket, or such car'on as he is. For all that, my merry to'gallant-man, kissin' goes by favor. There's a score of old sheet-anchor men for'ad that has weathered Cape Horn a dozen times; melted the grease out of their bodies in the East Indies, and been froze up in the arctic; and what are they now? Able seamen, Jack,—that's all. They don't get so much pay as you do, that never went out of sight of land in a man-of-war. You're lucky, Jack; and you ought to be thankful for what you've got."

"I am thankful, Tom. But why didn't the captain choose a cockswain from these sheet-anchor men?"

"'Cause kissin' goes by favor, my breezy little topman. But bless your heart, Jack, them old fellows aren't good for cockswains. They want lively, brisk, handsome little fellers like you for cockswains of the commodore's barge and the cap'n's gig. Besides, them fellers are gettin' old and stiff, and stow away grog enough to float a seventy-four. You've got what you desarve, Jack; and you ought to be satisfied."

"So I am; but I don't want any man to think that I was promoted when I didn't deserve it."

" You did desarve it."

" That's so!" added Bob Rushington with emphasis.

And so said the rest of the mess: for, while the argument was in progress, the crew had been piped to supper; and Jack had no reason to complain of a want of sympathy among his messmates.

The Harrisburg remained at Fortress Monroe five days; at the end of which time, she went to sea again. Though the prophets and wise men of the berth-deck indulged in all sorts of speculations in regard to the destination of the ship, nothing was known in regard to the future, except that she was headed to the southward. Whether she was going to serve as a blockader, or to engage in more active work, was as much a mystery as ever. If the quarter-deck was any wiser than the berth-deck, it preserved its own secrets with religious care.

Three days after she sailed, the ship approached the land again; and Jack learned that she was going into Port-Royal Harbor. A little later, he saw the forts, on either side of the bay, which had been captured by the squadron of Commodore Dupont. From the mizzen-top he saw the stars and stripes floating over them; and his heart beat a livelier pulsation as he recalled the glorious events of that heroic day.

The ship came to anchor in the harbor, and the captaiu's gig was again in demand. Jack saw a great many things which interested and instructed him; but no events of sufficient importance to be recorded in these pages occurred during his stay.

From Port Royal, the Harrisburg went to Key West on the following day; thence to Havana, where she exchanged salutes with the English, French, and Spanish men-of-war lying in the harbor; and Jack had a fine opportunity to observe the perfection of ceremonial observances which prevail in the navy. Admirals and commodores were as thick as snow-flakes at Christmas; and such a banging of great guns, such a dipping of ensigns, such a tossing of oars, even the old salts had never seen before. Every other man he met seemed to be an admiral; and he had nearly worn out his cap in touching it to the foul anchors that glittered upon the shoulders of those who passed his station.

The last time he pulled the captain off from the shore, he heard him tell a gentleman with him that the Harrisburg was ordered to Ship Island to relieve the flag-ship Niagara; and, the same day, she got under weigh again.

"We are in for't now, Jack. We shall have some music afore long," said Tom Longstone, when Jack reported his information to the old quarter-master. "I'll bet a month's pay we pitch into Mobile afore April Fools' Day."

"I hope so," replied Jack.

"Perhaps you won't feel so good about it when the time comes. You don't know what 'tis, Jack, to see round-shot smashin' through the sides of the ship, tearing off splinters, and scatteriu' 'em like kindlin'-wood all over the decks, knocking over the best men at the guns. We don't any on us know much about it."

"I'm ready for it, if we can only knock Mobile, or any other rebel place, in pieces. I hoped I should be in when Charleston was taken."

"Time enough yet, Jack."

If our hero could have known in what bloody and exciting scenes he was soon to engage, he would have been satisfied to spend the intervening time in preparing for the future. Every day the men were drilled at the guns, and in the use of the cutlass and boarding-pike ; so that, the longer the trying ordeal of battle was deferred, the better prepared were the crew to meet it.

After a passage of four days, the Harrisburg arrived at Ship Island ; which my young readers are aware is little more than a sand-bar off the eastern coast of Louisiana. She was now nearer the rebels than she had been before ; and certain little steamers, flaunting the Confederate flag, were occasionally seen near the land, as they came out to ascertain what Uncle Sam was doing at the island. They were very prudent, however ; and seldom placed themselves within range of the heavy guns on board the ships-of-war.

After the ship had been at this station about ten days, a boat-expedition was organized; though its object, as usual, was a profound secret to all except the officers. From various indications, the enterprise promised to be an exciting affair. The first, second, and third cutters were to compose the boat-party; and, besides the regular crews, a limited number of seamen were to engage in the expedition. Forthwith there was a great struggle among the men to obtain places in the boats; for there was hardly a man on board who did not wish to be counted in. The men had all been selected by Mr. Bankhead; and Jack Somers was terribly disappointed when he found that he was " left out in the cold."

Tom Longstone was to go in the first cutter, and our hero bemoaned to him his sad fate in being compelled to stay behind.

" Never mind, Jack; plenty of time yet. It will be your turn next," replied Tom in soothing tones.

" Let me go in your place. Tom," asked Jack, half in jest, and half in earnest.

" Can't do that," replied the veteran, shaking his head " If there's any chance for a fight, I musn't lose it. Besides, you may lose your number in the mess if you go."

" I'll risk that. Don't you think I can get a chance to go?"

" Perhaps you can find some one that will give you his chance, my little piper."

" Who wants to go?" said a voice at the mess-table behind them.

" I do," answered Jack promptly, and before he saw who asked the question.

" Jack Somers?"

" Yes."

Jack now found that the speaker was Sam Becket, his topmate, who had been disrated on account of the affair off the capes of Virginia. He had fully recovered from the effects of his involuntary bath on that eventful morning. Popular opinion on board the Harrisburg had set hard against him; and he had found that the way of the transgressor is hard. Since his recovery, he had performed his duty in surly silence. If he felt any gratitude towards his topmate for saving his life, he never manifested it by word or look; and Jack and his friends had hardly noticed him.

" You can have my place, Jack, if you want it bad," added Becket, without looking at the person he addressed.

" Thank you : I'm very much obliged to you, Becket," said Jack, astonished at this self-sacrifice on the part of his enemy.

" I owe you one for what you did that morning," continued the ex-cockswain of the captain's gig.

"That's handsome!" said Tom Longstone.

"I'd like to go myself," added Becket; "but I'll give way to Somers. He did better nor that by me."

"That's a fact, Becket. If it hadn't been for the lad, you'd 'a been fish-bait in twenty minutes."

"Nobody knows it better nor I do. I was wrong that night in the top, and I axes his pardon."

"There's my hand, Becket," said Jack heartily.

"You haven't any thing agin me, have you, Jack?" asked Becket, as he took the proffered hand.

"Not a thing."

"You are welcome to my chance in the first cutter."

"Thank you, Becket."

"But you must get leave of the first-lieutenant," added Tom. "How do you know but he has something for you to do? 'Spose the cap'n wants to go ashore: then where's his cockswain? Perhaps he kept you back on purpose."

Jack's ardor was a little dampened by this suggestion: but he determined to adopt it; for Tom's view seemed to be correct. Though the ship was at anchor, her fires were banked, and her regular watches were kept. The boat-expedition was to start very early in the morning; and Jack was fearful that he should have no opportunity to obtain the desired permission.

When the starboard watch was called at eight bells, he was so fortunate as to find Mr. Bankhead on deck; and he respectfully presented his petition. The first-lieutenant promised to consult the captain ; and the result was, that the permission was granted ; and Jack was as happy as though he were going to a feast, instead of to a work which might be bloody and fatal.

CHAPTER XIII.

THE BOAT-EXPEDITION.

ALL the starboard watch, ahoy!" piped the boatswain's mate at eight bells on the following morning.

Jack turned out of his hammock, eager to engage in the expedition which was to start at this time. Hastening to the spar-deck, he heard the order given to clear away the cutters. The men and material for the enterprise were ready. Boat-howitzers were placed in the bows of the cutters; a supply of ammunition, provisions, and water, was taken on board of them; and the men embarked.

Mr. Granger, the second-lieutenant, was to command the expedition, with the fourth-lieutenant in the third cutter, and a master's mate in the fourth. It was the first active service in which either officers or men had been engaged during the cruise; and every one, from the second-lieutenant down to the powder-boys, was anxious to distinguish himself, and each one felt competent to whip two or three rebels in any fair encounter. There was pluck enough in the expedition to have supplied three times as large a company : and it was fortunate for them and for the Government that Mr. Granger was a prudent and sensible man ; otherwise the expedition might have taken it into its head to attack the city of New Orleans or Mobile, or pitched into Fort Pike, Fort Gaines, or some other rebel stronghold in the vicinity.

When the boats were ready to start, Mr. Granger ordered the second and third cutters alongside the first, in which he was seated himself. The officers in command of the other boats had already been instructed in regard to their duties ; and Mr. Granger proceeded to give a few general directions for the conduct of the men. The oars had been " tossed," and the crews listened in respectful silence to the remarks of the commander of the expedition.

" Cast off ! " said the cockswains of the cutters ; and the three boats separated, so as to permit each to use its oars.

" Let fall ! " added the cockswains.   " Give way ! "

The cutters dashed away, the men pulling with a will. As yet, they knew not where they were going ; and, aside from the natural curiosity all men feel, it is not probable that they cared, provided they were introduced to some stirring scene which would enable them to do something for the old flag, and furnish an opportunity for the daring spirits to distinguish themselves in a hand-to-hand fight.

Jack Somers stowed himself away under the lee of Tom Longstone, who was in the same boat with him; partly because the old quartermaster wished "to keep an eye on him;" and partly because the veteran was a sage and a prophet, and Jack wanted the benefit of his observations and instructions.

"Do you know where we are going, Tom?" asked Jack in a low voice; for loud talking was not permitted.

"Haven't the least idea, my lad," replied Tom in a whisper.

"Where do you suppose?"

"The likes of you and me, my darling, are not to know any thing about it. Bless you, Jack, Mr. Granger hasn't asked my opinion about any thing, and hasn't even told me where we are going!"

"Can't you tell in what direction we are pulling?"

"As to the matter of that, my honey-bee, we are heading due north."

"What do you *think* we are going to do?"

"I have not the leastest idea in natur'. May be we are goin' to capter Mobile; that lays off here away somewhere . but I don't think we are, Jack."

"Of course we are not," replied Jack impatiently.

"May be, Fort Pike: I heard one of the jollies say there was such a battery or fort in here somewhere. I don't think we are, though."

"You know we are not, Tom."

" May be we are going across the country to strike New Orleans," chuckled Tom ; " but I don't believe we are."

" You know very well we are not going to do any thing of the kind. You are an old seaman. I didn't know but you could tell, from the arms and other things in the boat, what kind of work we are to perform."

" Well, my baby, seein' as how you want to know so bad, I'll give you my opinion. 'Taint worth much ; but old Tom's always ready to give the best he's got."

The veteran spoke in low tones ; and the seamen near him gathered closer around him, so as to hear the opinion of the sage of the first cutter. Tom took off his cap, scratched his bald head as if to stimulate his intellectual powers, and sharpen his judgment up to the requisite pitch for the important decision he was about to render.

" I don't know where we're goin', or what we're goin' to do, as I said before," continued Tom, when all heads were bent down to catch the words of wisdom when they should fall from his venerated lips. " Howsomever, in my opinion, we're goin' to take a look at the rebels, or else to attack some shore battery, or else some steamboat or sailing vessel. Now, my lads, you've got my opinion : so don't pester me no more."

Old Tom indulged in a low chuckle as he settled back on the thwart, and glanced around him to discover in the darkness how his opinion had been received.

"Bully for you, Tom! I thought you knowed all about this work," laughed an old sheet-anchor man.

Jack gave up in despair, and was obliged to content himself with knowing no more than the law allows. The men at the oars were relieved every hour; for it was a long pull before they reached the scene of operations. At eight o'clock, the expedition came into a broad bay extending into the mainland. The boats were passing between two headlands about two miles apart, when a cannon-shot dropped into the water a short distance ahead of the first cutter.

"There's music for you!" said Tom Longstone.

"There's some more!" added the sheet-anchor man.

This was the first time that Jack Somers had ever listened to the whizzing of a cannon-ball; and the sensation was decidedly novel, if not agreeable. It was different from what our sailor-boy had anticipated. One of the ugly missiles might hit the first cutter, and smash her in pieces, killing half her human freight. There was no chance to strike a blow in self-defence, or even to fire a shot in return from the howitzers; for the battery from which the shot came was situated on the headland on the port-hand, and more than a mile distant.

Mr. Granger being a prudent man, and unwilling to expose the boats' crews to the fire of the battery, gave orders for them to pull up into the favoring shelter of a small island, several of which appeared near the entrance to the bay. The fort then opened with shell; to whose hideous screaming, Jack and a majority of the party listened for the first time. The second-lieutenant landed upon the island, and with his glass made a careful examination of the battery and the shores of the bay.

"We're in the stocks!" said Tom Longstone with the peculiar low chuckle with which he often delivered himself.

"We shall not stay here long!" added Jack nervously; for the shells did not sound pleasantly to his ear.

"You aren't afraid, are you, my little lamb?" demanded Tom.

"Of course I'm not afraid," replied Jack with a deep blush; "but I don't like to lie here, and be shot at, without a chance of paying off the rebels in their own coin."

"It aren't pleasant to lay still under fire, my boy; but that's a part of a good seaman's duty, and he must take things as they come. Don't be alarmed, Jack: they won't hit you."

"They are just as likely to hit me as they are any one else. I should like something to do, if it's nothing more than pulling an oar."

"That's cause you're narvous, Jack."

Perhaps there were not many in the boats who were not nervous as they listened to the screaming shells. It was a new experience to them; and it is not in the nature of man to stand in the presence of death, without being moved by the peril. Some of the crew laughed, and made fun of the dangerous missiles as they screeched through the air, or burst at very inconvenient distances from them; but it is probable that those who laughed the loudest were the most afraid, and therefore struggled the hardest to avoid making an exhibition of their real feelings.

Tom Longstone and a few others had been under fire before; and they were as cool and self-possessed as though they had been on board a receiving-ship in a peaceful port. Mr. Granger, who had recently been promoted for gallant conduct, seemed to be perfectly calm, paying no attention to the shells which were dropping around him. The rebels in the fort had not yet got the range of the island; and their firing was not accurate, though it was rapidly improving. At last, the commander of the expedition finished his examination, and walked toward the boats.

The crews of the cutters watched him with eager interest: and most of them believed, perhaps some hoped, that the expedition was to be abandoned; for they did not see what three boats could do while exposed to the fire of the rebel battery, whose guns commanded the waters of the bay. Mr. Granger, Mr McBride, and the master's mate from the third cutter, held a short consultation on the shore, out of the hearing of the men. When it was ended, each returned to his boat, and orders were given to cast off. It was a moment of deep anxiety to all the men; for the question of success or failure rested upon the decision of the officers.

The boats shoved off from the land; and, when the men gave way, instead of going about, they were headed up the bay. There was a strong inclination to give three cheers manifested by the more ardent spirits; but it was quickly repressed by a sharp word from the second-lieutenant.

The boats were kept as much as possible within the shelter of the range of islands on the easterly side of the bay, and in a few moments they had passed out of reach of the shells; for the gunners in the fort, probably enveloped in their own smoke, had not discovered the change of position made by the boats.

"Steamer on the port-quarter, sir!" shouted Mr. McBride from the second cutter.

"I see her!" replied Mr. Granger.

"Now look out for squalls, my hearties!" said Tom Longstone in a low voice, as he glanced at the new enemy, which was just emerging from behind a headland in the direction indicated by the fourth-lieutenant.

"We shall have a fight yet!" added Jack uneasily; for, on a nearer approach, a hand-to-hand fight with the rebels was not quite so sentimental an affair as it had seemed to be at a distance.

We do not mean to accuse our hero of being afraid; but the terrible inactivity of the moment was almost insupportable. He wanted to pitch right in, and do "a big thing." He wanted something to do, so that he could prove to himself and his companions that he was no coward. To sit in the boat like a block of wood, and be shot at by the rebels, was wretched business; and he hoped Mr. Granger would pull out, and order the boats' crews to board the steamer, and not permit her to stand off and pelt them with shot and shell.

"It will be a smart fight too," added Tom.

"Ay, ay; that it will. The steamer's cut us off! I'll tell you what, Tom: Mr. Granger has got us into a tight place!" replied Grummet, the sheet-anchor man.

"Let him alone; he knows what he's about," answered the veteran.

"Don't ye see, Tom, the steamer can stand off, and whittle us up into inch-pieces; and we can't board, nor nothin'?"

"Leave all that to Mr. Granger," persisted Tom, whose long experience had begotten confidence in his officers.

Under the lee of one of the islands which rose higher above the water than the others, the men were ordered to lie on their oars. The fort still kept banging away at the island behind which the boats had first taken refuge. The steamer, which was a small river-boat, drawing no more water than the first cutter, came puffing across the bay, like a man with the asthma, towards the first island. She was a slow affair, and it took her some time to come within hailing distance of the .expedition. As she approached the man-of-war's boats, the fort, out of regard for her safety, ceased firing; which might have been done half an hour before, so far as any injury to the cutters was concerned.

"I tell you, Tom Longstone, we are booked for a rebel prison, as sure as you was born," said Grummet.

"Stopper your jaw!" replied Tom impatiently. "What are your officers for, if they are going for to send you to a rebel prison?"

"Don't you see that old snorter astarn of us, Tom? Are you goin' for to run away from a steamboat?"

"We aren't goin' for to run away from any thing that shows a rebel rag at its peak, — mind that, you old croaker!" added Tom. "You aren't afraid, are you, Jack?" continued he, putting his arm around his *protégé*, and hugging him like a baby.

"Of course I'm not afraid; only — only" —

"What, my bleating little lamb?"

"I wish the fun would commence."

"See that, Tom!" continued the sheet-anchor man. "D'ye see that gun on the t'gallant fo'castle? She is swinging it round."

"Let her swing it round," snarled Tom. "Now batten down your jaw-port and don't groan any more."

At this moment, an order was heard for the men to give way ; and, before the gun of the steamer was ready, the boats had doubled the island, and the men were lying upon their oars, with the high land between them and the steamer.

"See that !" said Tom triumphantly. "Mr. Granger knows all about it."

" Perhaps he do," replied Grummet doubtfully, as a shot from the steamer whizzed harmlessly over their heads.

CHAPTER XIV.

JACK ON THE LOOKOUT.

THE armament of the rebel steamer consisted of two guns, placed on the main-deck, forward of the boilers. The hull set so low in the water, that, while the island lay between the steamer and the boats of the expedition, she was powerless to do them any injury. Those in the first cutter could see the smoke-stack of the Wizard — which was the name of the steamer — over the island, while the crew of the latter could not even determine the position of the boats.

The battle — if the affair could be dignified by such a title — promised to be nothing but a game of hide-and-seek; for, when the Wizard moved, the boats dodged round the island, so as to escape her fire. It was "pull," and "lie on your oars," for half an hour. The rebel battery on shore could not interfere with the game, lest the steamer should suffer from its fire.

Tom Longstone sat upon the thwart, occasionally indulging in his inward chuckle, and apparently enjoying the sport as keenly as a live boy relishes a game of "ball" or "high-spy." Old Grummet was not at all satisfied with the position of affairs. He was a brave man, and ready to fight his gun while there was a plank to stand on ; but he was an inveterate croaker. He was always afraid that the officers had made some mistake, or that they did not see the whole of the ground. Once in a while, he was kind enough to suggest the manner in which all three boats were to be blown up, sunk, or captured. He could see a hundred ways to get into a bad scrape ; but he never troubled himself to consider how to get out of them.

"S'posin' another rebel steamer should come down upon us," growled Grummet: "where should we be then?"

"I reckon we should be just where we are now," replied Tom, who was the only man that ventured to confront the grim sheet-anchor man, as he doled out his dismal notes of foreboding.

"S'posin' a company of rebel infantry should show themselves on the main shore there, not twenty fathoms from where we were just now?"

"We'd have to give 'em a few charges of grape from that 'ere howitzer."

"There wouldn't be a man left of us if that should happen, Tom Longstone ; and you knows it."

"I should like to p'int that 'ere howitzer in among 'em, Grummet."

"Silence, forward!" said Mr. Granger in a low, stern tone.

Tom's body shook with his inward chuckle as he thought what an awful deprivation it would be for Grummet if he had to refrain from grumbling.

"Forward, there!" said the lieutenant. "I want a man who is light and smart."

"I sir!" exclaimed Jack, springing up from his position under the lee of the old quartermaster, and touching his cap.

Half a dozen others, answering to the description, sprang up at the same time, eager to perform any service which might be required of them.

"Somers, you'll do," replied Mr. Granger. "Come aft."

Jack passed along between the rowers to the stern-sheets, and again touched his cap to the commander of the expedition.

"Do you see the steamer?" asked Mr. Granger.

"Yes, sir," replied Jack, glancing at the Wizard's smoke-stack, which could still be seen over the little island.

"I will land you on the island; and you must creep on your face up to the highest part of the ground, and see if you can make out how many men there are on the steamer. Do you understand me, Somers?"

"I do, sir."

" Now mind your eye, and don't let them see you."

" Ay, ay, sir : I will be very careful."

" Now go forward, and be ready to jump ashore when the boat touches."

Jack saluted the lieutenant, and sprang forward to the bow of the cutter, proud and happy to be selected even for the humble duty to which he had been ordered.

" Good boy, Jack !" said Tom Longstone as our sailor-boy passed him on his way to the bow.

" What may that 'ere mean ?" queried Grummet.

" Fight !" replied Tom.

" He's goin' to board that steamer, as sure as I'm a Yankee," added Grummet, pulling out his cutlass from under the thwart, and passing his thumb along the edge.

" That's it : there's a hole in that millstone, least-wise," chuckled Tom.

" I s'pose he'd board a frigate if he fell foul of one."

" No doubt on't," laughed Tom.

" Give way, — easy !" said Mr. Granger ; and the boat swung in so that Jack Somers could jump ashore.

" Did you say good-by to the lad afore he went ashore?" continued Grummet : " 'cause that's the last you'll see of him."

Tom Longstone sprang to his feet at these words, and gazed earnestly at Jack and at all the surroundings on the island.

" Grummet, you're an old fool !" exclaimed Tom an

grily. "You frightened me more'n a whole frigate's broadside would. I thought the lad was killed for sartin."

"He will be, soon."

"Avast there! If you don't stop growling, I'll heave you overboard."

"Silence forward!" said Mr. Granger.

The command was obeyed, and the sheet-anchor man's savage reply was nipped in the bud. Tom was too much interested in the movements of his young friend on the island to give any further attention to his unhappy shipmate in the boat. Jack, as directed, crept on his stomach up the ascent of the island till his head had reached the highest point, from which he could look down on the low deck of the Wizard.

Our sailor-boy was a very good scholar for one who had enjoyed only the privileges of a district school; but it did not require a very profound knowledge of arithmetic to solve the problem which had been imposed upon him. The men in the rebel steamer were all gathered upon the forward-deck; and, according to our mathematician's estimate, they numbered about thirty. They would not stand still long enough to be counted with entire accuracy; but Jack satisfied himself that this was very nearly her force.

He was about to retire from his position, and report the result of the examination, when certain movements on board of the Wizard decided him to remain a few moments longer. The steamer had run up close to the island; and her deck-hands were now in the act of passing the gang-planks to the shore, evidently with the intention of landing her men. Jack did not want to see any more; but, retreating from his position with all haste, he leaped into the boat.

"Well, Somers?" demanded Mr. Granger in sharp, quick tones; for the speed which the scout had used in his return conveyed the impression that the whole expedition was in imminent danger.

"They have run the gang-planks ashore, sir; and I suppose they are going to land."

"How many men have they?"

"About thirty, sir."

"Did you count them?"

"As well as I could, sir."

"Are there a hundred of them?" asked Mr. Granger sharply.

"No, sir: the number won't vary half a dozen from what I said."

"Very well, Somers. Are you willing to go **up** again?"

"I am, sir," promptly replied Jack.

"Go, then. Are your pistols loaded?"

"Yes, sir."

"If the boats are in immediate danger, fire your pistol, and make **your way back as fast as you can.**"

Jack touched his cap, adjusted his pistol in his belt. and sprang forward to perform the important service intrusted to him.

"Keep your weather-eye wide open, Jack, my darling," said Tom Longstone as he passed the old seaman.

"Ay, ay, Tom!" replied the sailor-boy as he sprang to the stem of the cutter, and leaped ashore again.

He had not been absent more than five minutes from the crest of the island: but the rebels had been industrious during that short period; and one of the Wizard's guns, which was an ordinary field-piece, was on the gang-planks, ready to be rolled on shore.

Jack Somers was not a brigadier-general, nor was he a proficient in naval or military tactics; but the plan of the rebels was as transparent to him as though he had been a graduate of Annapolis or West Point. The information he had obtained was very important; and, without waiting to make any further observations, he hastened back to the boat, and reported the operations of the enemy.

He tried to keep cool, and not appear to be excited by the revelation he made. He thought he had something astounding to tell; and so he had, perhaps: but, to his intense astonishment, Mr. Granger did not appear to be alarmed. He did not rattle off any hasty orders such as he had read in naval romances.

In Jack's opinion, it was time something was done;

but Mr. Granger seemed to be provokingly indifferent to the importance of the announcement he had just made to him.

"You have done well, Somers," said the commander of the expedition; whereat Jack touched his cap, and would have blushed if he had not fully expected to see the rebels pitch into them the next minute. "Are you willing to go again?"

"I am, sir!" replied Jack as readily as before, though he was utterly confounded at the question.

"Go up once more, and see whether they are landing the other gun, Somers."

Our hero touched his cap again; for, in spite of the excitement of the moment, he did not forget his manners, and sprang ashore for the third time. Cautiously ascending the slope of the little hill, he again reached his position at its summit. The other gun had not been landed; the gang-planks had been hauled on board; and a squad of men had been sent on shore to work the field-piece already on the island. Jack wanted to know what the Wizard was going to do before he reported this time; and he determined to wait a moment longer, when this question would be decided.

The gunners on the island were only a few yards distant from him, crouching upon the ground; and none of them spoke above a whisper, lest their movements should be betrayed to the boats on the other side of the

island. Jack thought he was in a very ticklish situation; and, for his greater personal security, he drew
back a few feet, so that no inquisitive rebel should get
the range of his blue cap. As he did so, he glanced at
the navy revolver which he carried in his right hand
to assure himself that it was in readiness to give the
required signal if the occasion demanded it.

The pistol was all right; and, after waiting a moment,
he heard the splash of the Wizard's paddle. Advancing
again to the crest of the hillock, he raised his head to
obtain his final glance at the scene of operations. The
steamer was certainly moving off; but a more prominent
object, nearer to him, claimed all his attention at this
moment. Directly in front of him, and not three feet
distant, was a pair of rebel eyes, each of which seemed
to be as big as the rebel steamer.

The enemy, knowing and appreciating the value of
correct and seasonable information, had sent a man to
the crest of the hill to perform a service identical with
that which had devolved upon our hero. It would not
be of any use to stop and consider which of these scouts
was the most astonished as he gazed into the eager orbs
of the other; for the question presents too many difficulties for a just settlement. Both of them were astonished;
but, fortunately for Jack, he was in a better state of
preparation for the unexpected event than his adversary.

The rebels below were rolling up the field-piece where

it could be brought to bear upon the boats, and Jack considered himself fully justified in giving the signal for imminent danger; and his pistol being loaded with patent metallic cartridges, each of which contained its adjusted allowance of cold lead, he concluded to fire a shotted salute, as Lieutenant-General Grant has since done on several eminently proper occasions.

Jack was prompt and decided, — traits of character which he and his brother Tom inherited in common from three generations of shipmasters. He saw the pair of rebel eyes glaring upon him the first instant; and he raised his revolver, and fired the second. The cold lead, before mentioned, passed between the glowing orbs in front of him, crushing through the brain of their owner.

The sailor-boy felt a cold tremor creep through his veins as the rebel gunner convulsively sprang upward, and then dropped dead upon the ground. His self-possession did not forsake him; and, without stopping for further developments, he rushed down to the boat with all the speed he could command.

His face was almost as pale as that of the dead rebel on the hill when he leaped into the boat. His lip trembled; but it was with an emotion other than fear. He had slain a human being. He had seen his bullet enter the brain of a fellow-creature. His first experience of the awful solemnity of war was too minute in detail to be pleasant, or even exhilarating.

"Report, Somers, at once!" said Mr. Granger earnestly.

"The steamer is moving off, sir. There are twelve men and one gun on the island. They are moving up the gun to the top of the hill. I killed one of the men."

"Give way!" said Mr. Granger; and the boats moved out from the island.

CHAPTER XV.

THE C. S. STEAMER WIZARD.

SUCCESSFUL strategy owes as much to the stupidity and inertness of one party as it does to the shrewdness and activity of the other. If Mr. Granger had not been shrewd in discovering the purpose of the rebels, and active in defeating it, in a few minutes more they would probably have fired into the boats, and either sunk them, or driven them from their hiding-place under the lee of the island. Whoever commanded the rebels must have seen that the man-of-war boats could keep out of the way of the Wizard's gun by dodging round the island, and that the game of "hide-and-seek" would be prolonged till his Southern patience was entirely exhausted.

By landing the gun on the island, he expected to drive the boats away from their covert, and enable the steamer to destroy or capture them. From the information that Jack Somers had procured, it was further evident that the rebels indulged the hope of surprising the boat-expedition. The gunners whom he had seen were roll-

11

ing the field-piece up the slope with the utmost caution. Not one of them spoke a word ; and all of them crouched down, so that not a head should be seen over the crest of the island. The stealthy movements of the man whose eager eyes Jack had confronted furnished additional testimony on this point.

It is plain, then, that, if Mr. Granger had not thought to send a lookout-man to the high ground, he would have been caught in the trap which the enemy set for him. He had discovered the plan ; and he could now see the smoke-stack of the steamer receding from the island. She was to obtain a position so that she could open upon the boats the moment they were driven away from the shore by the piece she had landed. Mr. Granger did not become a victim of the enemy's strategy. His prudence and forethought had defeated it.

Almost all strategetic operations are attended with more or less risk. The movements uncover some assailable point. Mr. Granger was actually pleased with the strategy of the rebels on this occasion. He and his opponent had commenced a new game to determine which was the abler strategist. Thus far, he had exhibited neither the stupidity nor the inertness that belongs to the victim of successful strategy.

"Give way!" said Mr. Granger, glancing at the smoke-stack of the Wizard.

The men pulled the steady man-of-war stroke which

discipline had rendered so familiar to them. There was no hurry or nervousness in their movements. Not a man "crabbed his oar" or lost his stroke, though the race appeared to be for life, certainly for success. Mr. Granger sat in the stern-sheets as calm as a block of marble. His demeanor impressed the men with the belief that he knew what he was about. They had confidence in him, and were ready to run or fight as ordered, without asking a question or suggesting a doubt. If this was not true of all the blue-jackets, it certainly was of all but Grummet; and he growled more from the force of habit than from want of confidence in his officers.

After the boats had pulled a short distance, the order was given for the rowers to lie on their oars. The commander of the expedition kept one eye on the smoke-stack of the steamer; and as soon as she swung round, and headed towards the north side of the island, he was ready to develop his next movement.

"Give way with a will!" said he, as he gave orders to his cockswain in what direction to steer.

The boats were headed round the south end of the island, while the Wizard was going round the north end.

"Clear away your guns forward!" said Mr. Granger.

Old Grummet sprang to the howitzer in the first cutter. A grim smile lighted up his face as he adjusted the tackle, and put the piece in condition for instant use. Tom Longstone was with him, and the most perfect harmony now subsisted between them. While they were thus engaged, the officer in each boat detailed seven men to act as " boarders."

" Now, Jack, my beauty, you are goin' to see some fightin'," said Tom, when the gun was ready for use.

" That's so, Tom ; and I'm in for my share of it."

" So you be, Jack. I see you've got a cutlash."

" I'm one of the boarding-party."

" Now, stand right up to it, Jack, like a man."

" Oh ! you needn't be afraid of me. I've got my hand in already," replied Jack, as he glanced at the weapon he carried.

" Yes, and you'll be butchered like a young pig," sneered old Grummet. " It's worse nor murder to send little boys like that to board the lubbers on the island. Why don't he send men as is fit for such work ? "

" You needn't have any fears about me, Grummet. I'll do my share of the work : if I don't, you may call me a marine."

" You're a good boy enough, my lad ; but you aren't no more fit for such work than the Evil Sperit is for a missionary," added Grummet more graciously.

" All ready forward ? " said Mr. Granger.

" All ready, sir ! " answered Grummet, who was acting as captain of the gun.

The boats were now rounding the end of the island ; and a few more strokes of the oars brought them to a point where the officers could see the gun on shore, and the men who were putting it in position for use.

"Give way with a will!" shouted Mr. Granger, as he passed forward to the howitzer in the bow of the cutter.

The men redoubled their efforts at the oars, till they bent like reeds in their hands.

While they were making these preparations for the bold assault, the rebels on shore were not idle. They dragged the gun to a place where it commanded the boats; and, when the first cutter was within ten rods of the shore, a solid shot whizzed over her, and plunged into the water between the second and third cutters, which were only a short distance astern of her.

At this moment, Mr. Granger sighted the howitzer in the bow of his boat, and ordered the man at the lanyard to fire. At the same time, the second and third cutters followed the example of the first. The rebels, discovering the intention of the boats in season, threw themselves flat on the ground behind the crest of the island, and thus escaped all injury. The fire of neither party was effectual; and the gunners on the island, perhaps appreciating the celerity with which old man-of-war's-men handle a gun, instead of loading up their piece, and firing again, busied themselves in dragging it over the top of the island, where they could work it without being exposed to the fire of the boats.

While the rebels were tugging away at their gun, the

three cutters dashed up to the shore; for it was no part of Mr. Granger's plan to remain in the boats, and let the gunners knock them to pieces at their leisure. As the first cutter touched the island, he drew his sword, and put on a very business-like air, which Jack could not help admiring. He seemed to be as much at ease as though the success of his strategy had already been demonstrated, and his work actually accomplished.

"Boarders, away!" said he in his quick, sharp tones, as he leaped on shore, followed by the seven men from the first cutter who had been detailed for the purpose.

His party was immediately re-enforced by the fourteen men from the other boats; and, starting off at a run, they advanced towards the gun at the summit of the hill. Probably at this time the commander of the rebels discovered what an awful blunder he had made; and, very likely, visions of a court-martial began to dance before his vision. But, if no one made blunders in war, it would be a more trying and difficult game than it is at present.

The boarding-party rushed upon their prey; for, with two to one of the rebels, they could hardly be regarded in any other light. They saw the gleaming cutlasses of the blue-jackets, and the dash and fury with which they advanced. A few pistols were fired: but the resistance was brief and feeble; and, in less time than it would take to describe the operation, the rebels were borne down and captured. Two of the gunners were wounded,

Boarding the Wizard. Page 168.

and one of the boarding-party had a pistol ball through his right arm.

Twelve of the men were ordered to drag the gun down to the water, while six more marched the prisoners in the same direction. The latter were disarmed, and the ammunition for the field-piece thrown into the water. Four men, doubly armed, were detailed to guard the rebels; the assistant-surgeon was sent on shore to dress the wounds of the injured men; and the rest of the party returned to their places in the boats.

As soon as Mr. Granger had given his orders for the disposition of the prisoners and the wounded, — for he did not deem it advisable to encumber the boats with them in the more difficult and dangerous work yet to be performed by the expedition, — he returned to the first cutter. He had carefully watched the movements of the Wizard during these exciting moments. She was now sweeping round the south end of the island.

Mr. Granger had now a double duty to perform in protecting his party, and preventing the recapture of his prisoners on shore. There was apparently no opportunity for the practice of strategy; and it looked very much like a hand-to-hand fight for the possession of the steamer. The cool lieutenant in command gave his orders to Mr. McBride and the master's mate in charge of the third cutter, and in a few energetic words informed the men what he intended to do, and urged them to do their duty as American seamen.

His address was received with a lusty cheer, and the boats were ordered to cast off. The steamer continued on her course towards the place where the cutters had landed; her people probably being not yet fully aware of the extent of the catastrophe which had overtaken their auxiliary force on shore.

"Give way, my lads!" said Mr. Granger, when the boats had shoved off; and on they dashed towards the Wizard, which was now only a few rods distant.

Twelve men from each boat were ordered to act as boarders, and the guns in the bows were in readiness to open on the steamer. At the right time, the command was given to fire, and the howitzers sent their charges of grape into the Wizard. Before the people in the boats could ascertain the effect of the shot, the steamer returned the fire with solid shot. The ball struck the second cutter on the quarter; glancing off, however, so as to inflict but little damage.

"Give way lively, my lads!" shouted Mr. Granger.

"Now, my baby, don't you let 'em hurt you," said Tom Longstone. "We shall be aboard of 'em in half a minute more"

"I'll do my duty, Tom. If any thing happens to me, you will ask Mr. Bankhead to write to my mother, won't you?"

"Sartain, my lad; but you mustn't let 'em hurt you, my little infant. Keep your cutlash flying; and have your pistol handy for use, if you git in a tight place."

"Steady! Lie on your oars!" said Mr. Granger, whose boat was a little in advance of the others.

"See him!" added Tom, glancing at the officer in command. "Isn't he a darling? See how he does it! That man ought to be a commodore. See that! There comes the second cutter; and there goes the third cutter, —she is going to board her over the starn, while we take her on for'ard."

"Give way, my men!" said Mr. Granger in a deep, energetic tone, which seemed to electrify the muscles of the oarsmen. "All ready there, forward! Steady! Avast pulling!" he added, as the first cutter darted in under the port bow of the steamer.

"All ready, my darling!" said Tom Longstone in a low, encouraging tone; for he seemed to feel that it was part of his duty to keep up Jack's courage during this trying ordeal.

Our sailor-boy, however, needed no such stimulus. He was fully alive to the duty of the hour, —anxious to honor his flag, and distinguish himself. He had been in one slight brush with the rebels, and was fully prepared for the desperate work before him.

"Boarders away!" cried Mr. Granger.

"Boarders away!" shouted Mr. McBride, in the second cutter on the starboard bow, at the same instant.

The rebels on the deck of the Wizard were in readiness to repel boarders; and the first gallant tar who leaped on board fell back with a ball through his heart. The second was pierced with a bayonet; but he was followed by Tom Longstone, whose cutlass cleft the skull of the rebel who disputed his passage.

"Lay 'em aboard, my lads! Sweep the decks!" shouted Mr. Granger, as he gained a footing upon the forecastle of the Wizard.

Jack Somers was by the side of Tom; but he had scarcely reached the deck before he saw a rebel bayonet darting towards his heart. Turning it aside with a blow of his cutlass, he fired his pistol, and the man dropped.

"No pistols! Don't fire a pistol!" exclaimed Mr. Granger, turning round to see who had done so. "You will hit our own men on the starboard side!"

When the commander turned, a rebel soldier rushed upon him. He had lost his gun in the affray; and he sprang at the throat of Mr. Granger, evidently with the intention of wrenching his sword from his grasp. Jack saw the movement, and received the soldier upon the point of his cutlass, and beat him back.

The soldiers on board fought with desperate energy; but the determination of the seamen drove them back towards the stern of the steamer, where, by this time, the boarding-party from the third cutter had gained the deck. They saw their fate, if they persisted; and one by one they surrendered to the victors, and the Wizard was in possession of the cutters' men.

"Are you hurt, my dear?" demanded Tom Longstone when the fighting was finished.

"Not a bit, Tom. How is it with you?"

"Nothing to speak of, my lad: only a slash in the hand with a bagonet. The bloody rebel had near-a'most harpooned me like a dolphin, when I caught the tool in my hand," replied Tom, as he exhibited the wounded member. "Got a hankercher, Jack?"

The article was furnished; and Tom wrapped up his wound, and then seemed to forget all about it.

"The steamer is ours!" said Mr. Granger, after the last soldier and deck-hand had been secured.

"Hurrah!" yelled the blue-jackets; and the cry was taken up by the men in the boats, who had not been permitted to have an active part in the encounter.

CHAPTER XVI.

THE SHORE BATTERY.

THE engineer of the Wizard had stopped her when the combat commenced; for she was headed directly for the shore. During the fight, she had drifted up within a few feet of the island. Among the volunteers in the second cutter was one of the third assistant-engineers, to whom the charge of the machinery was immediately committed. The negro firemen of the steamer were not sorry for the change which had taken place in the ownership of the craft; and all of them, having no love for the rebel Confederacy, promptly offered to continue their labors in the firing department.

The intense exertions and excitement of the men had fatigued them very much; and, when the struggle was ended, they sat down wherever they could find a place to rest themselves and recover their breath. The men in the boats attended to the wounded of both parties. The first cutter brought off the assistant-surgeon from the island, and every thing was done that their condition required The sufferers were placed in the cabin, and included five sailors and eight rebels. Of the boats' crews, only one had been killed; and the bodies of three of the enemy lay upon the forward-deck of the Wizard.

"Somers, you did me a good turn in the action, which I shall not soon forget," said Mr. Granger, when the excitement had subsided.

Jack touched his cap, blushed, and stammered out that he hoped he had done his duty. He had tried to do the best he could.

"You have done nobly, my lad; and I shall have a good report of you for the captain, and a gentleman in the wardroom, who has a strong interest in your welfare."

"Thank you, sir!" replied Jack, blushing more deeply as he touched his cap again.

"The men all did well, — behaved admirably; but no one better than yourself, my lad," said he, turning to the seamen, who were seated in little groups on the deck of the steamer. "Our real work hasn't commenced yet."

"Hurrah!" shouted the blue-jackets, jumping to their feet, and displaying their readiness to engage the enemy wherever occasion might require.

"We came off to do a certain work; and we should have done it before this time, if this steamer hadn't come athwart our hawse. But I intend to do it before we return to the ship."

"Hurrah!" repeated the blue-jackets.

"I perceive you are all ready to stand by me, and see it through."

"Ay ay, sir!" responded the men in prompt and hearty tones.

"Then we will go to work at once."

The Wizard was run up to the island, the wounded men on shore conveyed to the cabin, and the field-piece placed in position on the forward-deck. In addition to this armament, two of the boat-howitzers were hoisted on board, and other preparations made, which indicated sharp work, and that Mr. Granger intended the steamer should be used for fighting purposes. The expedition was, to some extent, re-organized. Gun-crews were placed at the battery, and men detailed to serve in the boats, which were to be towed by the steamer.

Mr. Granger had noticed the strong friendship subsisting between Tom Longstone and Jack; and, when he made the former captain of one of the captured guns, he ordered Jack to serve as first train-tackle man, which gave him a position alongside the veteran.

"You'll do, quartermaster," said the commander. "I know I can trust you."

"Thank you, sir," replied Tom reverently. "I beg your honor's pardon; but I must ax permission to go and see the doctor for a couple of seconds."

"Are you wounded, my man?'

"Nothing to speak of, your honor : only a slash in the hand with a soger's bagonet. But I could work better if the doctor would put a bit of plaster on it."

"Go : we can spare you for an hour or more."

"Thank your honor; but I won't be gone above two minutes," answered Tom, saluting the officer, and running up the stairs to the cabin-deck.

"Goin' to lose this here steamer now we've got it," said the inevitable Grummet, who was captain of one of the howitzers, when Mr. Granger went up to the wheel-house to superintend the steering of the Wizard. "Well, she aren't fit for nothin' else," he added, as he glanced around him at the build of the steamer.

"She's a good enough boat, isn't she?" asked Jack.

"What's she good for? What was the lubber thinkin' of when he built such a top-heavy, top-sided consarn as this? I wouldn't trust the cap'n's monkey in her."

"She is a fresh-water steamer, built to run on the rivers and lakes about here."

"I wouldn't cross a mud-puddle in her. A five-knot breeze would blow her over. She looks more like a grocery-store nor she do like a wessel."

"This is the kind of steamer they use on all the Western rivers," added Jack, who had often seen pictures of this kind of craft in the illustrated newspapers; which, by the way, have done an important work in making up the history of this war.

"I don't care where they use 'em: they aren't ship-shape. They may do for sogers and marines, and such lubbers; but they aren't fit for sailors. Howsomever, there won't be much left of her in half an hour from now."

"Why not, Mr. Grummet?" asked Jack.

"Avast there! Don't you go for to *mistering* me. I aren't a dandy nor an officer," said Grummet fretfully.

"I meant no harm."

"I know you didn't, my lad; and, if you did, we can't afford to quarrel. Some of us will wake up in eternity in less nor an hour from now; and this crazy old craft will go to the bottom!"

"What makes you think so?"

"Think so? I knows it. Do you see that 'ere battery over there?"

"I've seen it before to-day."

"Do you expect this piece of shingle-work to stand up afore them guns?"

"I don't know; but I think Mr. Granger wouldn't take us in where there isn't a fair chance for us."

"The leftenant's a brave man; but he's hot-headed. Now, you mark my words, not one in five of us will ever get back to the ship; and the cap'n of the Harrisburg never'll set eyes on this ugly hulk of a steamboat."

"You forget that you told us once before to-day, we should come to a bad end."

" Didn't I tell you the truth?   There's Graves a-layin'
'here : his pipe's out."

" But he's the only man killed."

" Avast growling, Grummet!" said Tom, joining his
crew at the gun.   " The worse you makes it, Old Blower, the better it'll be for us_   When you says any thing's
goin' wrong, it always goes right."

" How's your hand, Tom?" asked Jack.

" Good as new: the doctor patched it up, and it's all
right now."

" I'm glad to hear it   How are our poor fellows in
the cabin?"

" All doing well but Jones , and the doctor says he'll
die, in spite of all he can do, poor fellow "

" Didn't I tell you so?" exclaimed Grummet.

" No, you didn't,— you old bruiser!   You aren't a
goin' for to frighten the boy with your ghost-yarns.   I
tell you " —

At that moment, a twenty-four-pound shot from the
battery, which the steamer was rapidly approaching,
dropped into the water on one side of her, and interrupted
the conversation.   All the steam that the Wizard's boilers would bear was now crowded upon her ; and, when
she had advanced a quarter of a mile farther, the order
was given for the battery on the forward-deck to open
upon the fort, which was an earthwork, mounting four
guns.

The firing was vigorously kept up on both sides. Two of the shots from the shore-battery struck the steamer, but without inflicting any serious injury. As each party had an equal number of guns, it was a fair thing; but the gunners in the fort were evidently not accustomed to their work, while the old man-of-war's men on the deck of the Wizard were perfectly at home at this business.

As the steamer approached nearer to the land, the fire from the fort was sensibly diminished; and Mr. Granger was confident that two of its guns had been disabled. The Wizard's course had been made by various angles, so as to disturb as much as possible the calculations of the gunners, and to prevent any chance shot from raking her. The two balls that had struck her, therefore, passed across her, instead of through her from end to end. Both went under the cabin, abaft the paddle-boxes; one of them crushing through the pine-wood partitions, and the other knocking off one of the quarter-pieces at the stern.

While the men were still busy at the guns, Mr. Granger came down from the wheel-house.

"Give it to them, my men!" said he with a smile, as he observed the vigor with which they worked. "We must hoist the stars and stripes on that battery."

"Hurrah!" shouted the gun crews.

"Ready with the gang-planks!" added the commander; and, at the same time, the bell from the wheel-house stopped the engine, and the boat struck the shore.

"Boarders, away!" shouted Mr. Granger, as the steamer touched the shore.

"Hurrah!" yelled the seamen, as they leaped ashore, and dashed up the hill to the spot where the battery was located.

On they flew, up the slope, and over the breastworks; when, after a short and decisive struggle, the victory was won. There were but few men in the fort,—only enough to man the guns,—and there was nothing very brilliant in the achievement. Jack Somers hardly found an opportunity to strike a blow. The rebel flag was pulled down, and the stars and stripes were run up in its place.

"Not so bad as it might be,—is it?" said Jack, with a smile, to Grummet.

"You haven't seen the end of it yet," persisted the grumbler.

"We've seen the end of this battery, at any rate."

It was quite true that they had not yet seen the end of the expedition; for, after a working-party had been detailed to transport the guns to the steamer, Mr. Granger ordered the first cutter to be manned, and immediately started up the bay in her. After pulling a short distance, they discovered the town which was known to be there; and, at a convenient place, the commander landed. Taking twenty men with him, he proceeded to examine the locality. On the road, which they soon reached, they captured two men, whom Mr. Granger questioned, and from whom, in spite of themselves, he obtained some valuable information.

Crossing the neck of land, they came to the water on the other side; and here Mr. Granger discovered that of which he had evidently been in search. It was a nondescript craft, which the rebels were converting into a ram; probably for the purpose of making a raid among the men-of-war at Ship Island. At the approach of the party, the mechanics who were at work upon her fled, as though the whole Federal army was sweeping down upon them. Mr. Granger gave directions for setting fire to the ram; and the seamen piled up heaps of chips and shavings in various parts of her, and applied the match.

The party remained long enough to insure the destruction of the clumsy contrivance; and then hastened back to the boat, which was about two miles distant.

When they reached the road which they had before crossed, a new and startling state of things menaced them. Rushing down the road, on the double-quick, was a company of infantry. They had just come in sight from behind a hotel used in summer for pleasure-seekers from New Orleans: and it was impossible to elude their observation; for the country was flat and open, and afforded no place for defence or concealment.

Jack could not help glancing at Mr. Granger to observe the effect of this discovery upon him; but he looked calm and unmoved, as he had all the morning.

" It's lucky old Grummet isn't here," said Tom.

" He told me we hadn't seen the end of it yet," replied Jack.   " What are we going to do?"

" Dunno, my darling."

" Shall we fight, or surrender?"

" Jest look at the leftenant afore you say surrender."

" They are three to our one."

" No matter, my boy, if they were ten to our one. Never say die!"

Jack couldn't exactly see how they were to proceed, with a company of fifty or sixty men in the very act of charging upon them; but he had unlimited confidence in his commander, and he was resolved to take things as they came.

" Halt!" shouted the captain of the rebel company.

Mr. Granger declined to obey, and ordered the men to move on towards the boat. The muskets of the soldiers were raised to their shoulders.

" Fall flat on the ground!" said the commander suddenly.

" Fire!" shouted the rebel officer at the moment, when all the seamen dropped as though they had been shot.

The bullets whistled over their heads; but not a man was injured. They jumped, and ran again with all their might towards the place where they had landed, closely pursued by the rebels.

Old Tom Longstone and some others of the party were

more accustomed to fighting than they were to running, and the consequence was, that the rebels gained rapidly upon them. But, in the midst of the race, Jack Somers, agile and fleet as he was, happened to be tripped by one of his companions, who was looking over his shoulder to see the pursuers. Before he could pick himself up, his party had left him, and the rebels were upon him.

CHAPTER XVII.

RETURN OF THE EXPEDITION.

PRECISELY what Jack's feelings were when he saw his friends pass on without him, and the rebels drawing near, it would be difficult to say. They were not pleasant; and it may have occurred to him that all the dismal forebodings of old Grummet were to be realized.

"Stand by that man!" said the rebel captain as he passed him.

The soldier to whom this order was given, was, no doubt, very glad to obey it; for Jack looked like a puny opponent, and there was a prospect of a sharp fight with the blue-jackets when they reached their boat. But the soldier made a slight mistake; for Jack had no intention of being made a prisoner by any single rebel in the Confederacy. He had a cutlass and a pistol; and he knew that his enemy's gun was not loaded.

Jack jumped up, and confronted the soldier as soon as he reached the spot; the main body still pursuing the sailors. He was a tall, stout fellow, and looked as ugly as a human being could look.

"Drop that cutlass!" said the rebel soldier as he placed himself in the attitude of "charge bayonets."

"Drop that gun!" replied Jack, elevating his large naval revolver.

"That's your game, is it, Yank?" added the rebel, retreating a few paces, evidently not pleased with the situation.

"That's my game, reb. I say, drop that gun, or there'll be a dead man round here somewhere."

"That's rather sharp, Yank!" replied the crest-fallen soldier, too proud to obey the order.

"I see you're not going to do what I told you: so we may as well finish this business before it gets any later, especially as I've got some tall running to do."

The soldier threw down the gun, and Jack picked it up. As he did so, he heard the report of fire-arms in the direction of the boat, and saw that the sailors, being hard pressed by their pursuers, had turned upon them.

"Take off that cartridge-box and the rest of your traps!" continued Jack.

The man obeyed; and Jack proceeded to load the musket, the rebel watching the operation in surly silence.

"Now, reb," said he, when he had returned the ramrod and capped the piece, "I want to see you run. Make tracks towards that hotel. If you turn to the right or the left, or look behind you, I shall just put

this bullet through you. Now, double-quick, forward,
march !"

The rebel could not do otherwise than obey ; and, to
do him full justice, he did obey the orders of his captor
to the letter. As soon as a reasonable distance lay between him and the soldier, Jack turned his attention to
the exciting events which were transpiring in the vicinity
of the first cutter.

The party had driven back the soldiers by an impetu-
ous charge upon them with cutlass and revolver, and
the rebels had taken time to reload their muskets. They
were now in line, firing upon the boat-party. Jack's
chance of escape was not yet first-rate ; for the rebels
were between him and his friends. He could not move
in that direction, and it was not prudent to remain where
he was. The only line of retreat open to him was the
road to the point on which the captured redoubt was
situated.

With the musket on his shoulder, and the cutlass and
pistol in his belt, he moved off in this direction, and
soon reached the road. While he was retreating with
due diligence, he heard the report of the first cutter's
howitzer, which assured him that his party had reached
the boat. He was exceedingly gratified at this result ;
though it might provoke the soldiers to pursue him,
when they were released from duty. To prevent any
such catastrophe as being recaptured, he quickened his

pace to a run, which soon brought him in sight of the fort.

Out of breath, and very much fatigued, he reached the battery, and reported himself to Mr. McBride. He told his story in full to the lieutenant, who, fearing that the first cutter's people might still be hard pressed by the rebels, immediately ordered the third cutter to pull up the bay to their assistance. Jack was sent in her as pilot, and to report himself to Mr. Granger. With the musket in his hand to verify his report, he stepped into the boat.

The third cutter reached the place where the party had landed. Mr. Granger's boat was there in charge of four men. The cockswain reported that the soldiers had been beaten off, and that the rest of the crew had gone upon shore again; where, or for what, he could not answer. Mr. Light, the master's mate, with most of his men, landed at once, and hastened towards the road to find them. They had proceeded but a short distance before they met the party returning to the boat.

"Why are you here, Mr. Light?" demanded Mr. Granger.

"We heard you were in trouble; and Mr. McBride sent me up to render assistance, if any were needed."

"We are all right now, though we have had two men killed, three wounded, and one captured. Young Somers was taken prisoner."

"I beg pardon, your honor," said Jack, stepping forward and touching his hat : "that's a mistake!"

"Somers!" exclaimed Mr. Granger.

"My darling!" exclaimed Tom Longstone, springing forward, and throwing his arms around him.

"Hurrah!" shouted the men, with whom Jack was a great favorite.

"How's this, Somers?" asked Mr. Granger, whose pleasant smile indicated the satisfaction which Jack's reappearance afforded him. "I thought you were taken by the rebels."

"No, sir : I wasn't taken. I took the rebel who was sent to capture me."

"How was that?"

"He ordered me to drop my cutlass; and I ordered him to drop his musket. As I had a loaded pistol in my hand, he had the worst of it. I picked up the gun, and loaded it. Then I told him to run up to the hotel yonder, or I would shoot him. He did so; and that's the last I saw of him. Here is the musket, sir."

"Why didn't you come down to the boat then?"

"Because the rebels were between you and me, sir. I was afraid I couldn't whip the whole of them: so I ran down to the fort."

"Bravo, Somers!" said Mr. Granger, laughing at the manner the story was told, no less than at the story itself.

The commander of the expedition then ordered the dead and the wounded men to be conveyed to the first cutter; and the boats returned to the steamer. The men were sad for the loss of their companions, and little was said on the passage. On their arrival at the point, all the brave fellows who had fallen during the day were reverently committed to the earth, prayers being said by Mr. Granger; while all who could be spared stood uncovered around the grave.

The work for the day was finished. The ram had been destroyed, an armed steamer captured, and some valuable information had been obtained by Mr. Granger. The result was entirely satisfactory to all, except old Grummet; and the expedition started on its return to the ship. The boats were all towed astern of the steamer, and the men had nothing to do but to talk over the events of the day.

It was three bells in the dog-watches, when the people on the deck of the Harrisburg discovered a steamer, with the stars and stripes over the stars and bars at her stern, approaching them. The arrival caused some excitement on board; and three stunning cheers welcomed the victors back to the ship. Captain Mainwright took Mr. Granger by the hand, and congratulated him upon the success of the expedition. That night there was such a spinning of yarns on board the Harrisburg as had never been known before. Every man who had been with the expedition was a hero; but Jack Somers was regarded as something better than a hero. He was commended by the officers, and lauded by the crew; and, if he had not been a very sensible young man, his head would have been turned by the lavish praise which was bestowed upon him.

Jack had a strong friend in the wardroom, — one who could command the ear of the captain; and, if our hero could have heard what was said about him by these distinguished persons in the cabin, he might well have been dazzled by the prospects in store for him. They were discussing a plan for his future advancement; which, in due time, will be revealed to our readers.

Our sailor-boy bore his honors with tolerable self-possession. His fame had extended beyond his own ship, and his position as cockswain of the captain's gig frequently brought him to the notice of the naval and military officers on the station. His modesty, however, prevented him from making a fool of himself; and, wherever he went, he was a universal favorite.

My readers must not suppose that there was no one else at Ship Island but Jack Somers, because he happens to be the central figure of our picture; or that the rest of the people there had nothing to do but to praise him. There was, at this time, a mighty expedition gathering there, which was destined to achieve one of the grandest and most brilliant operations recorded in the annals of war. Jack was only a very humble individual in the vast throng; and we doubt whether General Butler or Flag-officer Farragut ever heard that there was such a person.

It was fortunate for Jack that he did not consider him-self the greatest man in the fleet; as any self-sufficiency of that kind would have placed him in a very unpleasant position. He was still content to touch his cap to Mr. Midshipman Dickey, and to discharge all his duties on board with promptness and fidelity. In his letters to his mother, he related his adventures with the expedition: but Mr. Bankhead, in writing to his friends, gave a more glowing account of the affair; which, in due time, was conveyed to Pinchbrook.

"All hands up anchor, ahoy!" piped the boatswain, one morning, about a week after the boat-expedition.

Jack sprang to his place at the capstan, buoyant with hope that the day of action had again arrived. Every man at Ship Island knew that some stupendous enter-prise was about to be undertaken; though none but a few of the higher officers of the army and navy knew what it was.

"Where do you suppose we are going now, Tom?" asked Jack when the ship was fairly under way.

"Don't know, my bantling; but you may be sure, if there's any big thing to be done, this ship will be there," replied Tom. "We're headed to the south'ard."

" Perhaps we are going down to the Mississippi."

" Maybe we be, Jack."

That evening, the Harrisburg arrived at Pass à l'Outre; and, on the two following days, she made several attempts to cross the bar, and enter the Mississippi, but without success. She then went round to the Southwest Pass; where she crossed the bar, and proceeded up the river to Pilot Town.

At this place, Jack learned that the seamen in the navy have something to do besides drawing their pay and eating their "grub." The topmasts were sent down, and the ship stripped for action. Every thing not required for immediate service was sent on shore, and a guard of marines stationed there to protect the property. It was a hard day's work; and Jack's hammock never felt so good as it did that night when he was permitted to " turn in."

The guns were all shotted, in readiness for an attack; for the rebels had a fleet of rams and iron-clads up the river, with which they had already made one demonstration against the blockading-fleet. After these preparations were completed, the Harrisburg steamed up to the head of the Passes. But here she again mocked the eager expectations of the seamen; for no forward movement was made for a month.

There was occasionally an incident to vary the monotony of the scene. The arrival of the mortar-fleet, the discovery and destruction of a telegraph-wire extending across the river, afforded brief periods of excitement: but all were anxious to pour a few broadsides into Forts Jackson and St. Philip; for there was no longer any doubt that the reduction of these fortifications was the object of the expedition.

On the 16th of April, another fever of expectation was produced by the ship getting under way again, and going up to the head of the fleet, consisting of fifty-one men-of-war; where she anchored, much to the disappointment of the gallant tars. But the next week realized all their anticipations, and immortalized every man of them.

CHAPTER XVIII.

FORTS JACKSON AND ST. PHILIP.

UNDOUBTEDLY the hero of our story was a brave, smart, and patriotic young man; a good seaman, and fully devoted to his duty: but we do not wish any of our enthusiastic readers to suppose he captured Fort Jackson and Fort St. Philip alone, or even that he did any more than his fair share of the work. The river was full of ships, brigs, schooners, gunboats, and mortar-vessels. There were thousands of men, and hundreds of guns; and the history of those tremendous events would require a whole volume: so that we can only describe the part which our sailor-boy acted in the memorable scenes of that glorious occasion.

For nearly a week, the mortar-fleet shook the very earth with the roar of their ordnance; and the ponderous shells screamed through the atmosphere like "fiends in upper air." But no sensible impression seemed to be produced upon the forts. They still held out; and the intrepid flag-officer in command of the squadron prepared for more decided measures. The ships had been made ready for the severe work before them; and **every** heart in the fleet burned to meet the foe at closer quarters.

On the afternoon before the great battle, the flag-officer visited every ship in the squadron: and Jack Somers came to the conclusion that this act meant something; which was the unanimous opinion of all his top-mates. Every man on board the Harrisburg was in earnest, and longing for the decisive moment; but though there was a great deal of moving about in the fleet, a great many boats passing and repassing during the rest of the day, the men were piped to supper as usual, and the starboard-watch turned in at the proper time.

At three bells in the morning, all hands were called; and, shortly afterwards, the signal to get under way was made on board the flag-ship: but it was half-past three before the fleet was under way, owing to the difficulty which some of the ships experienced in "purchasing" their anchors. The drum beat to quarters; and the ships, in two lines, moved up the river. The chain which the rebels had extended across the river, supporting it upon hulks of vessels, had been partially removed, and the two lines of ships passed through. The "column of the Red" was commanded by Captain Bailey; and the "column of the Blue," by Farragut himself,—the former occupying the right, and the latter the left.

It was night; but the scene was illuminated by the

immense fires which the enemy had kindled on shore to assist the aim of the gunners in the forts, and by the fire-ships which were hurled down by the rebel squadron with the intention of destroying the Federal fleet by conflagration. The boat-brigade, which had been organized by Commodore Porter, fought these fire-fiends both obstinately and successfully, and not a ship was destroyed by them.

Before the Harrisburg reached the hulks, the forts opened fire upon the fleet. Shot and shell rained down upon the devoted vessels. The grandest and most terrible scene which the eye of man ever looked upon succeeded. The river seemed to be a molten sea of fire; while the roar of the cannon, the hissing of shot, and the screaming of shell, were enough to appall the stoutest heart.

When the order was given, the Harrisburg poured her broadside into Fort Jackson, which lay on the port hand. The ship was shaken down to her keel by the tremendous explosion, and Jack felt sure that the rebel works were blown to pieces; for it seemed to him that nothing which human hands had made could stand before such a tornado of iron hail. He attempted to look through the port, to observe the destruction which the broadside had caused; but the ship was enveloped in such a dense volume of smoke, that nothing could be seen. The sulphurous cloud rolled in at the port, and blinded him so that he could not even discern the man on the opposite side of the gun.

There was no time to look around him; for the gun-crew sprang to their duty with an energy which showed their zeal in the work before them. Almost in the twinkling of an eye, the ponderous piece was ready for a second discharge, and another broadside was poured into the fort. Again Jack tried to obtain a view of the fortification. His position as first-loader and second-boarder at the muzzle of the gun, when it was drawn in, placed him near the port, where he had an opportunity to see when there was any thing to be seen.

"Somers, ahoy!" shouted the first-captain of the gun. "Stand by, and take the cartridge!

"Ay, ay!" replied Jack as he sprang to his duty.

"What are you star-gazing out the port for? Keep both eyes peeled!"

Jack was reminded by these remarks that it was his duty to assist in knocking down the fort, and not to take notes for the future historian. But the scene was different from what he had anticipated; and it seemed hard to stand at the guns without the privilege of beholding the mischief they were doing. It was nothing but smoke, however, in every direction; and he might as well have been in the gloom of the forehold, so far as seeing any thing was concerned. He was nearly stunned by the awful roar of the broadside; and, when the captain of gun No. 9 shouted to him at the top of his lungs, his voice sounded like that of a pygmy in the distance. The words which he spoke himself did not seem to come from his own mouth.

In spite of the rebuke he had received, Jack Somers was thoroughly alive to his duty; and he worked with so much zeal, that he soon wiped out any imputation which his momentary neglect had produced.

At such a time as this, the splendid and punctilious discipline of the navy is exhibited to the best advantage. What to the casual observer, in the still waters of a peaceful harbor, may seem terribly formal and ridiculously precise, is the foundation of success in the ordeal of a mighty naval conflict. Every man knows his place, and has a definite duty assigned to him in case of any emergency that can happen. Every one of the gallant tars at gun No. 9 had a double, and some a triple, duty assigned to him. Every manœuvre of the piece was performed in order, with the utmost promptness and precision.

At quarters, the men are stationed on each side of the gun; and the same crew handle the gun on the opposite side of the ship, — a division consisting of three guns on the starboard, and three on the port-side. As the Harrisburg went up the river on this momentous occasion, her port-battery first engaged Fort Jackson; but when she reached Fort St. Philip, on the other side of the

river, her starboard-battery delivered the terrible broadside. The second-captain of gun No. 9, with his crew,
went over to the other side, and manned the other gun
No. 9.

Jack Somers, as we have before stated, was first-loader
and second-boarder. The man opposite to him was first-
boarder and second-loader. The next was a shot-and-
wad-man, who was also a pumpman and pikeman. The
third was a sponger, who was also a boarder. The
fourth was a crow-and-handspike-man, who was also a
fireman and sail-trimmer. The fifth was a train-tackle-
man, and also a boarder. The sixth was a captain of
the gun. The men on the opposite side had correspond-
ing duties; and each is designated by his proper ordinal,
as first-boarder, second-boarder, &c.

The gun is secured by three classes of ropes. The
breeching is the heavy piece of cable passing through an
eye at the breech of the gun, with each end fastened to the
side of the ship, which prevents the recoil from throwing
the piece out of position. The train-tackle is a rope
with double blocks, attached at one end to the carriage,
and at the other to a ring in the deck, by which the gun
is hauled back from the port, or secured for loading.
The side-tackles are the purchases attached to the side
of the carriage, by which the gun is drawn up to the
port.

Modern gun-carriages have but two wheels, the aftermost part resting on the deck. A handspike with rollers on the end, called a rolling handspike, by which the carriage is pried up and made to bear upon the rollers, is now used when the gun is to be run out at the port. The cartridges are brought up from below, one at a time, in a leathern bucket having a cover, which removes the liability to accident. Shot-stands are placed near the breech of the gun, to hold the balls, — five in each, — which are replenished as occasion requires.

The perfect discipline which prevailed on board the Harrisburg inspired every man with zeal and courage; for he knew that he was one wheel in the vast machine whose action was essential to the operation of the whole. Every one supported every other one, and was in turn supported by them; and entire confidence reigned throughout the ship.

The Harrisburg passed Fort Jackson, and poured her broadside into St. Philip. It was the same scene over again, but intensified by the hopes of success, and by the continued tension upon the nervous systems of its actors. But hardly had the ship passed the second fort before she got aground; and, at the same instant, the vessel seemed to be wrapped in flames. It was an awful moment to the devoted tars, who could not yet comprehend the nature or the extent of the calamity which had overtaken the ship; but, to their honor and glory, not one of them deserted his station. The port-battery still roared, as it poured its destructive missiles into the enemy.

An immense fire-raft had been pushed forward by one of the rebel rams; and the Harrisburg, in attempting to avoid it, had been run into shoal water, and grounded. The ship was on fire, the flames leaping up to her tops; and her destruction seemed to be inevitable. The firemen were called away, and, after exertions almost superhuman, the fire was extinguished, and the noble ship was then backed off from the shoal.

The severest part of the day's work was yet to come. What the officers saw was soon patent to all the crew, — that the river was swarming with rebel gunboats and iron-clads. The roar of battle increased; and the shot and shell crushed through the sides of the Harrisburg, scattering splinters and other missiles in every direction. Wounded men were borne down to the cockpit, where Dr. Sawsett was busily discharging the duties of his profession; and the dead lay silent and calm amid the awful din.

Still our noble ship continued to pour a terrible fire into the rebel vessels; and still her men, nerved to desperation by the thunder and the crash of battle, worked like heroes. Now she butted against a rebel ram, and now she poured her death-dealing broadsides into the iron-mailed vessels that assailed her.

Jack Somers was only a hero among heroes. Stunned

by the roar, blinded by the smoke, he maintained his position at gun No. 9, without knowing what was transpiring even a few feet from him. As the ship changed her place, he obtained an occasional glance at a rebel gunboat; and he saw one of them crushed like a paperbox by the great guns of the Pensacola.

Still he exerted himself to the utmost. When he saw a solid shot crush the head of poor Lawrence, — one of his topmates, — he felt dizzy for an instant; but, even from this shock, he recovered under the stimulus of the awful excitement.

Such a furious and destructive action could not long continue. The roar began to diminish; for the guns of the rebel fleet had been silenced. Of the fifteen which had appeared, eleven had been destroyed, driven ashore in a sinking condition, or sent to the bottom of the great river.

The columns of the Federal squadron moved on. Three or four vessels were missing. The Varuna had been sunk, after she had done deeds which immortalized her name and that of her heroic commander. The smoke cleared away, and the fleet steamed up the river. Silence reigned when the storm of battle had spent itself. The victory was complete; and cheer on cheer rent the air, and gave a thrill of inspiration to the poor fellows who had been wounded, as the grateful sounds reached their ears.

CHAPTER XIX.

QUARTERMASTER SOMERS.

AFTER passing the forts, the Harrisburg proceeded on her way up the river. On the following day, after many difficulties and delays, the fleet arrived at English Turn. Some of the light gunboats had been sent forward to cut the telegraph wires, and otherwise prepare the way for the more formidable squadron which was to follow. The intelligence of the approach of the terrible gunboats had already been conveyed to the city of New Orleans; and that reckless desperation which had so often characterized the movements of the rebels in times of extreme peril began to manifest itself in the wholesale destruction of property. Large cotton-ships, which had been freighted with the precious staple of the South to run the blockade, were set on fire, and came careering down the river, converting the mighty stream into a moving panorama of leaping flames.

The Mississippi was covered with burning vessels, and other valuable property, which the fiery sons of the South had made haste to destroy. The Harrisburg threaded her perilous path through these floating chariots of flame, till the roar of cannon was heard ahead of her. The ship had proceeded but a short distance farther, before the Cayuga, in which Captain Bailey was leading the way up the river, was discovered engaging the rebel earthworks on both shores.

The Harrisburg, being one of the fast ships, immediately crowded on all steam to assist the spunky little Cayuga in the unequal battle into which she had ventured. The ship was now within a mile of the batteries, which opened fire upon her, as well as upon the Brooklyn and Pensacola. As she approached the forts in a direct line, only the two guns on her topgallant-forecastle could be used; while the batteries were enabled to meet her with a raking fire during her approach.

The crew were at quarters; and the broadside guns had been loaded with shell, shrapnel, and grape, which are used only at short ranges. When the ship had approached sufficiently near, the order was given to keep her away. She rounded to, and her port battery poured into one of the forts a broadside which could not but be fearfully destructive among the gunners in the fort.

At the same time, the starboard battery of the Pensacola gave the fort on the other side of the river a broadside of the same material. The Brooklyn then passed between these two ships, and delivered her broadside;

which, being followed by others from the remaining vessels of the fleet, entirely silenced the guns in the earthworks. The action was short, but brilliant,—what Admiral Farragut has styled "one of the elegances of the
profession." Not all of the fleet could obtain a "pop"
at the batteries, so quickly were they silenced.

The Harrisburg continued on her course, the crew still
at quarters, in readiness to make the daylight shine
through any rebel works which should have the temerity
to dispute her advance. As she approached the city, the
artistic eye of Mr. Bankhead, who was standing in the
mizzen-rigging, giving directions to the quartermaster at
the wheel, so as to avoid the burning wrecks which were
borne down by the current of the mighty river, discerned
a beautiful little steamer, which had been set on fire, and
was drifting down with its fellows. It was not one of
those ungainly, top-heavy Western steamers, whose build
had called forth the criticisms of old Grummet; but she
was evidently a sea-going steamer, whose graceful lines
and symmetrical proportions would have filled the eye
of a professional yachtman.

The executive officer of the Harrisburg was a gentleman of exquisite taste in nautical affairs ; and the destruction of so fine a craft greatly disturbed his equanimity.
In fact, he was disposed to rescue the little steamer from
the " manifest destiny " which appeared to have overtaken her, especially as the fire had made but little prog

-ess. He immediately communicated the suggestion to Captain Mainwright, pointing out the value which the fine craft might be in the future operations of the fleet. Mr. Bankhead was satisfied that he could save the steamer; and the order was at once given for the attempt to be made.

"Strike two bells, quartermaster!" said the first-lieutenant. "Clear away the second cutter!"

"Two bells, sir!" repeated Tom Longstone, who was conning the wheel.

"Three bells, quartermaster!" continued Mr. Bankhead · the first signal being to stop her; the second, to back her

"Three bells, sir!"

By the time the little steamer had drifted down to the ship, the second cutter was in the water, manned by her regular crew. A dozen more men, with axes and buckets, were ordered into the boat. Mr. Bankhead, having a peculiar interest in the rescue of this elegant specimen of naval architecture, took charge of the expedition himself.

"Somers!" said he as he sprang upon the gangway.

"Ay, ay, sir!" shouted Jack in reply, as he sprang forward to answer the welcome summons.

"Take a bucket, and come into the boat."

"Ay, ay, sir!" answered our sailor-boy, pleased to be remembered when there was any difficult duty to be performed.

The boat dashed after the burning steamer; and, as she was now only a few fathoms astern of the ship, the bowman had his boat-hook fast to her before the oarsmen had pulled a dozen strokes. Jack, who had stowed himself in the bow of the cutter, was the first to leap on board. Rushing into the engine-room, he seized a shovel, and began to throw overboard the combustibles which had been piled up near the wood-work. There were a dozen pairs of ready hands to assist him.

The work of firing the steamer had been done in haste, and the chips and shavings were damp. The flames had therefore hardly been communicated to the wood-work; and, after a few moments of vigorous exertion with the buckets and the axes, the fire was completely subdued.

" Clear away that hawser on the forecastle!" said Mr. Bankhead. " Pass it into the boat."

" Ay, ay, sir!" answered Sam Becket, who happened to be nearest to him when the order was given, as he seized the end of the rope.

" Carry it over to the port-side," added the officer.

The cockswain in charge of the cutter was ordered to pull round to the other side of the steamer. By this time, half a dozen men had hold of the hawser, and were hauling it over as directed. Mr. Bankhead, who was now making signals with his hands for the ship to back down to the prize, incautiously stepped within the bight of the hawser, a portion of which had fallen into the water. He was standing on the plank-shear at the time; and, there being no railing for protection, he was suddenly and violently tripped up when the men hauled the rope over to the other side. By the operation, his legs were pulled out from under him; and, obeying the law of gravitation, he dropped head first into the river.

Unfortunately for Jack Somers, he was at this critical moment engaged in extinguishing the last remnants of fire in the cabin of the steamer, and lost this glorious opportunity of practising his favorite diversion of leaping overboard. We doubt not he would have done it, if he had witnessed the catastrophe; but, as he did not, an interesting and exciting incident for this chapter was thereby effectually spoiled.

Sam Becket, who had lost caste by falling overboard, was the nearest man to Mr. Bankhead when the accident happened; being at that moment engaged in clearing away the coils of the hawser in the middle of the deck. As the reader has a very indifferent opinion of Becket's Christian impulses, it is not to be supposed that he was moved by any lofty motives at this crisis in the affairs of the executive officer of the Harrisburg. It is reasonable to believe that he remembered how Jack had behaved on a similar occasion, and how much credit he had obtained by his promptness and courage. Be this as it may, Sam Becket plunged into the river, and swam towards Mr. Bankhead.

Though Becket was not an expert swimmer, he succeeded in reaching Mr. Bankhead as he rose, and grasped him by the collar, regardless of the dignity of his high office. It is quite probable, however, if a charred timber had not floated near him at this critical period, that both of them would have gone to the bottom together. Becket was clumsy in his operations; but he kept a firm hold upon the sufferer till the boat came up and rescued them.

Then it appeared that the first-lieutenant of the Harrisburg had struck his head in falling, which had inflicted a serious injury, and deprived him of consciousness. The ship had now backed down to the little steamer. A heave-line was thrown upon her deck, and the hawser hauled on board. The second cutter pulled immediately to the gangway; and Mr. Bankhead, still insensible, was conveyed to the deck, and thence to the wardroom, where Dr. Sawsett, full of interest and sympathy, hastened to his assistance. The hawser was secured, and the ship proceeded on her course with her prize in tow.

The Harrisburg, shortly after this accident, arrived before New Orleans, and anchored. The events connected with the surrender of the city are matters of history; and we shall confine our attention to the personages who have already been presented to the reader. Mr. Bankhead was not dangerously injured, though he was confined to his bed a few days; and Jack Somers was relieved of a heavy load of anxiety, when he saw him return to duty at the expiration of a week.

It need scarcely be said that Sam Becket had suddenly become a hero; that, from the neglect induced by his lost reputation, he had at once risen to the pinnacle of popularity. Men began to understand and appreciate him. They gave him due credit for the noble deed he had performed, without scrutinizing his motives. Mr. Bankhead had sent for him as soon as he was able to see him, and thanked him for the service he had rendered, besides giving him an intimation that he should be suitably rewarded in the future.

The first time that the executive officer appeared on deck, Jack Somers began to edge this way and that way, beating up towards the quarter-deck, till he found himself under the lee of the mainmast. It would have been quite evident, to any one who had watched our hero, that he desired to communicate with Mr. Bankhead; but he was very shy and sheepish in his movements. He was too familiar with the requisites of navy discipline to approach, and congratulate his powerful friend upon his recovery, as he would gladly have done. It was not to do any stupid thing of this kind which caused him to edge up to the mainmast: it was a purely business matter.

At last, when he had mustered the requisite degree

of boldness, he dashed briskly up to the first-lieutenant, and touched his cap. His face was covered with blushes, and he was as confused as a school-girl when she reads her first composition in public.

"Well, Somers?" said Mr. Bankhead kindly, as he smiled at the difficulties with which Jack was beset.

"I beg your honor's pardon!" stammered Jack, taking off his cap; "but I wanted to speak a word to you about Becket."

"What, Somers?"

"If you please, sir, I would like to see him rated as he was before that affair," added Jack, after a deal of stumbling and blundering.

"Cockswain of the captain's gig? Impossible! You would be disrated if that were done."

"Don't mind me, if you please, sir; and I would thank your honor more than any other man in the ship if it could be done."

"We may do something else for him; but I object to disrating you," replied Mr. Bankhead. "You are a good-hearted fellow, Somers; and you shall not suffer for it."

Jack argued like a lawyer; alleging that it would be peculiarly grateful to the feelings of his topmate to be restored to his old rating. It would wipe out the stain upon his character, and be better than any thing else that could possibly be done for him. At last, moved by all these arguments, Mr. Bankhead promised to submit the matter to Captain Mainwright.

Half an hour afterwards, the word was passed for Somers to appear at the mainmast; which is the high court of equity on board a man-of-war. The captain was there, and heard our sailor-boy repeat his request.

"Somers, why didn't you jump over after Mr. Bankhead?" said he in a quizzing tone.

"Because your honor told me not to jump overboard even after the best friend I had in the world. Besides, sir, I was not present when the accident happened."

"I grant his request, Mr. Bankhead; but Somers shall be rated as a quartermaster hereafter."

"Thank your honor!" exclaimed Jack, who, though happy to have Becket receive his due, was not at all anxious to lose his own rating as a petty officer.

Becket was sent for, and made as happy as a man could be by the restoration of his rating as cockswain of the captain's gig.

CHAPTER XX.

THE U. S. STEAMER MIDDY.

"I'M much obleeged to you, Jack Somers, for what you done," said Becket, as they sat down in the mizzen-top, on the evening after the conference at the mainmast.

"I knew, after what had happened, that the first-luff would want you to have your old place; and I thought I'd help him out a bit," replied Jack.

"It was handsome of you, Jack; and, with all my faults, I'm not mean enough to keep still after what you've done for me. You've been unanimous—no, that's not what the shore lubbers call it."

"Magnanimous," added Rushington, whose vocabulary was more extensive than that of the mass of man-of-war's-men.

"Ay, ay: that's the word. It's as long as a frigate's cable; but it's just what I meant. You saved my life, and you have always treated me handsomely, Somers. Now you've put me back just where I was before. I don't want to be foolish, Jack; but I'd do any thing in the world for you."

"Thank you, Becket. I'm glad I had a chance to do you a good turn."

"I've been a rough fellow, in my day; but you've taught me a lesson that all the parsons in the country couldn't have got into my noddle. By the way, Jack, do you know what I thought of you when we first come aboard the ship?"

"I haven't the least idea."

"Well, Jack, I thought you was one of them pious sort of lubbers that say long prayers, and go canting up and down the rigging, and shirk their duty whenever they get a chance, — one of them chaps that's always preaching what they don't practise."

"I don't see where you got such an idea as that of me."

"Nor I nuther, Jack; but I did get it: and I was determined to make you show your hand, or pick a quarrel with you. We had some talk about you in mess No. 2, and I told the boys I meant to show you up. I was rather taken aback when you wouldn't odd-and-even. You got the laugh on me, and I meant to sarve you out for it. You're a good fellow, Jack; and, what's more'n that, you're just my idee of a good Christian."

"I'm glad your opinion of me has changed," laughed Jack. "I'm sure I haven't lost any thing by being fair and just towards you. I'm a quartermaster now. and shall still wear my ' eagle, anchor, and star.' "

" Silence in the main-top ! " shouted the officer of the deck at this interesting point in the conversation.

The sharp rebuke of the officer of the deck was called forth by a disturbance in the main-top, where some extraordinary event appeared to have transpired. Some of the topmen were laughing, and some were swearing; and the aspect of the matter was, that a practical joke had just been perpetrated. The mizzen-top was at once deeply interested in the affairs of the main-top ; and the quarter-watch were exceedingly curious to learn the particulars. Jack Somers, whose new rating had relieved him from duty as a topman, came down to learn the facts, which were communicated to him by Ben Blinks.

The captain of the after-guard was an epicure, and had prepared, for his own especial use, a dish of dunderfunk, — a man-of-war delicacy which comes the nearest to what the Tremont House would serve up under the more pretentious title of " cracker-pudding " than any other dish that can be mentioned. It is made of " hard-tack " pounded up, with " slush " and molasses stirred in, and baked brown in a tin dish. The captain of the after-guard had no relish for the gross viands of the mess-table ; for he was a very nice young man. Indeed, all the after-guard are nice young men ; being selected for their trim and dandy appearance, because their duty lies on the quarter-deck, to haul the main-braces, to handle the spanker-sheet, brails, and vangs, and similar work in that part of the ship where the officers "most do congregate."

Spear, the captain of the after-guard, had duly prepared his dish of dunderfunk, and bribed the ship's cook to bake it for him. At the galley, or cooking-stove, of a large man-of-war, a marine is usually stationed, in busy times, to prevent any evil-disposed persons in the crew from indulging forbidden appetites. In other words, a roast chicken, duck, or goose, has been known to disappear from the galley in the most mysterious manner; but, of course, appropriated by some hungry tars who had not the spirit of the eighth commandment in their hearts. In this manner had Spear's dunderfunk taken to itself wings; and none better than he knew how vain a thing it would be to find the guilty purloiner of the delicious mess.

The captain of the after-guard was exceedingly wroth at first; but, when his anger had spent itself, he determined to wreak upon the thief or thieves a sweet revenge. The surgeon's steward kindly provided him with a quantity of ipecacuanha, which the malicious conspirator mixed up with pounded ship-biscuit, and put the dough in a baking-pan. The mess was duly slushed and sweetened, and committed to the care of the ship's cook, who, with half a dozen others, had been intrusted with the secret.

When the dunderfunk was properly cooked, it was placed in a tempting position; and the cook and marine cunningly afforded the victims abundant opportunity to pilfer the pudding. The half-dozen pairs of eyes that were watching for the issue of the plot presently saw a main-top-man slyly appropriate the dish, and carry it to the spar-deck. The fellow hung around the fife-rail of the mainmast for a time; but, as no one seemed to be watch-ing him, he attached to it a small cord which had been dropped down from the main-top for the purpose. It was then hoisted up by the accomplices of the thief, who immediately hastened up to share in the spoil.

The maintopmen partook greedily of the pudding; and, as the medicinal ingredient had been liberally sup-plied, the victims of the joke were soon in a suffering condition. Spear's interests were represented in the main-top by a friend; and, as soon as the thief and his accomplices began to be sick, he began to laugh so im-moderately, that the joke had to be explained. Not only the stomachs but the tempers of the victims rebelled. They were mad with everybody, and disgusted with themselves; and, while they swore and vowed vengeance upon the authors of the joke, those who had not par-taken laughed, till the din from the main-top constituted a breach of discipline, which called forth the sharp re-buke from the officer of the deck.

The history of the joke spread through the ship, and undoubtedly penetrated the sacred recesses of the cabin and wardroom. Every man on board was in a broad grin for the next twenty-four hours; and the victims of the plot became livid with rage when any one ventured to mention "dunderfunk emetics." We sincerely hope that the moral influence of the conspiracy was not lost upon them, and that it inspired in them a deep and lasting reverence for the eighth commandment.

We beg the reader's pardon for the intrusion of this nauseous incident in our story, which nothing but fidelity to the truth of history would have induced us to narrate. It is only a specimen of the practical jokes which men-of-war's-men play off upon each other, and which afford an agreeable, but not always salutary, relief from the monotony of life on board ship, especially in seasons of inactivity.

The Harrisburg had been somewhat injured by the shot and shell of the rebels in the two actions in which she had been engaged; and, while she remained at anchor opposite the city, her repairs were in progress. At the same time, by order of the flag-officer, the little steamer which had been rescued from the flames by the crew of the Harrisburg was refitted for service. A thirty-two-pounder was placed upon her forecastle, and a twenty-four-pounder on each side abaft the paddle-boxes; and she was suitably prepared for the accommodation of her fu-

ture officers and crew.   Her name was changed, and she
was henceforth to be known as the Middy.   Giving her
this undignified appellative was a freak of the naval officers in charge of the difficult task of finding a suitable
title for the new-born gunboat : but there was no small
degree of fitness in the name ; for the steamer was both
small and smart, which are supposed to be the represen-
tative characteristics of the young gentlemen whose official position is designated by the word.

The Middy made a trial trip when her repairs were
completed, and proved herself to be even more than had
been anticipated by her sanguine projector.   She went
down to Fort Jackson, and returned, making splendid
time, and working to the entire satisfaction of Mr. Bankhead, who had superintended her alterations.   On her
arrival from below, she came to anchor under the quarter
of the Harrisburg.

On the following day, great was the astonishment of
the crew when it was whispered through the ship that
Mr. Bankhead, at his own request, had been appointed
to the command of the little gunboat.   But the report
was received with incredulity.

"Don't you believe one word of it, my darling," said
Tom Longstone, to whom Jack had carried the astounding news.

"I hope it isn't true," added Jack, who was sorely
troubled at the idea of losing his wardroom friend.

" Not one word of it, my dear.   Do you suppose Mr. Bankhead is goin' for to let himself down into such a little craft as that?   Why, Jack, my boy. he ought to have the command of a sloop-of-war."

" But the Middy is a fine little vessel."

" No matter for that, my lad : she aren't big enough to hold a man like Mr. Bankhead.   If they should send off Mr. Dickey, or even Mr. McBride, I shouldn't so much wonder.   But to send off the fust-luff in a cockle-shell like that, — why, it aren't reasonable."

" But if he should go " —

" I tell you, my darling, he aren't goin'.   Why, I'd almost as soon think of the commodore's goin' in her himself ! "

" But officers are selected according to the service they have to perform, as well as to the size of the vessel.   The Middy may be ordered to duty which requires one of the best officers in the fleet."

" That may be, Jack," said Tom, taking off his cap, and rubbing his bald head.

" Suppose he should go, what will become of me ? "

" He aren't goin', I tell ye, my dear," persisted Tom. " You mought as well talk of the cap'n's goin' cockswain of the dingy ! "

Notwithstanding the very decided opinions of Quarter-master Longstone, Mr. Bankhead was detached from the Harrisburg, and ordered to the Middy.   The report passed from the wardroom to the steerage, and thence, through Mr. Bobstock, the boatswain, to Checks, sergeant of marines, who conveyed it to a ship's corporal, by whom it was disseminated through the ship, clothed with such an air of authority, that even Longstone and Grummet were compelled to believe.

"It may be so, Jack," said Tom.

"There can no longer be a doubt," added Jack.

"All I got to say is, if it is so, then the Middy's goin' to do a big thing somewhere."

"I wouldn't care, if I were only sure of going in her," continued Jack.

"Do you want to go off in the Middy, and leave me here, my darling? Haven't I watched over you like a baby? Haven't I mended your trousers, like your grandmother? Didn't I put that 'eagle, anchor, and star' in your blue frock? Haven't I nussed ye, and tended ye, and made a man-o'-war's-man of ye? And now you want to go for to leave me!"

"No, I don't want to leave you, Tom. I want you to go with me."

"You'd sartinly git killed in the fust action, if I wa'n't there to take care of ye."

"You shall be there, Tom. I won't leave the Harrisburg without you, if I can help it."

"Give us your flipper, my dear. I hain't got nobody in this world but you, Jack; and, if you cast off and leave me, I won't keer much what becomes of this old hulk."

"I will not leave you, if I can help it, Tom," replied Jack, much moved by the tenderness of the old man.

"I know you won't, Jack. I allus took you for an honest lad; and, if you desart me, I shall be disappinted, — that's all. Now read me a chapter in your mother's Testament, my darling."

Jack took the Testament from its place of concealment under the mess-table, and read — as he had often done before to the old quartermaster — a portion of a chapter. Tom, as was his habit, commented upon the text in man-of-war style. Our sailor-boy listened, but with only half his attention; for the Middy was still an anxious topic in his mind.

A week elapsed before any decided steps were taken in manning the Middy; and Jack was full of doubts and fears. In the mean time, the little steamer had taken in her ammunition, small-arms, provisions, and stores, and seemed to be entirely ready for a cruise.

We have continually spoken of the Middy as a little steamer; and so she was, when compared with the larger steamers of the fleet: but she was extensive enough to require the services of forty men, including petty-officers and marines, besides her officers and the engineers and firemen. Her crew was selected with great care from the squadron; and we are happy to inform our anxious readers that both Jack Somers and Tom Longstone were drafted into her, to their intense satisfaction.

Passed-midshipman Hayswell was appointed first-lieutenant, and Mr. Midshipman Dickey was ordered to the little gunboat in the capacity of second-lieutenant, — a promotion which added three inches to his height in a single instant.

The officers and crew of the Middy went on board, and at once made themselves comfortable in their new quarters.

CHAPTER XXI.

UP THE RIVER.

JACK SOMERS was delighted with the change which had been made in his position: not that he was dissatisfied with his duties on board the Harrisburg; but there was a prospect of being ordered to more active duty. The Middy was small and fast; and he was confident that her services would be in continual demand. Besides, Mr. Bankhead was now his captain; and he hoped he should have a better opportunity to distinguish himself.

Jack had hardly become accustomed to his new quarters in the Middy before a new character appeared on board, and one with whom the quartermasters were to become particularly intimate. He was a rough-looking man, and swore ever so much more than there was any need of; but he was not much worse than many of the crew. Jack Somers had not yet learned to swear. He was strongly tempted, sometimes, to use big words; but, when he observed that Mr. Bankhead and Mr. Granger never uttered an oath, he came to the conclusion that he could better afford to imitate them than the seamen who were less careful of their speech. Tom Longstone never used a profane word; and a long conversation with him, while the Harrisburg lay at anchor below the city, had fully confirmed all his previous resolutions.

Mr. Lunsley did swear; and his nose was very red, and his manners very coarse. Jack did not like him at all when he appeared at the wheel-house, where the two quartermasters were engaged in making things snug and orderly. He was the very antipodes of Mr Bankhead, who was a perfect gentleman in all his relations both with his inferiors and his superiors in rank. There was only one thing about him which Jack did like; and that was the rosette of " red, white, and blue," which he wore upon the lappel of his coat, indicating that he was a loyal man. In the midst of so many traitors, this was no small recommendation in a man who knew every bend and shoal of the Mississippi River.

" All hands, up anchor, ahoy!" passed through the Middy shortly after the appearance of Mr. Lunsley.

Tom Longstone and Jack were in the wheel-house with the pilot, who was smoking his cigar, and watching the operations of the sailors on the forecastle.

" Anchor's away, sir!" said the man who officiated in the capacity of boatswain, to Mr. Hayswell, who stood upon the hurricane-deck.

" Strike one bell, Jack!" added the lieutenant.

"One bell, sir!"

The Middy went ahead slowly; and, when the anchor had been placed on the forecastle, the four bells were struck, and she went ahead rapidly up the river Jack had the wheel, and received his directions from Mr. Lunsley, who continued to smoke his cigar and to swear, though he had nothing particular to swear at.

At the time of which we write, the country on both sides of the river was in possession of the enemy, who closely watched the stream, though they were very careful not to demonstrate upon any of the gunboats which passed up and down after the capture of New Orleans. Though the rebels could not successfully contest the possession of the river with the powerful naval armaments of the Government, it was their policy to impede the navigation as much as possible. Masked batteries had been planted at various points, and companies of light artillery and sharp-shooters were employed to annoy any steamers which had not the means of returning the fire.

Even the gunboats and larger vessels were annoyed by riflemen attempting to pick off any man who showed his head above the bulwarks, or appeared in the rigging. The Middy had been prepared for duty with a full knowledge of this state of things. Her wheel-house had been plated with iron sufficiently thick to resist a rifle-ball. Iron screens had been prepared to protect the men while working the guns.

The Middy continued on her course up the river, bearing the stars and stripes through the very midst of the discomfited rebels. The men were piped to dinner as usual; and no one on board seemed to consider that he was in the enemy's country, and surrounded by enterprising and spiteful foes. Tom was at dinner; and Jack was alone with Mr. Lunsley, who declared that he could not leave till the steamer had passed a certain difficult bend which he described.

"I think I can get along alone, after what you have said," added Jack, who had a great deal of confidence in his own ability.

"Perhaps you can, my little joker; but I don't trust this craft out of sight when there's a shoal ahead," replied the pilot; and of course he could not utter a remark of this length without interlarding it with half a dozen Mississippi oaths.

"Your directions are very plain, and I thought I understood them."

"But I have some pride in this business. I've run up and down this brook for ten years, and always had good luck. Now, if this steamer should get aground, some of your folks would call me a traitor, or some other pretty name of that sort."

"I think not, sir."

"I won't trust 'em, little joker. If you"—

The loyal philosophy which was contained in the

thought Mr. Lunsley was about to utter was forever lost upon our hero; for a cannon-shot at this instant whistled through the air, unpleasantly near the wheel-house.

"I know'd it!" said he, changing his tone and manner.

"Knew what?"

"I know'd there was a battery here."

"What did you run us upon it for, then?"

"We must go in the channel, any way, my joker. But may be you ain't afraid of cannon-balls?"

"Not particularly; though I have a wholesome respect for them when they are properly projected," replied Jack.

Another shot followed the first, and then a third. The crew were called to quarters, and Tom Longstone returned to the wheel-house. Captain Bankhead took his station on the hurricane-deck, by the side of the pilot; and Mr. Hayswell was on the forward-deck.

"Strike two bells, quartermaster," said the captain.

"Two bells, sir."

The boat stopped; for it was no part of Captain Bankhead's plan to have his vessel knocked to pieces without an adequate compensation. By his order, the thirty-two-pounder on the forecastle was discharged in the direction from which the shot came. Old Grummet was captain of this piece; and there was not a better gunner in the navy. The old man growled all the time; but he worked with an alacrity which spoke better for his zeal and courage than his words did. After half a dozen shells had been thrown into the thicket from which the firing had proceeded, the guns of the enemy appeared to be silenced; and the Middy again proceeded on her way.

She had been backed down the stream some distance; and, during the firing, the engine had worked just enough to keep her head up the river, and give her steerage-way. As she advanced, the thirty-two-pounder continued to discourse with the unseen rebels.

"We are all right now, Tom!" said Jack.

"Not yet, my darling. The rebel guns is short range; and, when we come up, they'll give us some more."

"You may depend on that," added Mr. Lunsley. "Starboard! quartermaster."

"Starboard, sir!" replied Tom.

"Steady!"

"Steady, sir!"

"Now we catch it again!" continued the pilot. "Starboard!"

"Starboard, sir!" replied Tom, as another shot passed over the forward-deck, so that the "wind" could be felt in the pilot-house.

Just then, Tom was called to assist in working one of the quarter-guns, and Jack was left alone at the wheel. The pilot kept well back behind the iron plates which shielded the helmsman.

"Hard-a-starboard!" said the pilot.

"You don't see where you are going, sir!" replied Jack.

The sun, which had been behind a cloud, at this moment came out, and the helmsman could distinctly see the bottom on the bow of the Middy. There was not four feet of water in the direction the pilot had ordered him to steer.

"Hard-a-starboard!" repeated the pilot sharply. "Do you think I don't know this river better than you do?

"But look, sir! I can see the bottom!'

At this moment, the thirty-two-pounder sent another shell into the thicket, the noise of which seemed to startle Lunsley, and he crouched back into his former position. He had risen with the intention of taking the wheel from the hands of the refractory quartermaster. Three or four more shots from the shore passed near the Middy: but she was still untouched, for her motion prevented the rebel gunners from obtaining the correct range.

"Hard-a-starboard the helm!" shouted Lunsley again, when he had quieted his nerves.

This time he did not wait for Jack to execute the order, but rose, and seized the spokes of the wheel, rolling it over in the direction indicated.

"Better mind what I say!" growled he with a volley of oaths, which made Jack's blood run cold.

"There's no water there!" exclaimed Tom, glancing

over the port-bow at the long shoal, which could be dis·
tinctly seen.

At the same time, mustering all the strength and nerve
of his slender frame, he heaved the wheel over to port
again, and thus prevented the Middy from grounding
while under the fire of the enemy's guns.

"Let go that wheel, you villain!" cried the pilot,
attempting to grasp him by the throat.

"What's the matter here?" demanded Captain Bankhead, opening the door of the pilot-house.

"This man is a traitor! He's trying to get the boat
aground!" replied Jack with energy.

"He lies!"

"Mind your helm, Somers!" said Captain Bankhead,
unable to comprehend the merits of the question.

"Shall I put her hard-a-starboard as he orders me?"
asked Jack. "You can see the bottom there, sir."

The captain glanced over the port-bow, and was satisfied that the quartermaster had spoken the truth.

"Steady!" said he.

"Steady, sir!" repeated Jack; which is the order
when the helm is to be kept as it is.

He looked at Lunsley, as he spoke, with a triumphant
expression upon his face. The pilot's face was as dark
as a thunder-cloud. The captain stepped out, apparently
satisfied that he could trust Jack, though he did not know
any thing about the river, better than the pilot, who knew
all about it.

A TRAITOR IN THE WHEEL-HOUSE. Page 231.

He had scarcely closed the door after he had withdrawn, when Lunsley sprang to the wheel again, and made a vigorous effort to throw it over as he had directed the wheelman to do. Jack braced his feet against the spokes underneath, and for a moment prevented the scoundrel from accomplishing his purpose. But the pilot was a powerful man, and Jack found himself defeated in his attempt by main strength to prevent the Middy from being thrown ashore. He did not give up the ship: and this was precisely what it would have amounted to, if she had got aground there; for the rebels could have knocked her to pieces in five minutes if she would only "hold still" long enough.

When he found he was not a match in physical strength for the burly pilot, he had the presence of mind to strike two bells, followed by three; which were the signals respectively to stop and back her. The traitor, finding the steamer was receding from the shoal, sprang forward towards the bell-pulls. There was a heavy hard-wood stick in the wheel-house, which had been used to pry up the iron screens into position. Jack grasped this weapon; and, as the pilot placed his hand upon the pull, he struck him a heavy blow upon the back of the head, which felled him to the deck.

Jack then rang two bells,—stop her; one bell,—ahead slow; four bells,—ahead, full speed.

CHAPTER XXII.

JACK ASHORE.

THE roar of the guns, and the busy scenes in every part of the steamer, had prevented any one from noticing the affair which had just transpired in the wheel-house. The Middy was completely enveloped in the smoke of her own guns; and, though Captain Bankhead was on the hurricane-deck, he had no knowledge of the important event which had saved his vessel from destruction. The stopping, backing, and going ahead again, had been noticed, of course; but they were supposed to have been occasioned by some difficulty in the navigation.

The battery which had opened upon the Middy was situated upon a point of land at a bend in the river, and on the port-hand. Near the land, there was a broad shoal; for the current, in turning this curve, would, by its natural law, sweep round to the opposite shore. As soon, therefore, as Jack found himself his own master in the wheel-house, he put the helm well a-port, and kept the steamer away from the dangerous ground.

Captain Bankhead, who was directing the action on deck, had passed the word for Tom Longstone as soon as he was conscious of any treachery on the part of Lunsley. Before Tom came up from below, he again opened the door of the wheel-house, where he discovered the prostrate form of the traitor.

"What's this, Somers?" demanded Captain Bankhead.

"He is a traitor, sir! He tried to take the wheel out of my hands, and throw the steamer on that shoal!" replied Jack in high excitement. "I knocked him down with this club, and kept her off."

"Good Heaven!" exclaimed the captain, who could not but be impressed by the danger he had just escaped. "You have done well, Jack. Here comes Longstone. Keep her off shore a few minutes longer, and we shall be clear of the battery."

"Ay, ay, sir. There is water enough for us anywhere on the starboard hand. We are all right now, sir."

"Keep her steady, Jack, and be very careful. Don't stop her again if you can help it."

"I will not, sir."

"Here, Longstone: roll this traitor out of the wheel-house, and then stand by with Somers."

"Ay, ay, sir;" and Tom pitched the carcass of the pilot out of the wheel-house, very much as though it had been the body of a dead dog.

"What's the matter, my darling?" asked Tom as he joined Jack at the wheel.

"Nothing particular, Tom. I'll tell you all about it, by and by," replied Jack, still keeping his eyes fixed upon the water ahead.

The clouds of smoke obstructed his vision; but he made the most of the brief intervals when the wind opened a clear space for him. He felt that the safety of the Middy depended as much upon him as upon the captain; for, if she got aground, it would insure her destruction in a very few moments. The rebels were improving in their practice, and two or three shots had struck the steamer. One had passed through the cabin on the main deck; and another had ploughed up several feet of the hurricane-deck, abaft the smoke-stack.

The Middy soon passed the most dangerous point, and the guns of the rebels had begun to fall short of the mark. Only the port-quarter gun of the steamer could be brought to bear upon the battery; and the action seemed to be over, unless Captain Bankhead chose to renew it.

"Where is that pilot?" asked the captain, opening the door of the wheel-house.

"I dunno, sir: I pitched him out on the hurricane-deck," replied Tom, stepping out to look for his victim.

"He is not here now."

"I dropped him down there," added Tom, pointing to

the place where he had deposited the senseless form of the pilot.

"We must find him before he has a chance to do any further mischief."

The captain and quartermaster walked aft to ascertain what had become of Lunsley, who had evidently come to his senses, and taken himself off. He was not on the hurricane-deck; and they were about to descend to the main-deck, when the pilot's canoe, which had been towing astern, was discovered some distance down the river, pulling towards the battery. The villain, who had in some measure recovered from the effects of Jack's blow, had crept down from the hurricane-deck during the excitement of the action, and taken to his canoe. A twenty-four-pound shot from one of the quarter-guns was sent after him; but the object was so small, and the distance so great, that the gunner failed to hit it.

The Middy was then put about, so as to bring the thirty-two-pounder to bear upon the battery, and again opened fire upon the rebels; for Captain Bankhead expressed his purpose to clean out the enemy from their position. As the battery did not reply, she was moved up nearer, so that one of the twenty-four-pounders could also command the spot. After firing for half an hour without eliciting any response from the rebels, the Middy went down the river again, and placed herself in different positions to tempt the enemy to renew the action; but the battery was still silent.

The quarter-boat on the starboard-side was then cleared away ; and Mr. Hayswell, the first-lieutenant, was ordered on shore to examine the position.

" Somers, you will go in the boat. Mr. Hayswell may want such a person as you are to assist him," said Captain Bankhead.

" Thank you, sir."

" Take a pistol and cutlass with you, and don't be reckless."

" Ay, ay, sir."

The boat contained twelve men besides the officer, and pulled to the nearest point of land, just below the battery, where it could be covered in case of necessity by the guns of the steamer. Mr. Hayswell with eight of the men landed, and cautiously made their way up to the battery. They found a rude earthwork ; but there was not a gun to be seen : and it was evident that the fort had been manned by a battery of light-artillery, which had decamped when the fire became too warm for the gunners.

A short distance from the thicket in which the gunners had been concealed, there was the mansion-house of a plantation, with its village of negro-huts in the vicinity. It was important to know in what direction the battery had gone ; for Mr. Hayswell concluded that it had gone farther up the river, to open upon the steamer from another position. The party, therefore, advanced towards the mansion, but with the utmost care, to avoid falling into an ambush or any other trap which the rebels might have set for them.

"Bress de Lord, massa! De jubilee am come!" shouted a negro, stepping out from a cabin as the party approached the negro-huts.

Mr. Hayswell at once proceeded to question the negro in regard to the battery which had occupied the earth-work. The man was very willing to give any information in his power; but unfortunately he knew nothing, except that the rebels had taken the road which he pointed out. It was a cross-road leading from the main highway; and the battery might have gone up or down the river, — he could not tell which. Mr. Hayswell then decided to visit the mansion-house, leaving the negro very much depressed in spirits because "de jubilee" had not yet come, and five hundred slaves were not to be carried off by the little Middy.

The people at the mansion-house were very uncommunicative. They did not know where the battery had gone; did not know there was any battery; had heard firing, but did not know what it meant; thought it best not to interfere with matters that did not concern them. Mr. Hayswell did not deem it prudent to continue his investigation any farther, and left the house. He had scarcely stepped off the veranda before a dense smoke was discovered some distance up the river. The cotton-burners, alarmed at the approach of the Union force, had probably set fire to a pile of the precious commodity. The smoke indicated in what direction the battery had gone; and Mr. Hayswell decided to reconnoitre that way: for it was the military force of the Confederacy which destroyed cotton; and there could be hardly a doubt that the party which had fired upon the Middy was the same that performed this work of destruction.

The boat-crew had advanced but a short distance before the lieutenant was startled by the roar of artillery in the direction of the earthwork, near the spot where he had landed. It did not proceed from the Middy's thirty-two-pounder.

"What does that mean?" said Mr. Hayswell as the party halted.

"I think the battery of artillery has got back to its old position, sir," replied Jack, who was the person addressed.

"If it has, we are in a bad situation."

"I'm afraid we are, sir!" added Jack, who wanted to ask Mr. Hayswell why he had wandered so far from his boat, since it did not make much difference where the battery had gone; but he was too well trained to ask an impertinent question.

"We must get back, if we can," added Mr. Hayswell, who seemed to be very much perplexed at the difficulty of his situation, as well he might have been.

He led his party down to the shore of the river, which Jack thought was the stupidest thing he could possibly do; for the earthwork was now between them and the boat. The Middy could not even be seen around the bend of the river. At last, when the situation seemed to be utterly hopeless, Jack ventured to suggest that they might pass round the battery, and reach the boat below, or at least escape capture till the Middy had time to shell out the rebels a second time.

Mr. Hayswell adopted the suggestion; and he party succeeded, with the help of the negro who was waiting for the jubilee, in making their way as far as the cross-road, which led from the principal highway to a landing-place on the river. While the boat-expedition were looking for the cotton-burners half a mile above, the rebel artillery company had returned by this road to their original position. Of course the enemy had a motive in leaving the earthwork, and a motive in returning to it. The subject was rather dark to Mr. Hayswell; but the fact was undeniable.

Meanwhile, the shells from the Middy were dropping into the earthwork, and doing terrible execution among the rebels. About the time our party reached the road, they had got about enough of it, and were on the point of retiring again, probably satisfied that they had "waked up the wrong customer" when they attacked the little Middy. Now, it was very unfortunate for our people on shore that this result had been reached at this particular moment; for the retreating graybacks instantly discovered the blue-jackets, and, with a whoop and a yell, dashed forward for the purpose of capturing them.

Resistance was useless; and Mr. Hayswell ordered the men to run for their lives; of which permission they promptly availed themselves. Most of them attempted to make a sweep round the road, and reach the boats, where the rebels followed them. Jack prudently retreated in another direction; and, reaching a gin-house, crawled in, and stowed himself away among the machinery.

The guns of the Middy still played a lively tune, and Jack was in hope that his companions had escaped. He remained in his concealment until he thought the rebels must have retired, and then crept out. No firing had been heard for some time; and he stealthily moved towards the river, confident that his progress would not be interrupted. But this was a day of mistakes; and our hero soon found that he had miscalculated his chances. The rebels had ceased firing, because their twelve-pounders only drew the steamer's fire, which they found too much for them, without injuring her.

While he was slowly and cautiously making his way towards the river, he was suddenly and very unexpectedly accosted by a couple of graybacks.

"Halt!" said one of them, stepping in front of our sailor-boy.

Jack did halt: he could not well help halting, unless he concluded to step over the rebels in his path. They had been concealed behind a mound of earth, and were either watching for him, or observing the movements of the Middy.

"Lay down your arms!" added the rebel speaker, elevating a musket, and taking aim at him.

Perhaps Jack was reckless; on the whole, we rather think he was: for, instead of obeying the order, he drew his revolver, and fired at the soldier who addressed him Of coarse, the grayback discharged his musket; and Jack felt something on his left shoulder very much like a saw drawn along the skin. But he was not killed,—he was sure of this,—and immediately fired another barrel of the revolver, which caused the assiduous rebel to drop. Yet Jack was sure he was not killed; for he heard him swear after he fell.

There was no time just then to balance probabilities: and our blue-jacket, concluding that the rebels were in force at the earthwork, decided to change his base; which is always considered a very difficult operation in the midst of an engagement. In the present instance, it consisted only of wheeling about, and running away in the opposite direction; which has often been the sum and substance of the same manœuvre when conducted on a larger scale.

Jack ran till he came to the mansion, being chased by the uninjured rebel of the couple. He dodged several times, and at last threw his pursuer off the track. As he doubled up under the lee of the big house, he saw a cellar-door open; through which, as the place looked inviting, he entered without asking permission.

CHAPTER XXIII.

THE PLANTER'S MANSION.

THE cellar into which Jack had entered appeared to be the storehouse of the plantation; for it was half filled with boxes and barrels, crates and cases, with demijohns, jugs, and canisters. In one corner, there was a small room partitioned off from the rest of the space, which our hero concluded was the depository for eatables, and for which reason he was very desirous of exploring it; for it will be remembered that the action had been commenced on board the Middy just as the hands were piped to dinner. Jack had eaten nothing since morning; and, as boys at his age are constitutionally predisposed to be hungry, he was now, in the middle of the afternoon, almost in a suffering condition.

He tried the door of the room in the corner of the cellar; but, to his grief, it was locked. Jack could not help thinking what a villanously bad practice it was to keep the pantry locked; but if he had considered the number of working negroes on the place, whose diet con-

sisted of a peck of corn and a small allowance of bacon
per week, he would have been satisfied with the wisdom
of the arrangement, and, for the sake of the negroes
aforesaid, have been content to remain hungry for the
present.

As he could not find any thing to eat, or even to
drink, — for the demijohns and jugs were either empty
or filled with oil or vinegar, — he was obliged to stow
himself away among the boxes and barrels, to wait for a
more convenient season to emerge from the gloom of his
hiding-place. He was alone, and there was nothing to
disturb his meditations. Of course, he could not help
reviewing the incidents of the afternoon, and wondering
how many of his companions had been killed, wounded,
and captured. As he had no data upon which to base
his calculations, his conclusions were not particularly
satisfactory. He was almost certain, however, that Mr.
Hayswell was a prisoner; but he contented himself with
the thought that he was no great loss to the Government,
after his mismanagement of the affair of the boat-party.

For the want of something better to do, in the gloom
and silence of the cellar, he went to sleep; as almost
any sailor is apt to do, when he has nothing to busy his
hands or occupy his mind. He is "broke of his rest,"
as the elderly ladies in the country say; and it is just as
natural for him to go to sleep as it is for him to "splice
the main-brace." Jack went to sleep. He had not eaten

any thing to give him the nightmare, and his bed was hard, cold, and uncomfortable. His position was rather cramped; and these things, combined, caused him to dream.

An old horse, thin, spavined, and afflicted with the heaves, covered all over with stars and bars, slowly came round, and began making stern-way till his heels were within reach of the dreamer. He thought it was about time to retire, but found himself unable to move. The old horse deliberately raised his heels, and kicked him in the head. He tried to cry out, and tried to beat a retreat; both of which, for some mysterious reason, he was unable to do. The dilapidated old nag continued to pound away till his head seemed to be mashed to a jelly, and, when it appeared to him that the end of all things had come, he waked up in a violent perspiration, trembling from head to foot with the agony he had endured during his slumbers

It was as dark as Egypt; but there was no old horse present. He felt around him, and the boxes and barrels among which he had stowed himself recalled his bewildered senses, and informed him where he was. He rubbed his eyes, and renewed the vision which had just faded from his consciousness. The old horse was, without doubt, the Southern Confederacy; a fact sufficiently certified by the stars and bars he wore. Jack could not help laughing at the sorry figure of the miserable creature ; but, when he thought what awful blows the typical beast had given him, he concluded that the Confederacy, though a one-horse affair, was not to be despised.

Jack had seen a dream-book on board the Harrisburg; but what the significance of dreaming about horses, and especially about such a miserable beast as that which had occupied his slumbering mind, might be, he could not tell. In truth, he had not much faith in dreams; yet he could hardly escape the conclusion, that such a remarkable vision must mean something. If not actually a captive in the hands of the rebels, he was certainly in a fair way of becoming such; and he was afraid the dream foreshadowed his own fate in the hands of the enemy: but he hoped, if he was doomed to a rebel prison, that the old horse would not kick quite so hard as he had in his dream.

It was very dark in the cellar now; and Jack groped his way out from the boxes and barrels which had concealed him, and felt his way in the direction of the door by which he had entered. It was closed, locked, and the key removed. He could not open it by any art or device of his fertile ingenuity; and it was patent to him that his retreat by the door was cut off. But there must be, according to the natural rule of architecture, some means of getting into the cellar other than from the outside of the house. This was a comfortable reflection; and he groped about the dark place till he found the

As a matter of precaution, he seated himself on the first step, and, while he was listening for any sounds which might reach him from the rooms above, loaded the two barrels of his pistol which had been discharged at the rebels. There were footsteps to be heard in one of the rooms over him; but the entry was apparently unoccupied. When the pistol had been prepared for use, he cautiously ascended the steps, opened the door, and passed into the principal hall of the mansion.

The front door was now before him. On each side of it, there was a room opening into the hall. Jack's intention was to pass out of the house by the main entrance; but, unfortunately, one of the doors at the side of it was open. The room was lighted, and there were persons in it engaged in conversation. It was not safe to run the gantlet of this open door; and Jack was obliged to seek a passage in some other direction, or wait till the parlor-door should be closed.

To facilitate the ease and silence of his movements, our hero slipped off his shoes; and, tying them together by the strings, secured them in his belt. Thus prepared, he commenced exploring the premises. There was a door in the rear of the house; but this was locked, and the key removed. Adjoining the two front rooms, there were two other rooms; one of which Jack concluded, from the pleasant odors saluting him in that direction, was the dining-room. He looked in at the key-hole. The room was lighted, and the table seemed to be in readiness for the family. There were no servants present ; and Jack concluded that they had gone to the cook-house, which in the Southern States, our readers are aware, is usually located at some little distance from the mansion.

The hungry intruder ventured to open the door, using extreme care in the operation. On the table, there were a pair of cold roast chickens, ham, bread, cake, and other nice things, which proved to be an unconquerable temptation to the unwelcome visitor. Without ceremony, he confiscated one of the chickens and a quantity of bread, — soft-tack, in the vernacular of the blue-jackets ; and, his mouth watering at the savory anticipations the feast excited, he beat a hasty but well-conducted retreat.

As the hall was an exposed place, he thought of returning to the cellar to discuss this supply of viands ; but, as he passed the door of the apartment opposite the dining-room, he glanced through the key-hole. It was not lighted ; and, with the same care he had before used, he opened the door. It was a starlight evening, and sufficient light came through the windows to enable him to see that the room was the planter's library. But he had hardly entered the apartment before he heard footsteps in the hall. Darting towards a door which he descried in the dim light, he opened it, and shut himself in, just as a person entered from the hall. It was as dark as Erebus in his new quarters; but Jack, after placing his pistols in a position for instant service, felt around him, and ascertained that he had taken refuge in a large closet, which contained stacks of old papers, pamphlets, and books. Hanging on one side were sundry articles of clothing; but our hero hoped they would not be wanted till he had departed. He had not dared to latch the door behind him, lest the noise should attract the attention of the person who had entered. Pushing it open a little, he found that the library had been lighted; and the servant who had performed this service was seated in an easy-chair, occupied with his own reflections. He was a sleek, well-fed negro, dressed like a gentleman; and apparently had no interest whatever in the "jubilee" for which the field-hands in the huts were impatiently praying.

The fellow was evidently waiting for the planter to finish his supper and take possession of the library. He sat there as composed and contented as though he had been the owner of the library. He was certainly unconscious that he was, just at that moment, very much in Jack's way; for the latter wanted a chance to open the window, and jump out. Jack was provoked at the indifference of the gentlemanly servant, and even considered the propriety of giving him one of the bullets in his revolver: but he rejected this suggestion, as it would have been nothing less than murder; for the fellow was as harmless as he was fat and lazy.

Then he thought he would "appear" to the negro, and, in the confusion which ensued, escape by the front door; but, as this would subject him to a pursuit, he decided to remain quiet, even at the risk of having to stay in the closet till the planter had retired for the night. He concluded, after mature deliberation, that this would not be a very terrible calamity; for the old horse of his dreams could hardly reach him in that comfortable position. One thing, however, he regarded in the light of a calamity; and that was his empty, gnawing, rebellious stomach, which was protesting in its own eloquent language against the deprivations to which it had been cruelly subjected since seven-bells in the morning-watch. Whatever happened, he was determined to attend to the claims of this discomfited organ.

Carefully pulling the door to, he detached a wing from the carcass of the chicken, and devoured it. The drumstick and second joint were next depleted of every edible particle; and, in due time, the disintegrated skeleton of the fowl lay in a heap upon a pile of pamphlets, stripped as clean as the buzzards could have picked it. The three large slices of bread also disappeared, and Jack felt better. Nothing was needed but a cup of tea or coffee to complete the feast. Perhaps the negro exquisite in the easy-chair thought there were rats in the planter's closet when he heard the chicken-bones crack; but, luckily for Jack, he was too indolent to investigate the cause of the strange noises.

Our hero felt perfectly contented at this point of our narrative. I don't think he would have cared a straw if the servant, or even the master, had opened the closet door when he had finished his supper; for there is something in a full stomach which inspires confidence. If it should ever be our lot to become a brigadier-general, we should never take our brigade into battle except upon a full stomach. Jack again pushed the door open a little, so that he could see into the library. Suddenly the sleek black rose from the easy-chair as though he had received a charge of electricity through his back-bone, and the planter with another gentleman entered the apartment. Of course, the colored gentleman retired.

"Have a cigar, Litchfield," said the planter

"Thank'e," replied the guest; for such he appeared to be. "I always smoke when I get a chance."

"Eh, Mr. Litchfield?" thought Jack, when he heard that voice, and recognized it as belonging to Lunsley, the pilot. "So you change your name as well as your colors."

The gentlemen in the library talked about the Rebellion, and especially about the affair of the Middy: and Jack learned that the first-lieutenant and four of the men had been captured; that the others had escaped to the boat, and reached the steamer, which still lay at anchor off the earthwork.

"Well, I suppose it's about time for me to start," said Litchfield, *alias* Lunsley, after they had conversed about the event for half an hour. "But I don't quite understand the cotton matter yet."

The planter then proceeded, after closing the hall-door, and declaring that no negro must hear a word about the business, to describe the place where a large steamer, loaded with cotton, was concealed in a bayou some miles above. He was afraid the Union gunboats would discover and appropriate the valuable cargo, or that the Confederate cotton-burners would destroy it. Between these two fires, he was terribly perplexed. He had chartered a steamer, and intended to run his cotton up the Red River, where it would be safe for the present. Lunsley agreed to pilot the boat up, and manage the enterprise.

"But it must be done to-night. That Yankee gunboat will have it in the morning, if you don't," said the planter.

"It shall be forty miles up the river before daylight," replied the pilot.

"Perhaps not!" said Jack to himself, as the two gentlemen left the study.

CHAPTER XXIV.

A NIGHT-EXPEDITION.

JACK SOMERS was troubled with a strong desire to get his hands upon that Mr. Litchfield, *alias* Lunsley; or, failing in that, to bring his pistol to bear upon some vital part of his corporeal being. The wretch was a traitor, and had worn Union colors to obtain the favor of the naval officers, that he might betray his trust into the hands of his employers. It was evident to him now that Litchfield had never intended to take the Middy above this point; for he knew of the existence of the earthwork. It was his purpose to get her aground, where the battery could knock her to pieces. It also looked very much as though he had come up for the purpose of taking charge of the cotton-steamer which the planter had intrusted to his care.

Jack waited but a moment, after the gentlemen had left the room, before he emerged from his hiding-place; and, carefully opening the window, jumped out upon the veranda. He took the precaution to close the window, that no suspicions might be awakened. He was now free : the old horse had not yet hit him on the head ; and he was disposed to believe the old adage, that dreams go by contraries. But Jack was too wise a lad to crow before he had got out of the woods.

The conversation between the pilot and the planter, to which he had listened, placed in his possession some valuable information, of which he now purposed to avail himself. The light-battery was still in the vicinity, and a squad of rebels was at the earthwork watching the Middy. Instead, therefore, of going to the point where he had landed, he made his way directly to the river, hoping that he should be able to find a boat. He could discover no craft of any sort ; and was compelled to resort to a log, upon which he boldly put off.

The current carried him down the stream, after he had pushed out from the shore ; and, when he had rounded the bend, he discovered the Middy at anchor on the edge of the shoal. By a vigorous application of the board he used as a paddle, he contrived to navigate the log so as to bring it up under the bow of the steamer. The watch hailed him ; but his well-known voice was all that was needed to secure him assistance in getting on board.

" Why, Jack, my darling ! " cried Tom Longstone, as the veteran threw his arms around him, " I guv you up for lost ! "

" I'm all right, Tom. Who's officer of the deck ? "

" Mr. Dickey, up there," replied Tom, pointing to the hurricane-deck.

" Come on board, sir," added Jack, touching his cap to Mr. Dickey. " If you please, sir, I would like to see the captain."

" Come up, then."

" Where away now, Jack, my dear? Can't you tell us any thing about it?"

" Not now, Tom ; there'll be more fun by and by : but don't say a word," whispered Jack as he ascended to the hurricane-deck.

" So you got off, Somers !" said Mr. Dickey with a degree of condescension which was indeed quite remark-able.

" Yes, sir : I stowed myself away in a dark place till night, and then came off."

" Have you seen Mr. Hayswell?"

" No, sir : he was taken, and they have sent him off somewhere. If you please, sir, I would like to see the captain about something of great importance."

" The captain ! I'm acting first-lieutenant of this ship ; and you are aware that all communications must pass through me," added Mr. Dickey with sublime impor-tance.

" I beg your honor's pardon," added Jack with a clever stroke of policy. " There's something to be done right off; and I only wanted to save time."

"State your business to me at once, then," continued the acting first-lieutenant of the Middy.

Fortunately, however, Mr. Dickey's high flight was disturbed by the appearance of Captain Bankhead himself, who at once recognized Jack, dark as it was.

"Somers!" exclaimed he, greatly astonished.

"Come on board, sir," answered Jack, touching his cap.

"But you were captured?"

"No, sir: not quite.   I came very near it."

"Come into the wheel-house, and tell me all about it," added Captain Bankhead, leading the way.

Jack told his story as rapidly as possible, including that part relating to the cotton-steamer.   The latter portion of the narrative was particularly interesting to Captain Bankhead, who was much dispirited by the loss of his first-lieutenant and five men ; for it now appeared that one had been killed in the boat.   The capture of the steamer, laden with cotton, would heal his wounded pride, and enable him to return to the fleet with flying colors.

Mr. Dickey was called in ; and Jack stated with great care all the particulars in relation to the cotton-steamer. The captain proposed at once to get up his anchor, and hasten to the mouth of the bayou where the boat was concealed.

"I beg your honor's pardon," interposed Jack very

reverently; "but the battery is on duty somewhere about here, and men are watching the steamer from the earthwork."

"Very good, Jack," said the captain with a smile. "You are right. If you have any suggestions to make, I will hear them; for I find you have got a long head for so small a body."

"I think the first cutter, with a howitzer and twenty men, would do the business in first-rate style," replied Jack.

"But, Somers, you must be used up after such a hard day's work."

"Not at all, sir: I am as fresh as though I had just come out of my hammock."

"Because you must go in the boat, if we conclude to take the steamer in that manner."

"I am all ready, sir."

"Mr. Dickey, clear away the first cutter, and have a howitzer ready for her!" added the captain.

The commander of the Middy seemed to be much troubled when his little first-lieutenant had gone to execute the order. He did not speak for some time; and, as it was not proper to submit his doubts to a quartermaster, we must add that the want of a suitable officer to conduct the expedition was the occasion of his perplexity. Mr. Dickey was the only officer who was available for the important duty, and it was not proper that the captain should go himself.

Mr. Dickey was young, brave, and smart in a double sense; but he was hardly qualified to execute so difficult an undertaking. Captain Bankhead had seen one expedition fail for want of discretion on the part of an officer; and he was very much inclined to leave Mr. Dickey in charge of the Middy, and perform the duty himself. This plan was rejected; for the steamer herself might be captured in his absence. There was no alternative but to commit the charge of the expedition to Mr. Dickey; and accordingly that little officer was duly instructed for the purpose.

The best men on board were detailed to form his crew, all of them armed to the teeth. Mr. Dickey was solemnly charged to be prudent, and to act with vigor and determination. The chief-engineer was ordered to go in the boat, as his services would be required in case the enterprise should be successful. Mr. Dickey was directed to consult with him in any emergency.

Captain Bankhead had decided to make a demonstration with the Middy in order to cover up the movements of the boat-party. The anchor was weighed, and she stood over to the other side of the river, where, under the shadow of the high bank, the boat cast off, and pulled up the river with muffled oars. The Middy was then headed down the river; and those who were watching no doubt congratulated themselves that they had driven her off.

Curled up in the bow of the cutter, Jack Somers related his adventures to Tom Longstone, who was one of the party. He spoke in whispers; and Tom did not speak at all, so deeply was he absorbed in the exciting story.

The oarsmen pulled for two hours against the current, when she was in the vicinity of the bayou where the cotton-steamer lay. Of course, none of the party knew precisely where to find the mouth of the stream they were to ascend. Jack Somers was in the bow of the cutter, on the lookout for any thing like an opening in the bank of the river. The boat still kept under the shadow of the left bank of the river; and Mr. Dickey had carefully observed his instructions to preserve entire silence.

While Jack was on the watch, straining his eyes to find the bayou, he discovered a light on the opposite shore; and, when the boat had advanced a little farther, he clearly discerned the opening for which he had been in search. But the light was ominous. It was clearly a lantern in the hands of a man, as its occasional motion plainly showed.

Jack Somers promptly concluded that the light meant something, and that it was some kind of a signal for the cotton-steamer. As the man who carried it could not possibly have seen the cutter, the meaning of the light was easily read. The signal-man had, of course, been instructed to show the light if there was nothing to interfere with the passage of the cotton-boat.

Our hero saw that this was delicate business to manage, and he was very much afraid that Mr. Dickey would spoil every thing by his self-sufficiency. He had a suggestion; but he hardly dared to offer it, lest it should be rejected: but there was no time to spare; for the cutter was now passing the bayou.

Creeping aft between the oarsmen, he touched his cap in the darkness, and "begged his honor's pardon; but there was a light on the bank."

"What of it?" demanded Mr. Dickey.

"Here's the place, your honor," added Jack in a whisper. "There is a man with a light on the bank. If your honor will please to order the men to lie on their oars."

Mr. Dickey did give the order; for he had been submissively addressed as "your honor;" and nothing more than that could possibly be expected of a quartermaster. Jack then explained the probable meaning of the light, and hinted, in a very respectful but roundabout way, that the man who carried it must be disposed of before the boat entered the bayou. He did not say this in so many words; and, happily, Mr. Dickey did not take offence at the suggestion.

"We will pull over to the other side, and land a couple of men, who can silence him, and keep the signal flying," said Mr. Dickey, who fully believed that he had given utterance to an original idea, so carefully had Jack worded his hint.

The boat dropped down stream about half a mile, and then crossed over. Jack begged permission to be one of the two men who were to execute the important duty of capturing the signal-man; adding, that it would enable him to verify some of the information he had obtained on shore. Mr. Dickey was graciously pleased to grant his request, for the reason stated; and, when a signal for the boat to approach had been agreed upon, he landed with his companion.

"Have you got your pipe with you, Raymond?" asked Jack as they touched the bank.

"Of course I've got my pipe. D'ye want to smoke, Jack?"

"No, I never smoke." And Jack proceeded to explain his plan to his shipmate.

A fifteen-minutes' walk brought them to the junction of the bayou with the main river, where they found the signal-man.

"Has that boat come down yet?" demanded Jack, pointing up the bayou.

"What boat?" replied the man.

"That cotton-boat: we are going up in her."

"She hain't come down yet. Why don't you go up where she is, if you are goin' in her?"

"Didn't know where to find her. Come along, Raymond: we shall find her now easy enough," added Jack as he moved off.

"Avast a minute till I light my pipe by this 'ere lantern," replied Raymond as he had been instructed. "Lend us your glim a moment."

"You'll put it out."

"No, I won't."

The signal-man permitted him to take the lantern: whereupon Jack sprang upon him, and bore him to the ground. The movement was so sudden, that he had no chance to resist. Raymond came to Jack's assistance; placing his pistol at the fellow's temple, which caused him to beg for his life. With a rope which had been brought for the purpose they tied him hand and foot, and fastened him to a tree.

Jack assured the unfortunate rebel that he should not be harmed, if he made no noise; but he instructed Raymond to shoot him if he opened his mouth or attempted to escape. Our hero then took the lantern, and waved it three times, — which was the signal for the boat to advance; then giving it to his companion, who was to remain, he hastened down to the water to board the cutter as she entered the bayou.

CHAPTER XXV.

THE CAPTURE OF THE KENSHAW.

JACK SOMERS sat down on a log at the mouth of the bayou to await the arrival of the cutter. He was entirely satisfied with what had been done thus far, and every thing was certainly working right; but he would have felt much safer in regard to the future if such a man as Mr. Granger had been in command of the expedition. Mr. Dickey was no older than himself, and had a higher respect for his own personal dignity than for any thing else. Any indiscretion might ruin the whole affair, and return the party to the Middy empty-handed and crest-fallen. Jack hoped for the best; and, when the boat appeared, he jumped on board, and reported to Mr. Dickey the success of his mission.

"Very well, Somers. You have behaved yourself with great gallantry, and I shall take occasion to report your good conduct to the captain," replied Mr. Dickey.

"Thank your honor," added Jack, removing his cap,

though he could not help "laughing in his sleeve" at the magnificent bearing of the young officer.

"It is a great satisfaction to an officer to have men upon whom he can rely, when difficult and dangerous service is to be performed," continued Mr. Dickey, addressing the engineer.

"Yes, sir," responded that officer,—a man of forty, who had seen more service before Mr. Dickey was born than the latter had ever performed.

Jack Somers resumed his position in the bow of the boat, on the lookout now for the cotton-steamer. After the expedition had proceeded a couple of miles or more, a second lantern was discovered on shore, which was evidently another signal for the pilot. Jack reported the fact to Mr. Dickey; and that gentleman was by this time so well trained, that he knew exactly what to do. Our hero and another man were ordered to land, and secure the signal-man. The work was accomplished, and the lantern hung upon a branch of a tree; for Jack concluded that another man could not be spared for such inactivity as simply holding a lantern.

This signal was displayed at a bend in the bayou; and, when the cutter came up to the curve, the blazing fires of the cotton-steamer were discovered at the distance of less than half a mile. Mr. Dickey at once became excited by the brilliant prospect before him. A smart dash, and the valuable prize would be his own; and what a joy it would be to report the success of his mission!

"Give way, my lads!" said Mr. Dickey, warming up with the enthusiasm of the moment.

"He'll spoil the whole of it!" groaned Jack in the ear of Tom Longstone. "We shall have to sneak back like whipped chickens!"

"Why, no, my darling. We can board her, and carry her decks at one pull," whispered Tom.

"We may do that; but the rebels will set the prize on fire, disable her engine, and run her aground, or something of that sort, as soon as they see us coming. We ought to pounce upon them like cats, when they are not thinking."

"Here comes the engineer," added Tom as Mr. Gordon came forward to obtain a better view of the scene of operations.

Jack ventured to suggest to him what he had just said to Tom; and the engineer volunteered to open the subject to Mr. Dickey. The result was that the men were ordered to lie on their oars. The boat was then moved into a recess in the bank, where it was concealed by overhanging bushes.

"Now, my lads," said Mr. Dickey, when he had placed the boat to his satisfaction, "I expect every man to do his duty. We shall board that steamer as she comes down, and carry her in the twinkling of an eye"

"Ay, ay, sir!" replied the crew in a low tone.

" Silence, men ! "

The cotton-steamer was now in motion. The signal-lantern at the bend below assured her pilot that every thing was ready ; and she came forward very slowly. Her great furnaces, which were opened occasionally when the firemen threw in wood, cast a broad glare upon the dark waters of the bayou. Every heart in the cutter was beating wild with expectation as she advanced. She was now within a few rods of the boat. Her forward-deck was but a few inches above the surface of the water, presenting a most inviting prospect for a boarding-party.

" All ready, my lads ! " said Mr. Dickey in a low tone. " Give way ! '

The boat dashed forward ; and Jack, with the painter in his hand, leaped on board, and made it fast to a cleat on the forecastle. Tom Longstone was by his side ; and, as Mr. Dickey had not thought to make a particular distribution of his characters for the exciting drama which was now acting, the two quartermasters, animated probably by the instinct of their profession, rushed up the stairs to the boiler-deck, and thence to the hurricane-deck ; from which Jack, outstripping his companion, bounded into the wheel-house, where, with pistol in hand, he confronted the astonished Litchfield, *alias* Lunsley.

" Surrender, or you are a dead man ! " shouted Jack.

" Who are you ? " demanded the pilot with a horrid oath.

"Do you surrender? or shall I blow your brains out?" yelled Jack, as Tom Longstone tumbled into the wheel-house.

At this moment, the boat stopped; for Mr. Gordon, the engineer, had prudently taken possession of the machinery as soon as he came on board, to prevent the pilot from running the boat aground.

"Mind the helm, Jack, and I'll settle this 'ere chap," said Tom, as he approached the pilot, and thrust his pistol in his face.

"Who are you?" growled Lunsley, retreating into the corner of the wheel-house.

"I'll larn ye who I am, you black-hearted traitor!" added Tom, as he seized him by the collar.

"Hands off, my old joker!" replied the pilot, shaking off his grasp; for he was a powerful man.

"All right, my hearty! If you don't surrender like a Christian, I'll send you down to Davy Jones!"

Tom evidently intended to put a pistol-ball through his head; but Jack begged him not to cheat the gallows of its due. After some further parley, Lunsley concluded to surrender, and gave up his pistols, which he had had no opportunity to take from his pockets. He was handed over to a couple of marines, and secured in a safe place.

The cotton-steamer had now come to a dead stand. All the white men on board had been secured, including the captain, mate, clerk, engineers, and two pilots. The firemen were negroes; and, being by nature loyal, they were not molested.

"Our victory is complete," said Mr. Dickey, who had now made his way to the wheel-house.

"I beg your honor's pardon," said Jack; "but there's a battery of artillery on shore, and we had better not stay up here too long."

"I don't ask your advice, quartermaster," replied the commander of the expedition.

"I beg your honor's pardon," added Jack with becoming humility.

Mr. Dickey walked down the hurricane-deck, and back, and then returned to the wheel-house.

"Strike one bell, quartermaster!" added he.

Jack obeyed the order, and the steamer started.

"Will your honor please to give me the course I am to steer?" asked Jack meekly.

"Down the stream, of course!" replied Mr. Dickey nervously.

"I am no pilot, sir, for these waters; and she may stick hard and fast before we go ahead five fathoms."

"Strike two bells, quartermaster!"

"Two bells, sir!" repeated Jack.

"We have no pilot, certainly," said Mr. Dickey more nervously; "but we must go ahead."

"If your honor would send the boat ahead to sound, we could work her down very well," suggested Jack, when he saw that the accomplished Mr. Dickey was absolutely at his wits' end for an expedient.

The commander was graciously pleased to adopt this plan; and Tom Longstone was ordered to take one of the steamer's lanterns, and sound out the channel in the boat. The veteran quartermaster took the lead from the forecastle, and proceeded to execute the order.

Mr. Dickey placed himself at Jack's side at the wheel, and the steamer went ahead again. Her progress was necessarily very slow: but the lantern in the cutter was a safe guide; and, in due time, she reached the mouth of the bayou. The boat was then recalled, Raymond taken on board, and the steamer emerged into the great river. The commander was relieved from his nervous anxiety, and his remarks became more brilliant, though he displayed less of the self-sufficiency of his nature than might have been expected under the circumstances. The events of the night had inspired him with no small degree of respect for Quartermaster Somers, and he was less haughty than on former occasions.

The cotton-steamer had proceeded but a short distance down the river before the Middy was discovered steaming up. It is quite likely that Captain Bankhead suffered a great deal during the absence of the expedition, from anxiety for the safety of his men. The appearance of the prize must have been a great relief to him; for it removed from his mind a burden equal in weight to the whole cargo of cotton.

The Middy ran up alongside the Kenshaw, — which was the cotton-steamer's name, — after hailing her, and learning that she was indeed the expected prize.

"Captain Bankhead, I have the honor to report the entire success of the expedition," said Mr. Dickey, as he stepped on board the Middy.

"I congratulate you upon your success, Mr. Dickey," replied the captain, grasping the hand of the proud and happy young officer. "I have been trembling for you every moment since your departure."

"I am happy to say, sir, that every thing has worked to my entire satisfaction. The men behaved themselves with great discretion and gallantry; and I would particularly recommend Quartermaster Somers to your favor."

"Somers again!" laughed Captain Bankhead.

"He conducted himself with remarkable skill and gallantry, sir; and his conduct merits my entire approbation. I take great pleasure in reporting his excellent conduct to you, sir; and trust that his merit will not be overlooked."

"It shall not be, Mr. Dickey. He shall be particularly mentioned in my despatch to the flag-officer," replied the captain, who could hardly help laughing at the high-flown speech of Mr. Dickey.

The Kenshaw was run up to the bank of the river, and moored to a tree; for Captain Bankhead did not think it prudent to start for New Orleans without a pilot. The Middy came to anchor in a position where she could defend her from any attack from the shore.

Litchfield, the pilot, had been put in irons, and conveyed on board the Middy. He was silent and sullen, refusing to answer any questions put to him by the captain. In the morning, however, he appeared to be more tractable, and expressed his regret for his past conduct.

"I'm true to the Gover'ment, cap'n, and have been from the beginning," said he.

"And for that reason you attempted to destroy my vessel!"

"No, sir: I only wanted to get that steamer out, and take her down to New Orleans. You haven't any pilot on board now, cap'n; and, if you will only trust me, I'll take the Kenshaw down for you, and prove that I'm a true man."

"Very well: I will trust you," replied Captain Bankhead.

"You will find that I'm all right."

The pilot's irons were taken off, and he was ordered into the boat. Mr. Dickey was appointed to the command of the Kenshaw as prize-master, and Jack was to go in her as wheelman. Captain Bankhead accompanied the party to the steamer; and, on boarding her, proceeded at once to the wheel-house, followed by Luns-ley. Two marines, armed with muskets and pistols, were placed in the apartment.

"Somers," said the captain, "you will remain at the wheel during the passage down. The pilot will give you your steering directions. If the boat gets aground, you will immediately order the marines to shoot him!"

"Ay, ay, sir," replied Jack.

"You needn't take all that trouble, cap'n. I shall do my duty, honor bright," added Lunsley.

"You have a strong inducement for doing it," an-swered the captain as he left the wheel-house.

Mr. Dickey gave his orders, and the great furnaces of the Kenshaw blazed with renewed vigor. The fasts were cast off, and the steamer commenced her downward trip to New Orleans. The Middy kept close astern of her, with her guns shotted in readiness to defend her in case of an attack.

Jack Somers kept his station at the wheel-house for seven long hours, his breakfast and dinner being brought up to him. Lunsley said very little on the passage. He was apparently studying his chances to escape from the strong grip which held him in abeyance: but there sat the marines, pistol in hand, during the entire trip; and certain death was the penalty of even a suspicion of treachery.

At one o'clock, the Kenshaw made her landing at the

Levee in New Orleans. The pilot was immediately delivered over to General Butler for safe keeping; and
Jack, who had not slept a wink during the preceding
night, appropriated the captain's stateroom to his own
use, and turned in

18

CHAPTER XXVI

THE UNION REFUGEES.

A FOUR-HOURS' nap renovated Jack's exhausted frame; and he was ready to take another job of piloting, if one had presented. Towards evening, Captain Bankhead visited the prize; and one of the boat's crew handed Jack a letter from home. It was a joyous missive; for it contained the intelligence of his father's escape from the rebels, and his return to Pinchbrook. On the last page were a few lines written in the well-known heavy hand of Captain Somers, in which he encouraged his son to do his duty to the country faithfully, and to stand by the old flag to the last. The old gentleman declared his intention of going into the navy in some capacity, as soon as he had recovered from the effects of his campaign in Virginia.

The letter also contained tidings from " Tom Somers in the Army," who had been promoted to the rank of sergeant for meritorious conduct. The people in Pinchbrook were all well, and every thing was in a prosperous condition at the cottage.

"All right!" said Jack, as he folded up the letter, and put it in his pocket, to be read over and over again. "They shall hear from *me* one of these days. Well, God bless the old gentleman! He is one of the right sort, and ought to have the command of one of these gunboats. I suppose little Dickey, who don't know enough to go into the house when it rains, could get a vessel as quick again as my father, who has tumbled about on the ocean all his lifetime."

Mr. Dickey obtained a great deal of credit for the skilful manner in which he had brought in the Kenshaw; and there was a strong probability that he would be promoted for his good conduct on that occasion. The facts in the case were not explained. Tom Longstone could not tell the captain, that, if it had not been for Jack's suggestions, the whole affair must have been a failure. Mr. Gordon, the engineer, might have said so; but he was a prudent man, and minded his own business. Probably it was just as well that nothing of the kind was said; for Mr. Dickey's faults were those which age would correct. He was a good fellow with his equals, and was as brave as a lion in the presence of his country's foes.

The crew of the prize-steamer were sent on board the Middy on the day after her arrival, with a fine prospect before them of pocketing a very handsome allowance of prize-money, after the Kenshaw and her cargo had passed through all the meshes of red-tape with which the law surrounds a naval prize.

The little steamer was repaired and strengthened where she had been found to be weak; and, at the expiration of a fortnight, she was ready for another cruise. An addition was made to her crew. Mr. Hayswell's place was supplied by Mr. McBride, the fourth-lieutenant of the Harrisburg; and a pilot of known loyalty was put on board. Thus prepared, the little Middy again sailed upon a cruise up the river. This time she attended the Harrisburg and other ships of the fleet, and went up as far as Vicksburg. Natchez, Baton Rouge, and other cities on the river, had surrendered, after more or less display of force.

Vicksburg proved to be " a hard nut to crack." The batteries which defended the city were located on high bluffs, where the guns of the fleet were unable to reach them. The water was falling, and the larger ships had experienced much difficulty in getting up. The Harrisburg had been compelled to lighter her battery and coal over some of the shoals. In the face of these difficulties, operations were suspended until a rise of the river should favor their renewal; and the larger vessels of the fleet returned to New Orleans or Baton Rouge.

The gunboats had command of the river, however. below Vicksburg; and the iron-clads belonging to the squadron of Commodore Porter had run the gantlet of the heavy batteries at that place. During the summer, the fleet inflicted severe injury upon the rebels at various points; and all the efforts of the latter to regain possession of the river were unavailing. The Arkansas, which had forced a passage through the Union fleet at Vicksburg, was destroyed, Grand Gulf bombarded, and the enemy terribly punished at Baton Rouge.

In the midst of such events as these, Jack Somers passed the season. The Middy was ordered to watch the banks of the river, to protect the transports which conveyed troops and stores to the fleet and the army, and generally to annoy the enemy as opportunity was presented. At one time she narrowly avoided a broadside from the Arkansas; and, at another, escaped by superior running from the Webb and Music, — the two consorts of the rebel iron-clad.

Later in the season, when the river began to rise, the Middy was ordered to make a reconnoissance up the Red River; and she started upon the perilous duty. This river had been the hiding-place for rebel gunboats and cotton-steamers; and the Middy had not proceeded many miles before she was attacked by a battery of light-artillery, which she repulsed without difficulty, and proceeded on her way.

" I don't think we shall make a very long trip in this direction," said Mr. Deane, the pilot.

" I suppose we have only come up to take a look, and find out what there is here," replied Jack, who was at the wheel.

"There's a steamer round that bend," added the pilot. "I see her smoke-stacks."

"There's a chance for a prize, then. Very likely she is a rebel gunboat, — one of the cotton-clads."

"Well, we shall soon find out."

He had hardly uttered the words before a shot from a concealed battery struck the wheel-house, tearing the roof completely off, and scattering the splinters in every direction.

"That's a close shave," said Jack. "Are you hurt, Mr. Deane?"

"Not at all," replied he, shaking off the pine-wood which had fallen upon him. "But I shouldn't like to try it over again."

"Two shots never go in the same place. We are safe for the rest of the day."

The order was given by the captain to stop and back her; but, before the Middy could get out of range, half a dozen more shot fell unpleasantly near to her. The guns in the fort were heavy, long-range pieces; and it would be madness for the little steamer to attempt to go any farther. She therefore put about, and commenced her return trip. She had proceeded but a few miles towards the Mississippi, when a white flag was discovered on the shore, around which were gathered some forty or fifty men. They hailed the steamer, and asked to be taken off.

The Middy's wheels were stopped, and Captain Bankhead desired to know who and what they were.

"We are all Union men," replied the spokesman of the party ; "and we want to get out of this region."

"Where are you from?"

"We came from up the river. We have been robbed by the rebels of every thing we had : some of the Unionists have been murdered ; and we want to get inside the Union lines."

"Where are your families?" demanded Captain Bankhead.

"We had to leave them ; but the rebels don't meddle with the women and children. We haven't had any thing to eat for two days."

The bow of the Middy was run up to the shore : but the captain seemed to have some doubts in regard to the party ; for a portion of them were armed with guns, pistols, and other weapons. He questioned them still further in regard to their antecedents, and finally permitted them to come on board ; taking the precaution to disarm them as they passed the gang-plank. They were provided with food, of which they partook with ravenous appetites.

Their clothing was in a very dilapidated condition ; and their appearance certainly confirmed their story, that they had suffered every imaginable hardship. Many of them proposed at once to enlist in the Union army, or enter the navy, as the captain might elect. They professed to be very anxious to avenge the indignities to which they had been subjected, and desired to join any force which should have for its object the subjugation of their State.

The man who had spoken for them was an intelligent and gentlemanly person ; but the majority of the party were coarse and rude in their manners, belonging to the lowest stratum of Western society.

" I say, Jack, my dear, I don't like the looks of them bloody vill'ns on the main-deck," said Tom Longstone in a low tone when he came up to relieve the wheel at dinner-time.

" Why not ? "

" Stop my grub if I don't believe they are rebels at heart, Jack ! "

" What makes you think so ? "

" I don't like the looks of them. The sharks would dodge such a crowd ! "

" They have seen hard times."

" I don't mind their dress, Jack ; but they look ugly about the eyes."

" Is that all you have against them ? "

" No ; shiver my timbers if it is. I seen 'em whispering together more'n decent men ought to."

Jack went down to his dinner ; and, being off duty afterwards, he took the opportunity to examine the refugees. They were certainly whispering together; and he noticed that their spokesman frequently passed from one squad to another about the deck. Their movements were suspicious; and Jack very much desired to know what their head man had to say in this confidential manner.

The refugees were congregated on the deck around the wind-sail by which fresh air was introduced to the fire-room below the main-deck. Dunnett, the leader, was seated near this wind-sail at that moment, talking to a group around him; and Jack's curiosity was so thoroughly stimulated, that he could not resist the temptation to become one of his hearers.

Descending to the fire-room, he procured a short ladder used in oiling the engine; and, running it up the hatch through which the wind-sail passed, he ascended till his head was above the deck. He was now right in the midst of the squad, and could distinctly hear every word that was said.

" When I whistle, every man will do his share of the work," said Dunnett in a whisper. " Half the crew are below : put the hatch on, and keep them there ; then we can easily conquer the rest."

Jack did not wait to hear any more. He was only afraid that the plot would be executed before he could communicate the information to the officers. Coming up from the fire-room, he hastened to find Mr. McBride, who was then officer of the deck. In a few words, he informed him of the conspiracy. The captain was then made acquainted with the alarming facts; but not a word was yet said to any other person.

Captain Bankhead was prompt and decided. The watch on deck were ordered to the quarter-guns in a quiet way. They had been loaded with case-shot during the action with the light battery. The charge of one was given to Tom Longstone, while the other was in care of Raymond.

At the same time, a plank in the bulkhead between the forecastle — where part of the men were at the time — and the fire-room was knocked out. Through this opening the seamen passed into the fire-room, and thence into the after-cabin, where they were armed with cutlasses and pistols. They were ordered to stay behind the paddle-boxes, where they could not be seen by the conspirators. The two quarter-guns were in readiness to be slung round in an instant, so as to command the passage on each side of the engine.

The preparations were all completed; but Dunnett did not yet give his signal for the attack. The crew of the Middy were impatient for operations to commence; and, after some further time had elapsed, the captain began to think that Jack had been deceived, and that his passengers were honest and loyal men.

The fact was, that Dunnett had been waiting for a bet

ter disposition of the crew for his purpose ; but, when he had waited till his patience was exhausted as well as that of the captain, he gave the designated whistle.

A couple of the rebels sprang to the hatch, and closed it ; perfectly confident, no doubt, that they were imprisoning at least half the seamen of the Middy. Others rushed to the wheel-house and to the engine-room, where, of course, they overpowered the pilot and the engineer. Having secured these points, they formed in a body, and moved aft. It now appeared that they were armed with bowie-knives ; but, believing they were to encounter only half their number, they advanced with entire confidence.

CHAPTER XXVII.

THE CONSPIRACY ON BOARD THE MIDDY.

"SWING round the guns!" said Captain Bankhead; and, when the rebels advanced, they were confronted by the black muzzles of the twenty-four-pounders.

"There! what do you think of that, my beauties?" added Tom Longstone, who stood with the lock-string in his hand, ready to scatter the iron hail among the conspirators.

"Silence!" commanded the captain.

The rebels, seeing what kind of a trap they had fallen into, began to retreat.

"Halt!" shouted the captain in a voice of thunder. "If a man of you moves, I will give the order to fire!"

There was no mistaking this insinuating request; and the party stood in dumb amazement before the frowning guns. It was impossible for them to help seeing, that, if they made any movement, it would result in the certain destruction of half their number. Their plans had certainly been well laid; and nothing but the discovery of them interfered with their success. Expecting an easy victory, they were confounded to find the whole project suddenly ruined.

Dunnett looked savagely discontented with the result; and Captain Bankhead was afraid he would be rash enough to rush upon the guns, and sacrifice his party. It would have been a terrible necessity to him to give the order for the destruction of so many human beings as must have followed the discharge of the twenty-four-pounders, especially as the engineers and two seamen were also exposed to the fire.

" You understand the matter now," said Captain Bankhead, after the rebels had stared at the guns long enough to understand the situation. "It only remains for you to surrender."

" Never !" yelled Dunnett, stamping his foot with rage.

" Very well : you can take your choice."

The villain looked behind him, glancing at the shore ahead of the steamer. He evidently had something to hope for ; as the rebels had the wheel and engine in their power, and could take the Middy where they pleased. Captain Bankhead then nipped this hope in the bud by sending Mr. McBride, with Jack Somers and two marines, to recover the wheel-house.

Unfortunately, the rebels who had captured Mr. Deane, the pilot, had taken his pistols from him ; and the two men at the wheel were thus supplied with weapons. The lieutenant and his men were equally well armed, it is true; but the capture of the rebels involved the loss of some life, which a prudent officer should always avoid if possible. There was no other way, however; for the Confederates at the wheel, beginning to understand the state of affairs below, were putting the steamer about, probably with the intention of running her under the guns of some battery in the vicinity.

Mr. McBride ordered the marines to advance, and take the men at the wheel. They obeyed; but the rebels were prompt and decided in their resistance, and one of the marines fell. The other, intimidated by the fall of his companion, discharged his musket, and retreated. Jack, seeing how matters were going, climbed upon the top of the pilot's stateroom,—which was a continuation of the wheel-house,—and advanced towards the scene of action.

"Shoot them, Somers!" said Mr. McBride, fearful that Jack might attempt to compromise the matter.

"Ay, ay, sir!" replied our sailor-boy, lying down upon his stomach, and creeping forward, with his revolver in his hand.

The lieutenant then approached the wheel-house with the marine, ready to take advantage of the panic which the other movement might occasion; though they did not show themselves to the enemy. Jack had now reached a point where he could see the rebels; for, as the reader remembers, the roof of the wheel-house had been blown off by the shot from the battery on shore. The two men were crouching behind the door, pistols in hand, ready to repel an assault in that direction. Jack took deliberate aim at the man who had one hand on the wheel, and fired. The wretch uttered an oath, and let go his hold, which caused the wheel to roll over; for the steamer was in the act of coming about. His companion, dismayed by this unexpected assault, turned to see whence it came, and to be in readiness to repel it. As he did so, Mr. McBride fired his pistol, but missed his aim.

The rebel, finding himself attacked in front and in flank, and not knowing from what direction the next assault might come, crouched down in the corner of the wheel-house, and cried for " quarter." Jack Somers then dropped into the apartment from the broken roof, and grasped the wheel, while Mr. McBride and the marine seized the discomfited rebel. Mr. Deane, who had been thrust into the pilot's state-room for safe keeping, was called out; and the Middy, which had nearly run into the bank of the river during the affray, was again headed down stream.

The steamer was now a " house divided against itself," having a Union pilot and a rebel engineer. The latter soon manifested his opposition to the dominant power in the wheel-house by stopping the engine. Mr. McBride, after the wounded rebel and the wounded marine had been placed in the pilot's room, left the hurricane-deck to report to the captain on the quarter.

While these events were transpiring, Captain Bankhead had been parleying with Dunnett, endeavoring to prevent the scene of bloodshed which must follow more decided operations. When the rebel engineer stopped the engine at a signal from the chief conspirator, it was plain that no further temporizing must be allowed.

"I give you two minutes to surrender!" said the captain sternly. "At the end of that time, we shall fire upon you!"

"And blow your boat all to pieces!" sneered Dunnett, who evidently did not believe Captain Bankhead would put his threat into execution, except in self-defence.

"Whatever happens, we shall fire!" said the captain, taking out his watch.

Dunnett waited with compressed lips and glaring eyes until the captain announced that the time had nearly expired.

"Lie down, boys!" shouted the rebel leader; and, suiting the action to the words, he threw himself flat upon the deck, and the others followed his example.

Without any orders from the captain, Tom Longstone and Raymond depressed the muzzles of the guns till they pointed into the midst of the two groups in the passage-ways.

"Those who wish to surrender, come aft!" said Captain Bankhead in a loud tone, so that all the rebels could hear him.

Before Dunnett could counteract the effects of this invitation upon his party, the miserable rebels began to crawl aft; for it was not in the nature of man to face the muzzles of those terrible guns, which at any instant might tear them in pieces. It was folly and madness to stand up or lie down in range of such savage persecutors.

The movement soon became general; and, as the rebels came aft, they were disarmed and secured by the seamen.

"Cowards!" yelled Dunnett. "Will you desert me? Will you put your necks into a halter?"

The words hissed from his mouth in the fearful rage he exhibited when he saw himself deserted by nearly all his party. He was a desperate man, and evidently had no regard for his own life or the lives of his men. He had risen from his recumbent posture when the stampede of his forces became general. Finding his words had no effect upon his frightened followers, he began to flourish his bowie-knife, and threatened to take the life of any one who accepted the captain's offer.

The force of example was potent; and apparently there were not more than half a dozen who were willing to stand by him in his reckless measures. The battle among the rebels themselves had actually commenced; and the desperado had stabbed two or three of his mis-

erable crew, when Captain Bankhead considered it time
for him to interfere.   He ordered six marines to advance
with bayonets, under the direction of Mr. Dickey, to be
supported by half the crew with cutlasses and pistols.

Mr. Dickey, with his sword drawn, advanced valiantly
to the charge.   Dunnett, and the half-dozen rebels who
still adhered to his failing fortunes, retreated to the bow
of the steamer, passing over the wounded and frightened
ones who had been vainly striving to escape the fury of
their own leader.

"Come on, my men!" shouted Mr. Dickey, who led
the way ten feet ahead of the marines, when the rebels
fled from the heavy force sent to capture them.

He rushed forward, flourishing his sword in the air exactly as he had seen the weapon displayed in pictures of
such desperate affrays.   Dunnett, probably inspired with
a supreme contempt for this puny antagonist, and more
likely with a desire to wreak his vengeance upon the
authors of his discomfiture, advanced upon him; and the
captain trembled for the fate of his little officer.   But
Mr. Dickey parried the blow of the bowie-knife with the
trusty blade, which had hitherto been only an ornament
in his hand; and, stepping back a pace or two, he drew
his pistol, and fired.   Dunnett fell.   The marines then
charged upon the others who supported him.   Disheart-
ened by the fate of their chief, they gave way, and,
throwing down their knives, were made prisoners.   The

battle was ended, and the Middy still remained in possession of the original officers and crew.

"Mr. Dickey, you have done nobly!" said Captain Bankhead, when the gallant tars had given the cheers which are almost irrepressible after a victory.

"Hurrah!" shouted the crew, as the captain took the hand of his second-lieutenant.

"Thank you, sir. I have only endeavored to do my duty," replied Mr. Dickey.

"You have done it bravely; and I thank you for your valuable services, which, I assure you, I shall not fail to embody in my report to the flag-officer."

"I am very grateful to you, sir, both for the opportunity you afforded me of serving the cause, and for your kind appreciation of my humble endeavors to do my duty," added Mr. Dickey.

"But there is another man on board who ought to be remembered at this time, — one who ferreted out this plot, and gave me the information in time to prevent its execution. Where is Somers?"

"Somers again!" exclaimed Mr. Dickey, facetiously repeating the captain's words on a former occasion.

"I am here, sir," said Jack, who, after the engine started, had come down from the wheel-house to witness the exciting events transpiring on the main-deck. — "I am here, sir; but" —

"Hurrah!" shouted the crew.

"The credit does not belong to me, Captain Bankhead," continued Jack. "It was Tom Longstone"—

"Vast heavin', my darling!" interposed that veteran. "It was Jack Somers, your honor. Don't believe a word he says about me, sir."

"It was Longstone who first found out about it, sir. He told me when he came up to relieve the wheel, at dinner-time."

"Hurrah!" shouted the crew, swinging their caps in honor of the veteran quartermaster.

"Silence, my lads!" said the captain.

"Who climbed up the wind-sail, and heard what the lubbers had to say?" persisted Tom stoutly.

"We owe our safety to both of you; and both of you have behaved very handsomely during the affair."

"Somers certainly has," added Mr. McBride, who now reported the events which had taken place at the wheel-house.

"Somers again!" added Mr. Dickey.

Jack blushed, and was glad when the orders were given to dispose of the rebel prisoners. Dunnett was the only man killed during the exciting affray; the ball from Mr. Dickey's pistol passing through his head. The marine wounded on the hurricane-deck was in a critical condition. The ball from Jack's pistol had passed through the rebel's shoulder; but his wound was not mortal. Three of the desperadoes, stabbed by Dunnett and his immediate supporters, appeared not to be dangerously hurt. All of these sufferers were placed in the cabin, and the surgeon was already attending to them.

When the usual order and quiet of the steamer had been restored, Captain Bankhead examined the prisoners in relation to the desperate enterprise they had undertaken. It was ascertained that Dunnett was a lieutenant in the light battery which had fired upon the Middy in her passage up the river, and that the men were, most of them, members of the company. Dunnett had suggested the plot, and selected the men to carry it out. Knowing that the steamer would soon be beaten back by the heavy battery above, he had awaited her return, and hailed her under cover of a flag of truce. They had been provided with bowie-knives, which they had concealed about their persons, though they had not expected to be deprived of their guns and pistols. The wariness of Captain Bankhead had prevented the earlier execution of the treacherous scheme, which could hardly have failed of ultimate success if the suspicions of Tom Longstone and the investigations of Jack Somers had not disclosed it in season to prevent its accomplishment.

The Middy reached the Mississippi at dark, and joined the fleet which was blockading the mouth of the Red River. The next day, she reported to the flag-officer at Baton Rouge, and was ordered to New Orleans for repairs.

CHAPTER XXVIII.

THE MIDDY ON THE BLOCKADE.

THE Middy arrived at New Orleans about the middle of August, where she was immediately followed by the Harrisburg. The little steamer was then hauled up at Algiers, opposite the city, and completely dismantled for the purpose of making certain repairs and alterations, to adapt her to a different service from that in which she had before been engaged. Her officers returned to the ship, with the exception of Mr. Dickey, who remained in charge of the crew. The Harrisburg then departed for Ship Island.

During the session of Congress, the navy had been re-organized; and Jack learned that his friend Mr. Bankhead was now a commander. Flag-officer Farragut was henceforth to be known as a rear-admiral. Mr. Dickey had been promoted to the new rank of ensign. Mr. McBride was still a lieutenant; but his name was much nearer the head of the list than before.

Our sailor-boy was rejoiced at the promotion of his friends; but he was heartily disgusted when he learned, a few days later, that Captain Bankhead had been ordered to the command of a gunboat in the Eastern Gulf Squadron, and that by no possibility could he obtain a berth in the same vessel. He poured out his sorrows in dubious strains to his friend Tom Longstone, who did all he could to comfort him.

"I've got enough of this fresh-water duty!" said Jack. "I want to see the blue sea again, and be tumbled about in a gale once more. I suppose we can get back into the Harrisburg again, if we want to do so."

"Don't you do it, my darling. We have done very well in this 'ere trim little craft."

"But I don't want to paddle about here in fresh water all my days; though I wouldn't mind it if Captain Bankhead were to remain in command."

"See here, Jack: do you mind what them 'ere men are doin'?" continued Tom, pointing to the shipwrights at work on the forecastle of the Middy.

"They are putting up bulwarks, of course."

"That means that we are going to sea, my bantling."

"But who is going to command her? That is the question."

"I dunno, Jack."

"Mr. Dickey, very likely."

"Perhaps he be: he's a ensign now!" added Tom with one of his inward chuckles. "What a lubberly name that is to give an officer in the United-States Navy! It aren't much better nor callin' him a marine."

The supposition in regard to Mr. Ensign Dickey proved not to be correct; for the command of the Middy was given to Lieutenant McBride: but the aspiring little gentleman was to serve as executive officer, while an acting ensign — Mr. Brackett — was attached to her as second-lieutenant. The repairs and alterations were completed, her quota of officers reported to the captain, and the Middy was again ready for duty.

"All hands, up anchor, ahoy!" piped the acting-boatswain one fine morning about the middle of September.

"Here's a letter which Commander Bankhead requested me to deliver to you, Somers," said Captain McBride, who had just come on board with his orders, having arrived the night before from Ship Island.

"Thank you, sir," replied Jack, as he received the letter through the window of the wheel-house.

"You had better open it before we get off; for it may contain an official document," added the captain. "I have been expecting an order to send you ashore; but I hope there is nothing of the kind there."

"Nothing, sir."

"Anchor away, sir!" reported the boatswain.

"Strike one bell, quartermaster!" said Mr. Dickey.

"One bell, sir!" replied Tom Longstone.

There was a pilot on board, who had already received his instructions; and, as Tom had the helm, Jack was at liberty to read his letter, which was an object of no little interest to him. Captain Bankhead informed him that he was waiting an opportunity to join his ship, and that they should probably meet again in a few weeks; for the Middy had been transferred to the Eastern Gulf Squadron.

"I hope you will continue to conduct yourself with the same heroism, and devotion to your country's cause, which have heretofore distinguished you," the writer continued; "for I have high hopes of your future. Your character has, thus far, been above reproach; and I am satisfied that you will continue to keep it pure and unsullied. I have just written to your mother a long story about you, in which I told her that you never gambled, drank liquor, or swore; that, when you had a day's liberty in New Orleans, you returned with no vices clinging to you; that your shipmates love you for your virtues; that you frequently read your Testament; and are, in every respect, what I would have you. It is easier to be brave in battle than it is to be a good man.

"But I have not written this letter to tell you what a good boy you have been; though it was exceedingly pleasant to be able to give your mother so good an account of you. I desired to inform you that I have represented your case to the admiral, and others who have influence at Washington. I hope to procure for you a warrant as a midshipman in the navy. I think I could obtain a commission for you as an acting-ensign; but you are not a navigator, and I wish to have you well instructed. You must go to the Naval School for a time; and, as your education has not been neglected, you need remain there but a few months. The admiral warmly seconds my views; and I doubt not, as a special favor to him, the request we make will be granted.

"Now, my dear boy, be true to yourself, your country, and God, and I shall hope to see you an officer in the regular navy — not a volunteer — in a few months. I have taken all this pains, and am willing to accept a warrant, when I could procure a commission for you, in order that you may not be thrown out of the service when the war closes; of which, Heaven knows, there seems to be no present prospect. I shall expect to see you when the Middy arrives; but I may be gone before she comes.

"Good-by, Jack; and remember me to Tom Longstone.

"Your devoted friend,

"John Bankhead."

Jack was bewildered by the contents of this kind letter, and glanced at his collar to see if there was not already an anchor upon it. "Midshipman Somers" did not sound badly; and our hero's face was wreathed in smiles as the thought passed through his mind. A delightful prospect was certainly before him; and he resolved to be good and true to the end, that he might be worthy of such friends as Commander Bankhead.

"What's in the letter, my dear?" demanded Tom bluntly, as Jack went forward to look out at the window.

"Captain Bankhead desires to be remembered to you, Tom."

"God bless his honor!" exclaimed the old quarter-master, lifting his cap.

"Starboard!" said the pilot.

"Starboard, sir!" repeated Tom.

"Steady!"

"Steady, sir!"

"Well, Somers," said Captain McBride, stopping at the side of the window of the wheel-house, "did the letter please you?"

"Very much, sir," replied Jack. "Will you please to read it, sir?"

Captain McBride, in spite of the traditions of the navy, had ventured to be quite familiar with the quarter-masters of the Middy; for both of them were trusty men, and had more than once won the approbation of the officers. He took the letter, and read it through.

"I knew something about this matter before, Somers; and I congratulate you upon the bright prospect before you"

"Thank you, sir," replied Jack, touching his cap; for

he was determined that this familiarity in his case should not breed contempt.

"I don't know much about your education, Somers. What have you studied?" asked the captain.

"I've only been to the common school, sir; but I went through with what they called the high-school course."

"Have you studied Latin?"

"No, sir," laughed Jack; "but I have studied algebra and geometry."

"Well, Somers, I'll give you my opinion, and you may take it for what it is worth. I've got some books in my cabin; and, while we are lying at anchor, I recommend you to overhaul your studies, and brush them up. You have plenty of time to spare."

"I thank you, sir: I shall certainly do so."

"You and Longstone have the wheel-house all to yourselves after we have discharged the pilot; and there is nothing to prevent your making good use of your time."

"I shall do so, sir."

"And, if you want any assistance, I will cheerfully afford it," added the captain as he walked aft.

"Thank you, sir. You are very kind."

"God bless your honor!" ejaculated Tom Longstone, who felt just as though all these favors were conferred upon himself. "What's in the wind, my darling?"

"Port!" said the pilot.

"Port, sir!" repeated Tom.

"Steady!" added the pilot, who was determined that the wheelman should not do any talking while upon duty.

"Steady, sir!" repeated Tom.

But Jack, who sympathized with his friend in his impatience to know what the important letter contained, took the helm, and handed the document to Tom, who sat down in the corner, and proceeded to study out its contents.

"Is it a middy, my darling?" exclaimed the veteran when he had finished the letter. "I touch my hat to your honor."

"Not yet, Tom."

"Starboard!" said the pilot.

"Starboard, sir!" added Jack.

"No talking at the helm!" said the pilot testily. "If you say another word, I'll report you to the officer of the deck."

Tom took the helm again, and Jack went below. In the course of the day, the captain gave him several works on geometry, gunnery, and mathematics in general, which he carefully deposited in the closet in the wheel-house.

In the afternoon, the Middy went through Pass à l'Outre, and, before evening, was rolling about in the swells of the Gulf; but she was a good sea-boat, and the motion was rather refreshing to the old salts on board. Before daylight, she came to anchor near the Harrisburg. Visits were interchanged between the ship and the Middy during the day; but Jack was disappointed to find that Captain Baukhead had gone the day before.

At sunset, the Middy departed for the eastward, and, on the following day, reported to the acting admiral commanding the Eastern Gulf Squadron. Captain McBride received his orders, and immediately sailed again for the station, which was near the mouth of the Suwannee River, in Florida. Tom Longstone expressed his disgust when he found, as he supposed, that the steamer was actually engaged in the blockading service; but Jack was too busy with his books to object to this life of inactivity.

After they had lain on the station a few days, and Jack's head was as full of lines and angles, projectiles and parabolas, as a professor's, an incident occurred which broke up the monotony of the blockader's life. Jack was standing at the window of the wheel-house, running over in his mind a difficult problem in geometry which had perplexed him during the day. It was a dark and foggy evening, and no lights were allowed; for it was just the time to tempt a blockade-runner into a daring deed: but Jack was an earnest student, and he did not cease to study because he could not use his book.

As he meditated upon the mysterious problem, he thought he heard the splashing of a steamer's paddles in the water, between the Middy and the shore. The sound drove all the mathematics out of his head; and he soon satisfied himself that the splashing was not an illusion. He immediately reported the fact to Mr. Dickey, who communicated it to Captain McBride. The cable was instantly slipped and buoyed, and the Middy was in motion. The fog was so dense, that nothing could be seen; but, after going at full speed for fifteen minutes in the direction of the mouth of the river, she was stopped, and her officers listened attentively for the sounds. They could now be distinctly heard; and the Middy continued the chase in the fog and darkness. She approached the mouth of the river, sounding her way, and stopping frequently to listen to the splashing of the steamer's wheels, which could be more distinctly heard at every pause.

"Hullo, de steamer!" said a voice, close aboard of her, at one of these stoppages.

A negro in a skiff now emerged from a dense volume of fog, and came alongside.

"May I come on board, massa?" said he. "I'm pilot, massa: knows ebery foot ob de riber."

"Ay, ay; come on board!" replied the captain.

"You go mos' aground, massa! No water ober dar," added the man as he pointed over on the port-bow. "How much water do you draw, massa?"

"We can carry up about five feet," replied Captain McBride.

"Golly, massa! jus' five foot on de bar at high water, — dat's all!" grinned the negro.

"Are there any batteries up the river?"

"Yes, sir: tree guns up dar. Mos' on de bar now, massa cap'n."

"We will remain here till high water, Mr. Dickey," added the captain.

"Dis chile want to run away awful bad, massa," said the visitor. "Good pilot, massa: knows all about de Keys, and all about here."

"I am glad to see you, then. What steamer was that which just went up the river?"

"Don't know, massa: 'speck it was de 'Lympus. She done run de blockade from de Keys."

The Middy remained where she was, and the pilot was taken below to be fed and clothed.

CHAPTER XXIX.

THE BLOCKADE-RUNNER.

THE water on that portion of the coast of Florida to which the Middy had been ordered is very shallow. The shoals extend out from the land about sixteen miles; and, six miles from shore, there was not, in many places, more than a foot of water between the Middy's keel and the bottom. Her light draught, and weatherly qualities, had been her principal recommendations for the service on which she had been sent; but, for in-shore duty, she was well-nigh useless without a pilot, which she had, thus far, been unable to obtain.

The Suwannee River has two outlets. In front of these there is a long, circular reef, outside of which the Middy lay. The blockade-runner had approached from the direction of Cedar Keys, and entered the river by the most southern of the two outlets, passing inside of the Middy.

The negro who had boarded the steamer said he had been after oysters. He had been on the lookout for a

Government vessel for weeks; for, as he had declared, he " wanted to run away very bad."   Hundreds of slaves had come off to the fleet in various places; and Clem — this was the negro's name — said there were thousands more who wanted to escape from slavery.   There was no difficulty in believing all this, and nothing very strange in Clem's coming off just when and where he did.   His color was a sufficient guaranty for his loyalty, but not for his skill as a pilot in those difficult and dangerous waters.

Captain McBride gave him some supper, and supplied him with clothing; for the poor fellow was not very far from naked.   He questioned him very closely in regard to his knowledge of the navigation of the river and the contiguous waters.   Clem answered that he had been a fireman on a river-steamer for ten years; had been fishing and oystering for five more; and, finally, that he had several times piloted a steamer, drawing three or four feet of water, from the Keys to Clay Landing; and he wished he " was jes as sartin of gwine to heaben as he was of gwine frew dem channels."

The Middy started, in the fog and darkness, to pass the bar; though not till the captain had carefully consulted all his authorities on board in regard to the channel, and ascertained that the spring-tides were then prevailing.

" I'm going to trust you, Clem," said the captain, as

he conducted him to the wheel-house; "but woe betide you if you get us into trouble!"

"Golly, massa! What's dis nigger gwine to git you into trouble fur? I kin take de steamboat up to Clay Landin'; and dat's fur as five foot kin go. Git you into trouble, massa cap'n! Golly! I guess dis chile git hisself into trouble fus. Yah, yah! What you s'pose ole massa say if he cotch Clem takin' Yankee gunboat up de riber? I s'peck he broke his back if he cotch him, jes as shore as you was a white man!"

"Well, never mind that now," added Captain McBride, who could not help seeing the force of the black pilot's argument. "Go into the wheel-house now, and tell the quartermaster how to steer."

"Sar!" exclaimed Clem, opening his mouth from ear to ear.

"Give these men your orders, and they will observe them."

"Clem gib dese gemmen de orders?"

"Certainly."

"Cotch Clem doin' such a t'ing as dat, massa cap'n! Nigger gib orders to de white man! Yah, yah, yah!" and the pilot doubled up and laughed till the waistbands of his new trousers were in danger of being ruptured.

"Come, Clem, we are losing the tide," said the captain

"Yes, sar!" exclaimed he, springing to the wheel. "Whar does you stroke dem bells?"

"Here," said Jack, pointing out the bell-pulls.

"If de gemman gib dis chile de wheel, he can steer hisself all alone."

"Give him the wheel, quartermaster," added the captain.

The black pilot stuck his head out of the window, as though he was trying to peer through the fog and gloom of the night. It certainly looked very hopeless; but the negro snuffed the air half a dozen times, and then confidently struck the bell to go ahead.

"Have you got your bearings?" demanded the captain nervously; for it looked like dubious business to go over a bar, with not more than six feet of water on it, in such a night as that.

"Yes, massa cap'n: I smell um," replied Clem gravely.

"You smell them, you black rascal! What do you mean by that?" roared the captain angrily; for he was disturbed by a strong suspicion that Clem was making game of him.

"Golly, massa cap'n, you frighten dis nigger out of his wits; and he won't know de channel from de reef!"

"What do you mean by saying that you *smell* your bearings?"

"Yes, massa, dat's so: I smell de rotten isters ober on de point dar."

The Middy now went ahead slowly. Clem was as confident as though it had been broad daylight, with a clear sky above him. Tom Longstone heaved the lead constantly.

"Quarter, less two!" said he as the steamer began to move.

"Dat's all right dar," said the black pilot. "Dis chile kin tell you de depf hisself, widout no soundin'."

"And a half, one!" added Tom with emphasis.

"Yes, sar; and, de nex' time you frow, find jes one fadom."

"By the mark, one!" roared Tom, who thought it was about time to strike two bells.

"Rite on de bar, massa," said Clem, thrusting his head out of the side-window, and taking three long snuffs. "Dar's de pint ober dar."

"By the mark, one!" repeated Tom as he threw the lead again.

"Needn't soun' no more down dar. Dis chile knows all about it hisself," cried Clem, who appeared to think that the precaution was an imputation upon his skill or his loyalty.

But Tom did not suspend the operation; and soon the depth increased to eight feet.

"All right now, massa cap'n," said Clem a few minutes later, as he fixed his eye on the compass.

The binnacle-lamp had been lighted: but it was not to be supposed that Clem knew any thing about the compass; yet great was the astonishment of the captain when it was observed that now he steered entirely by that instrument.

'What is your course, Clem?" asked Captain Mc-Bride.

" No'th-east by no'th, massa," replied the black pilot.

" Can you box the compass?"

" Yes, sar. no'th, no'th by east, nor'-nor'-east, no'th-east by no'th, nor'-east, no'th-east by east, east-nor'-east, east by no'th, east," chattered Clem without hesitation.

" That will do   Where did you learn that?"

" 'Board vessel down t' de Keys."

Clem was certainly a prize ; and Captain McBride was duly grateful that this "intelligent contraband" had concluded to run away at the precise time he did.

" Steamer on the port-bow !" shouted the lookout on the forecastle.

" Dems 'em, massa cap'n ; and de fort's right ober dar," said Clem, pointing out of the window.

" We had better not wake up the fort, if we can help it," said the captain.

" I think not, sir," added Mr. Dickey.

The fog was not quite so dense up the river as it had been outside ; and the blockade-runner could be distinctly seen, at anchor. But there was a great deal of confusion on board of her, as it now appeared from the noise which reached the Middy. Probably her captain was not a little surprised to find a United-States steamer at his heels on such a night and in such a place; and it must be acknowledged that Captain McBride was scarcely less surprised.

"Can you run alongside that steamer?" asked the captain of the pilot.

"No, sar: dat steamer don't draw no more'n four foot ob water."

"Clear away the first cutter, Mr. Dickey!" added the captain. "Send Mr. Brackett to board the steamer."

In a few moments, the first cutter, as the starboard quarter boat was designated, was pulling towards the blockade-runner. It contained, besides the second-lieutenant, an engineer, a master's mate, and fifteen seamen, all armed to the teeth. As the boat approached the prize, a rocket went up from her forecastle, and she began to move up the river again. But, before she had got full headway on, Mr. Brackett boarded her. No resistance was made, though some of the crew jumped overboard, and swam towards the shore.

The rocket had done its work, and the battery opened fire; but the aim of the gunners seemed to be half a mile farther up the river, and no notice was taken of the firing by the Middy. The prize was brought alongside the steamer, and her crew put in irons to prevent them from doing mischief. Mr. Brackett was directed to remain on board of her with his prize-crew; and Jack was ordered to her wheel, with instructions to follow the

Middy. Both vessels reached the bar in safety; but there was not water enough for the little gunboat to go over, and she was compelled to anchor. The Olympus — for Clem had been correct in his supposition — was supplied with provisions and stores, and ordered to Key West. An engineer and two first-class firemen were sent on board, who, with her negro firemen, formed a sufficient force for the engine. The master's mate and six seamen also went in her.

The Olympus was a river-steamer of light draught. She was loaded with a valuable cargo of hardware and clothing, which she had just brought up from Cedar Keys, where it had been landed by a schooner hailing from Nassau. Captain McBride had some doubts whether she would reach Key West; but nothing else could be done with her; and he had full confidence in Mr. Brackett's skill and prudence. She was fortunately favored with good weather; and, at the end of three weeks, the prize-crew returned to the Middy by a vessel bound to Pensacola.

"Now, massa cap'n," said Clem, when the Olympus had departed, "dar's two boats loaded with cotton up de riber, wat's gwine down to de Keys to load de schooners dar."

"Where are they?"

"Up to Clay Landing, massa."

"Can we go up there?"

"Yes, sar, 'pose de fort let you go."

"We can take care of the fort."

"And de gorillas, massa?"

"The what?"

"Dem fellers dat goes about on hoss-back cutting people froats,—dem dat fired on de boats down to de Keys."

"Oh! the guerillas?"

"Yes, sar."

"We can take care of them too."

"Take de gumboat right up dar, den; but de gorillas done shoot de man at de wheel!" added Clem with a shudder.

"Well, we have iron screens to protect the helmsman."

The Middy remained at her anchorage above the bar till the forenoon of the next day, when a southerly wind, which had prevailed for several days, had raised the water nearly two feet above the ordinary level of high tide. The fog had disappeared; and, under these favorable circumstances, the little gunboat sailed on her cruise up the river, where no armed steamer had gone before. The iron screens had been put up to protect the gunners and the helmsman, and every preparation made for a stormy time.

Clem was now as lively as though he had been going to a ball instead of a battle. He opened his mouth wide enough to shame the alligators, and seemed to rejoice continually at his good fortune in escaping to the "gumboat." From the paymaster's stores he had been rigged out in a complete suit of seaman's clothes; and the change of dress certainly wrought a marvellous revolution in his personal appearance. He was apparently forty years of age, as black as charcoal, and very far from being a handsome man. He had no knowledge of any thing except what related to his particular sphere of duty. He didn't know what caused the war; but he was sure it would free the slaves. He had been down to Key West several times in a schooner; but his travels did not appear to have enlarged his understanding. He was always good-natured, docile, and funny. He could not speak without exciting a laugh; and at once became a favorite with both officers and crew, all of whom had a high respect for him on account of his skill as a pilot.

Clem took his place at the wheel; and the Middy ascended the river, with the American flag flying at the stern, to the intense disgust of "Secesh" on its banks. In due time, the fort opened upon her very spitefully; but its guns proved to be miserably inefficient in range, which suggested to Captain McBride his proper course. Dropping his anchor with a spring on the cable, out of reach of the enemy's guns, he proceeded in a leisurely manner to knock the works to pieces with his thirty-two-pounder and one quarter-gun.

CHAPTER XXX.

ON THE SUWANNEE RIVER.

THE superiority of the Middy's metal over that of the fort was soon manifest, not only to those on board the steamer, but to the occupants of the works, and the latter displayed their appreciation of the fact by running away This important part of the enterprise being disposed of, the gunboat proceeded up the river. On her passage, she was continually assailed by riflemen on the banks of the river; but the bullets struck harmlessly upon the iron screens which protected the wheel-house and the gun-crews.

Clem performed his share of the work to the admiration of the officers. Safely ensconced behind the iron plates of his quarters, he shouted with delight when the rifle-balls struck the screens.

"Golly! dis jes like a skeeter-bar!" cried he with his long chattering laugh. "You hears de skeeters buzz on de outside: but dey can't come in, nohow; no, sar! Yah, yah, yah!"

"Shut your mouth, blackee, afore any one falls into it," added Tom Longstone.

"Yah, yah, yah!" added Clem, peering through the sight-holes in the front screens. "Dar's de steamers!"

"I see them," said Jack. "There are hundreds of people on shore."

Just then, a shot from the thirty-two-pounder fell near them, and they fled. At the same time, the quarter-guns opened with canister; and not a human being could be seen in any direction. Captain McBride was afraid that the rebels would set fire to the steamers when their capture became inevitable, especially as the Middy could not run up into the shallow water, where they were moored to the shore.

Mr. Dickey was ordered to get out the first cutter, and, with a strong force, proceed to the steamers; the Middy all the time playing upon the shore with grape and canister to keep the rebels at a respectful distance. Jack Somers asked permission to go in the boat; and, as Mr. Dickey knew the value of his services, his request was readily granted. The boat dashed in under the stern of the nearest steamer; but the painter had scarcely been made fast before a volley of rifle-balls was discharged into the midst of the crew by a gang of rebels concealed among the cotton-bales.

"I am wounded!" groaned Mr. Dickey, sinking back in the stern-sheets of the boat, just as he had risen to board the steamer. "Lead on, Somers; don't mind me!" added the intrepid young officer as the seamen hesitated.

"Come on, boys! come on!" shouted Jack, leaping on board the cotton-boat.

"Ay, ay!" added the men with a cheer as they followed our hero.

The rebels who had fired the volley had formed a casemate among the cotton-bales, at the stern of the steamer. As soon as Jack discovered the position of the enemy, he ordered the cockswain of the first cutter to cast off, and pull away from his exposed situation. The order was obeyed, the four men in the boat moving her up under the lee of the steamer's paddles. One man had been killed, and one wounded, besides the first-lieutenant.

Jack had fourteen men with him; and of course he lost no time in placing them out of the reach of the rebel riflemen at the stern of the boat. As the guns of the Middy protected his party from assault in the direction of the shore, our hero was in no haste to finish the affair. He took time to consider the best means of driving the enemy from their lair without the loss of any of his men.

Climbing up to the top of the mass of cotton-bales, he soon found a way to their stronghold, which was open at the top. But it was not safe to approach the den; for the rebels were ready to fire the moment they discovered a blue-jacket.

"Bear a hand here, my lads!" said Jack in a low tone, when a happy thought took possession of his mind. "Roll up this bale!"

"Ay, ay!" replied the men promptly, as they saw at a glance what Jack intended to do. "Now she rises!"

The bale did rise, was rolled over two or three times, and then tumbled down into the lair of the rebels. From the groans and the oaths that followed this novel assault, it was plain that some of the boat's defenders had been crushed under the bale.

"Up with another!" shouted Jack.

"Ay, ay, Somers! Here she goes!"

But the rebels did not wait for another. They leaped from their dangerous quarters, and fled to the shore, — those who were able to do so. An examination of the den showed that two of the rebels had been badly injured by the fall of the bale. As the seamen were all on the top of the pile, they were unable to prevent the escape of the others, if they had been disposed to do so.

Not another rebel could be found, after a diligent search in every part of the steamer; and the victory was complete. The fasts were cast off; and, while a dozen men pushed her off from the landing-place with poles, Jack, with the rest of the men, pulled off to the Middy with the wounded officer and seamen. Mr. Dickey was evidently very badly injured, — a bullet having passed through his side. He was faint, and appeared to be rapidly sinking.

"Somers again!" said he with a gentle smile, in recognition of the service which Jack had rendered.

"How do you feel, sir?"

"Very bad: there is a hole in my side big enough for an alligator to crawl in," he replied languidly

Jack could not smile at this conceit, for Mr. Dickey looked as though he was dying.

"I ought to have taken you on board before, sir."

"No, Somers: you did just right, and just what I ordered you to do."

The cutter came alongside the Middy, and the wounded officer was tenderly conveyed to the cabin, where the surgeon proceeded to examine his wound. Before his decision could be reached, the captain ordered off the cutter to secure the other steamer. It was fully manned again, and placed in charge of Mr. Scott, the master's mate, and the only remaining officer who was available for this duty. Captain McBride would willingly have given Jack the command of this expedition; but it was hardly in order to send a petty-officer upon such duty.

As the boat pulled over to the steamer, Jack informed Mr. Scott of the manner in which the first steamer had been defended: so that officer was prepared for an ambush. But all doubts on this point were soon settled by the discovery of a broad sheet of flame rising from the steamer's forecastle. The rebels, who were concealed in various hiding-places near the landing, had improved the opportunity while the boat returned to the Middy, and set her on fire.

The first cutter dashed up to the cotton-boat, and her crew leaped on board. The fire had made but little progress. By rolling a few of the bales overboard, and a diligent use of the buckets, the flames were extinguished. During these operations, an occasional shot had been fired by the rebels from their concealment in the storehouses on the shore; but the distance was too great for effective firing, and no one had been hit.

Mr. Scott, while the cutter was coming off, expressed his astonishment that the enemy had not burned the boats on the appearance of the Middy; but it seemed, from the plan they had adopted to defend them, that they were confident of beating off the steamer's boats. A further reason was now manifest to the party, consisting of a company of artillery, having four guns, which now appeared on the shore, dashing down to the landing-place at the utmost speed of the horses.

"We must abandon her!" exclaimed Mr. Scott when this new array of force was discovered.

"I hope not, sir!" replied Jack. "We can tow her off with the boat, or carry a long line to the Middy."

"Cast off the fasts, Somers!" shouted Mr. Scott in an excited tone. "Pass that hawser into the boat! Lively, my men!"

Jack rushed forward to let go the steamer's fasts. The rebel company were wheeling their guns into position, and there was yet imminent danger. Our sailor-boy, foreseeing that the long hawser would be necessary in hauling off the steamer, considered it necessary to cast off the end on shore so as to save the line. For this purpose he sprang over the gang-plank, and had unfastened the rope, when a bullet from the rifle of one of the concealed rebels passed through the fleshy part of his left thigh. He dropped upon the ground, just as the steamer began to recede from the land.

All the boat-party were in the cutter or in the afterpart of the steamer, so that the catastrophe which had overtaken him was not discovered till it was too late to remedy it. Jack, with admirable presence of mind, tied his handkerchief tightly around his leg. He rose, and attempted to walk down to the water; but he found himself unable to do so.

By this time, the artillery company had unlimbered their pieces, and were pouring a steady fire into the Middy and the first cutter; to which she was replying with shell from her thirty-two, and canister from one of the twenty-fours. Mr. Scott was still on board of the steamer, with a portion of the men. He had attached the hawser which Jack had saved to the tow-line, so that the Middy soon had both her prizes in hand; with which, having accomplished the work for which she had come, she steamed down the river.

Jack had crawled a short distance from the landing-place to shelter himself from the fire of the Middy's guns; but, as soon as the action ceased, he was waited upon by at least fifty rebels. They were not in the best humor imaginable, and not disposed to treat the wounded quartermaster with the kindness due to a brave but unfortunate enemy. He was taken to a shed, and laid upon some cotton-bales. A doctor who was present dressed his wound, and declared that he would be fit to be hung in a week; which was certainly very consoling to the sufferer.

While he lay there surrounded by a knot of rebels, he had an opportunity to learn their opinions. They were vexed, disappointed, and angry, and bestowed unmeasured abuse upon the artillery company for not coming sooner. This battery had been in the vicinity of the keys to guard that place from a boat-attack, which was expected. On the appearance of the Middy on the preceding night, it had been sent for, and had been momentarily expected during the forenoon. This was the principal reason why the steamers had not been burned.

Jack Somers found himself to be an object of great curiosity. He was visited by all the men, women, and children in the place, all of whom were anxious to look upon one of the "terrible Yankees." The sufferer was not a very dangerous-looking person, especially in his present exhausted condition; and those who came to scoff at him found their admiration and sympathy excited rather than their hatred. He was pale, but he was handsome; and the ladies expressed their surprise that such a pretty boy should be a "horrid Yank."

Among those who came were Major Sandford, a rich planter residing near the landing, and his wife and daughter. The latter, a girl of fifteen, was touched to the heart by the sad, pale face of Jack. She thought it was a terrible thing for such a nice-looking young man to lie wounded and suffering upon a heap of cotton-bales.

"What is your name, poor fellow?" said she.

"John Somers, miss," answered Jack.

"What did you come down here to kill our people for?" added she.

"Because they are rebels and traitors!" replied he faintly

We don't know whether Miss Edith Sandford liked this answer or not; but she protested with all her might against the little Yankee's lying on cotton-bales, where he was, in such a dreadful condition. She insisted that her father should take him home, and treat him like a human being. She was an only daughter; and, though Major Sandford had a great many objections, he finally consented, and Jack was paroled for this purpose

He was conveyed in a wagon to the house of the planter; a good room was provided for him, and Edith saw that he was tenderly nursed. At the expiration of a fortnight, he was able to walk out.

" I wish you wasn't a Yankee," said Edith one day, as they walked in front of the mansion.

" I wish you wasn't a rebel," replied Jack.

" I'm not a rebel, any more than you are ! " exclaimed she, with a very pretty pout upon her interesting countenance.

" We won't talk politics then," laughed Jack. " I suppose my time here is about out, and I must soon be sent to a rebel prison."

" To prison? Oh, no ! they won't send a nice young man like you to prison."

" But they will, Miss Edith."

" Why don't you run off, then ? "

" I would not break my parole."

" I thought a Yankee would do any thing that is mean ? "

" I think not."

It was plain that Edith was much interested in Jack ; and she was not the first young lady who had been moved in the same direction : not that she indulged in " moonshine " at his expense ; but she pitied him. She wept when the captain of the artillery company insisted that his prisoner should be sent off ; for he did not believe in treating Yankees like gentlemen. No reasonable excuse could be offered for resisting this claim ; and Jack, after giving up his parole, was taken into custody. He was sent to a barrack a few miles farther inland, where three others, captured from a boat-expedition at Cedar Keys, were confined. They were to remain here till an opportunity offered to send them to a prison-camp.

Jack decided not to wait for this opportunity; but one night he made his way through the roof of the barrack, and, under the guidance of a negro who was panting for the " day of jubilee," reached the coast, near the mouth of the Suwannee. After starving, and suffering from cold and storms, for a week, they found a dug-out, with which they pulled off to the Middy.

" Somers again ! " said Mr. Dickey as he climbed over the bulwark.

Mr. Dickey was not dead, and gave him a warm hand as he stepped upon deck.

" My darling ! " cried Tom Longstone. " I was sure you was dead ! "

" Not yet, Tom. I was wounded ; but I am pretty well now."

Jack had been absent four weeks, and had suffered a great deal during the last part of this time ; but it was worth while to endure a great deal for such a welcome as was extended to him by officers and crew. After he had taken his supper, he told his story, and listened to a narrative of the events which had taken place on board during his absence. The cotton-steamers had been sent to Key West, and the officers and men who went in them had just returned. Mr. Dickey had been very low, and was not expected to live for a week. He was now able only to walk about the deck. Clem had taken the Middy through every conceivable channel where there was water enough to float her, and was still a favorite on board.

"Now, Somers, if you have finished your yarn, I want to see you," said Captain McBride at a later hour in the evening. "Here is your warrant as a midshipman; and you are ordered to the Naval Academy, after a thirty-days' leave of absence. Here is a letter from Captain Bankhead."

"Thank you, sir!" exclaimed Jack as he took the papers.

"A supply-steamer will be along in a few days, and you will leave in her," added the captain.

Jack was bewildered by this intelligence; for the prospect of seeing Pinchbrook in a few days, and embracing his mother, shaking hands with his father, and spinning yarns to the rest of the folks, was very delightful. The two days he remained on board the Middy, he spent with Tom in the wheel-house. The veteran could hardly reconcile himself to part with his young friend; but, as it was for Jack's advancement, he put a cheerful face upon the matter.

The supply-steamer arrived; and Jack, after thanking the captain for his kindness and shaking hands with officers and crew, went on board: and thus ended the career of Jack Somers in the navy as an ordinary seaman.

CHAPTER XXXI.

HOMEWARD BOUND.

JACK SOMERS was compelled to remain at Key West three weeks before he could find a vessel bound to the North; and the important documents which he carried burned in his pocket. He wanted to show them to Captain Barney, to his mother, and to all his friends in Pinchbrook. They were the evidences of his good conduct, of his skill and bravery; and, though Jack was a modest young man, he was proud of his record. He had served his country faithfully and zealously; and he was grateful to his friends for their high appreciation of his services.

During those three weeks of idleness, Jack applied himself closely to the study of navigation; using a book which Captain McBride had kindly presented to him. He felt that he had not a moment to waste, and that his future success depended upon the zeal and energy with which he devoted himself to his studies. He was anxious to secure a high rank in the Naval School; and he was willing to purchase his anticipated position by hard work.

He was already a thorough seaman. Tom Longstone had been a patient teacher, and he had learned all that belongs to an able seaman's duty. He was perfectly familiar with the practical part of gunnery; was thoroughly posted in all the technicalities of the ship and its batteries. Of the science of gunnery he knew only what he had learned from his books since the Middy sailed from New Orleans. He had thus obtained a measure of knowledge in regard to the practical details of his profession, to the attainment of which the young gentlemen in the Naval School must devote months or years. But Jack had not acquired all this information during the single year he had been in the navy: he had simply added to his previous knowledge by close attention to his duty.

Busy as he was with his studies, he found time to write a long letter to Captain Bankhead, informing him of the reception of his warrant, and expressing his gratitude for the friendly interest he had ever manifested in his welfare. "I shall always think the trip we made to Fort Warren on that dark November night, a year ago, was the luckiest cruise I ever made," wrote Jack in the letter; "for it gave me a friend who has done more for me than I could ever have done for myself."

Jack wrote this; but I am sure that Captain Bankhead neither would nor could have done what he did, if our hero had not deserved such distinguished favors,—if he had not been a good boy and a good seaman. He had several weeks before received letters from home, informing him that his brother had been promoted to a lieutenancy. Tom was a commissioned officer, and was therefore some months, if not years, ahead of him in the race for distinction ; but both of them, while they had a just and proper regard for the honors of their respective professions, were better satisfied to have served their country in its hour of trial than they were to receive their merited promotion.

Jack wanted very much to get home ; but he was so busy with his studies, that he had no time to be impatient at the delay. When an opportunity to depart was presented, he was much less elated than his half-dozen impatient companions who had nothing to occupy their minds. The men who were to go North were sent on board of an old steamer, which was hardly seaworthy, and which was going to New York for repairs.

The voyage was prosperous till the steamer reached the latitude of Cape Hatteras, where she was overtaken by one of the severe gales which prevail in that region. The vessel leaked badly, and shipped great seas, till she was in imminent danger of foundering. It required the utmost exertion of all hands to keep her afloat ; but the men worked zealously and cheerfully, till an accident to the engine seemed to deprive them of all hope of ever seeing the land again.

The ship rolled and pitched heavily in the head-seas for a time; and, at every roll, it seemed as though her back must be broken. By almost superhuman efforts on the part of the crew, sufficient sail was set to keep her head up to the sea, and she worked easier. Jack had just come down from the fore-topsail-yard, completely exhausted by the violence of his exertions. Life-lines had been extended along the deck for the men to hold on by when the seas swept over the decks. Jack had grasped one of these ropes just as the ship felt her helm; when a great combing billow broke over the bow, sweeping a flood of water towards the stern.

The second-lieutenant of the steamer, who had been forward superintending the setting of the sail, was in front of him, and, either by accident or carelessness, lost his hold upon the life-line. The mass of water bore him along, as though he had been a feather, towards a hole which the sea had stove in the bulwarks. Perceiving the perilous situation of the officer, Jack seized the inner fake of a rope, flemished on the deck, and sprang towards the lieutenant. Passing the line around his body, he followed the rolling billow, and succeeded in securing a hold upon the officer's leg, just as he was sliding over the plank-shear into the sea.

Jack would certainly have gone with him, if his attentive shipmates had not grasped the other end of the line by which he had secured himself. Another sea rolled over them before they could recover their perpendicular positions; but Jack held on to the leg of the officer, and the men hauled them both up to the life-line.

"Your name?" demanded the lieutenant, when he had regained his feet.

"Somers, sir."

"Well, Somers, this is a bad time to plank the deck," he added with a smile, as he emptied the salt water from his mouth.

"Very bad, sir."

"You shall hear from me again, Somers," added the officer as he walked aft.

After the crew of the old steamer had endured more than we have room to describe, the gale broke; and, favored with better weather, the engine was repaired, and she proceeded on her voyage, very much to the satisfaction of those who had lost all hope of ever reaching the land.

The next day, while the ship was rolling heavily through the sea which had not yet subsided, Jack, who had just been relieved from duty at the pumps, was accosted by Mr. Waldron, the second-lieutenant, whom he had saved from an ocean-grave.

"Somers, you saved my life yesterday: what can I do for you?" said he.

"Thank you, sir: I'm not in want of any thing just now," replied Jack, touching his cap.

"Your time is out, I suppose?"

" Yes, sir."

" Do you quit the navy?"

" No, sir."

" Well, then, my lad, you shall have a better berth than you had before. I think I have influence enough to procure a good rating."

" Thank you, sir," replied Jack.

" You look as though you would make a good topman. What do you say to being captain of the main-top?"

" Thank you, sir: I have been rated as cockswain of the captain's gig and as a quartermaster."

" Is that so? Then I may not be able to do any thing better in that direction."

Jack thought it would be a good joke to show him his midshipman's warrant at this point of the conversation; and accordingly he produced the precious document.

" What are you doing forward with this paper in your pocket?" asked the astonished lieutenant.

" I had no uniform, sir, and was in no condition to appear as an officer."

" You shall swing your hammock in the steerage for the rest of the voyage, at least. If you are.a brother-officer, I need not think of rewarding you," laughed Mr. Waldron.

" I hope not, sir."

Jack was immediately presented to the captain, who ordered him to carry his bag into the steerage, greatly to the astonishment of his late companions, who had no suspicion that they had messed with so distinguished an individual as a midshipman. The steamer rolled along on her voyage, and at last arrived at New York.

Jack lost no time in proceeding to Boston, though not till he had arranged for a meeting with Mr. Waldron at some future time; for the grateful officer insisted upon continuing the acquaintance so fortunately begun. It was about sunset when the sailor-boy reached Pinchbrook.

" Hallo, Jack, my hearty ! " said a familiar voice as he stepped from the car.

" Captain Barney ! "

" Ay, ay, my lad ! But where do you come from? We did not expect you back yet a while," added the old gentleman, still wringing our hero's hand.

Jack briefly informed his good friend where he had come from.

" Well, Jack " —

" I beg your pardon, Captain Barney: call me Mr. Somers, if you please," laughed Jack.

" Eh ? "

" Mr. Midshipman Somers is my present designation '

" Whew ! " whistled the old sailor.

" I have won my warrant."

" Well, *Mr.* Somers " —

" Avast, captain: that will do. You may call me Jack, now ; for I don't know the sound of my own name with such a long handle to it."

" Come down to the house with me, Jack."

" Oh, no, sir ! not now. I must go up and see mother —
and father : I haven't seen him for nearly two years."

" Never mind : come down to the house. You will
scare your mother out of her wits if you bolt in upon
her like a harpoon into a whale. I'll put the horse in,
and take you up pretty soon."

" I want to see her at once."

" And frighten her into a fit ! "

" She don't have fits : at any rate, she would only have
a fit of gladness at seeing me."

Captain Barney persisted, apparently firm in the belief
that Mrs. Somers would go into hysterics if her son presented himself too suddenly. It would be better to
break the news gradually to her. Jack could not help
himself, and walked home with Captain Barney. He
was conducted to the library as the bell rang for tea.

" Come, Jack, now come out and have some supper
with me," said the captain.

" No, sir : decidedly, I cannot. What would my
mother say if I took tea in Pinchbrook before I went
home?" replied Jack emphatically

" Well, come out and look at the folks, at any rate ;
and then, if you insist on going, I will harness right
up."

Jack began to protest that he would not go, even to
look at the folks ; when Captain Barney took him by the

arm, and gently forced him through the door leading to the dining-room.

"Why, John Somers!" exclaimed a voice which Jack could not possibly mistake.

"Why, Jack, my boy! is that you?" added another voice equally familiar to his ear.

In another moment our sailor-boy was in the arms of his mother, who hugged and kissed him as though he were still an infant. Mr. Midshipman Somers, regardless of the dignity of an officer in the United-States Navy, wept like a baby. His "top-lights" were flooded, in spite of all his efforts to suppress the rising tide; but we are happy to say that Mrs. Somers did not go into hysterics, "conniptions," or any thing of the sort. Like a sensible woman, she did not even faint.

Captain Somers took the hand of his brave boy, and gave him a sailor's hearty welcome home. The whole family, it appeared, were taking tea at the hospitable mansion of the retired shipmaster, who had got up a surprise for Jack as well as for his mother.

"Don't you think my mother will be frightened into a fit, Captain Barney?" said Jack, when the first greetings were over. "You meant to throw me into a fit."

"Well, Jack, I had no more idea of seeing you than I had of seeing Jeff. Davis. I went up after my newspaper; for I can't eat my supper till I've seen the news; but I didn't expect to bring you back with me."

"I'll forgive you this time."

"Next time you come home, I suppose you'll be an admiral."

"I hope not; for I shall be older than you are, then."

I need not tell my readers what a happy evening was spent at Captain Barney's, nor how late Jack and his parents sat up that night in reviewing the events of the year. Tom's letters were all brought out and read; and Jack could not help taking a little walk about the house, though the Pinchbrook clock was striking twelve.

"Eight bells! All the starboard-watch, ahoy!" said Jack, as he kissed his mother, and went to his old chamber in the attic of the cottage.

A few days after his return, Jack put on his uniform; and certain young ladies declared that he was even a "handsomer fellow than his brother Tom;" for patriotic young ladies have a high regard for blue coats and bright buttons.

At the expiration of his furlough, Jack reported at the Naval School; and here — leaving him as a bright example of what a young man may accomplish by being true to himself, true to his country, and true to God — here properly ends the eventful history of "THE SAILOR BOY," though not of "JACK SOMERS IN THE NAVY."